# Firebird

A Desert Air Force Novel

**Melvyn Fickling**

**By the same Author**

Bluebirds: A Battle of Britain Novel

Blackbirds: A London Blitz Novel

Falcons: A Siege of Malta Novel

Farewell to the Glory Boys: A Battle of Arras Novel

Cover art © Altimeter Aviation Photography
Author Portrait by Moff Moffat
www.melvynfickling.com

Dedicated to Louise Robinson with love

# Chapter 1

## Friday, 14 August 1942 – Ta'Qali Airfield, Malta

The sky lightened from purple to deep blue as the sun roused from its eastern vault. Bisected by the horizon, it slanted its primal beams through the streamers of dust that swirled behind the Spitfires running up their engines on the airfield.

Bryan Hale swung his aircraft onto the runway and trundled forward for twenty yards. He squeezed on the brakes and dropped the throttle to idle. He looked into his mirror to check progress behind him. A Spitfire stood stationary on the perimeter, its propeller windmilling to a halt. It looked like Ben Steven's aircraft. As groundcrew moved in to drag the fighter out of the way, Ben stood up in the cockpit, waving at Bryan and making slashing motions across his throat. Bryan waved an arm from his open canopy in reluctant acknowledgement; he'd be flying with no wingman today.

The wireless buzzed into life, cutting through Bryan's annoyance: *'Fighter Control to Falcon Squadron, you're clear for take-off. Once airborne, take heading two-four-zero. Good luck.'*

The order released the waiting fighters into action. Throttles slid open, engines swelled and the rippling streamers lashed into blinding pennants. Bryan banged his canopy shut against the buffeting airflow. Releasing the brakes, he followed the rest of Falcon Squadron along the dust-plumed runway and into the air.

Squadron Leader Copeland banked the formation into the south-westerly heading and powered into a steady climb as the Dingli Cliffs dropped away to the empty sea below them. At their backs, the sun's disc finally broke free of the horizon; rising with languid serenity, it flushed the soft, golden dawn with a brighter luminance.

*'Fighter Control to Falcon Squadron, we're tracking two formations of bandits. You are on a converging course. Maintain angels.'*

The squadron levelled out and Bryan scanned the horizon through the blur of his spinning propeller. Dead ahead, a dark anomaly appeared through the glare on the sparkling water; four large ships, grouped dangerously close and seemingly stationary, sat exposed in the flat blue wilderness. This was the ragged remains of the convoy centred around the oil tanker that meant so much to Malta's hopes of continued resistance.

'*Falcon Leader to Falcon Aircraft,*' Copeland called. '*Bandits at two o'clock. Tally-ho!*'

The squadron banked gently to starboard and Bryan picked up the enemy formations. The foremost moved with the stodgy pace of bombers, their fixed undercarriage and deep, creased wings identified them as Stuka dive-bombers. Behind, and a good deal higher, a gaggle of 109 fighters shadowed them to their target.

Falcon Squadron lanced towards the bombers. Bryan edged out to starboard, loosening up space to manoeuvre as the squat, ugly silhouettes of the dive-bombers grew larger. A wave of panic infected the enemy formation and it split apart, breaking in all directions. Bryan squeezed off a one-second burst at a huge gull-winged shape that barrelled across his vision before he broke through the melee and banked left to seek another target.

'*Look out!*' An unrecognisable voice. '*109s coming down now!*'

Bryan reversed his bank to gain clear sky and looked upwards for the danger. Bright orange motes of tracer streamed down towards him followed by two huge black shapes that flashed past either side of his fuselage. Bryan hauled his turn into the opposite direction to throw them off. A Stuka wallowed into view in front of him. He throttled back, lined up and fired. Hits peppered the enemy's tail cascading tiny shards backwards into its slipstream. The Stuka's rear gunner fired back, squirting a spiral of tracer that looped and swung dangerously close to Bryan's canopy. The dive-bomber lurched into a violent side-slip and Bryan dived away to regain airspeed.

Ahead, a Spitfire dropped through the air in a slow, flat spin, like a monstrous maple seed. The letters on the side flashed clearly into view as it rotated; they were Copeland's. Above the stricken aircraft, a parachute opened, pristine white against the blue.

Bryan pulled into a wide bank and scanned the sky. A German fighter levelled out from a diving turn and flew towards the parachutist. Gun flashes sparkled along it wings and cowling. Bryan craned his neck back in time to see the figure in the harness jerk under many impacts. Something hose-like draped away from the man, looping and glistening in the sunlight. The 109 barrelled past a few feet above the parachute's canopy. Propeller wash folded the fabric into itself and the parachute collapsed and twisted, streaming behind the plummeting pilot like a tangled shroud.

Bryan howled with impotent rage and kicked his Spitfire into pursuit behind the diving Messerschmitt, pushing his throttle full against the gate. His quarry sped north for home, trading away his altitude for speed. The German levelled out a few hundred feet above the sea and weaved gently back and forth as he fled, keeping a wary mirror-eye on his pursuer. Bryan levelled out behind him, growling under his breath and rocking against his straps, willing the gap to close.

A detonation against the armour behind Bryan's seat punched the air out of his chest and jolted his head forward. Gasping against his empty lungs he screwed his face around in confusion. A hammer blow shattered his canopy and three concussions smashed into the nose ahead of the windshield. The engine rattled in mechanical agonies for a few seconds, then seized with a sickening jolt that jerked through the airframe.

A disconnected roar filled the sudden silence and Bryan looked up as the sky-blue underside of a 109 slid into place above him. Oil streaks feathered down its length and the malevolent white-edged crosses of the black knights filled its wings. It hung there for a moment, then wallowed over to the right, dropping down to fly alongside him. Mesmerised, Bryan watched its manoeuvre and found himself looking across at the pilot. The man lifted his goggles, as if removing a mask, and met Bryan's gaze. The German blinked impassively then turned his head away, surging his aircraft forward towards home.

Smoke feathered out of the Spitfire's crippled engine and seeped into the cockpit. Bryan watched the German pulling away as his own aircraft slowed and dipped into a silent, shallow dive.

'Shit.'

Bryan eased a fraction back on the stick to level out the descent, and checked the altimeter. He had enough height in hand to bail-out, and his speed had been high before his engine stopped. No need to panic. He pulled at the canopy, exhaling in quiet relief as it slid back smoothly. He fingered his parachute harness buckle to make sure it was solid. Keeping a tight grip on the control column, he undid his straps and squirmed his shoulders up the seatback. He bent one leg up to get his foot onto the seat, then the other foot, so he was squatting with his arm stretched between his knees and fingertip grip on the control column. He drew a deep breath to steady himself. Then, in one fluid motion, he pushed the stick forward, straightened his legs and dove out the cockpit's starboard side.

The tailplane rapped against his right boot, sending a concussive flash of pain up his leg and sending him into a spin through the void. The now-diving Spitfire flashed through his swirling vision twice before his groping fingers found and pulled the parachute release ring. Fabric swirled and flapped for a moment behind and above his head, then the cords whipped and tightened and his harness jerked painfully into his crotch to arrest his fall. He hung limp and spent as the untwisting cords rotated him in serene revolutions.

A short distance below him, Bryan's Spitfire swallow-dived into the clear Mediterranean water, raising only a brief plume of foam to mark its passing. That same water now rushed closer to claim the machine's pilot. Bryan took a deep breath and held it. He released his harness as he plunged feet-first into the swell, wriggling out of the canvas webbing as he kicked himself back to the surface. Panting against the shock of the cooler temperature, he leaned back and trod water while he found the mouthpiece and inflated his Mae West life vest.

Pain throbbed up his calf from his injured foot and he lifted it above the surface. There was no blood, but he could feel his flesh swelling against the thin leather of his desert boots. He let his leg sink back under the water and, using his hands as paddles, rotated his body to survey the horizon. There was nothing to see, except the slightest suggestion of a smoke smudge in the sky, too far away to guess the distance. That smoke could only be rising from the ships in the convoy, those ships were travelling south towards Malta, and Bryan had been chasing his enemy northwards when he was bounced. He bobbed on the slight swell as the minutes ticked by, watching the smudge dissipate and eventually vanish.

'Shit,' he muttered.

\*\*\*

The sun climbed higher as Bryan scanned the southern skies for aircraft. Surely someone had seen his parachute and they'd send a big fat floatplane out to look for him. But nothing moved apart from a few wispy clouds extruded across the vault by high-altitude winds. He closed his eyes against the flashing glare from the water's surface. The pain from his foot devolved into a steady throb, rising and falling with mechanical regularity, and his tongue became sticky with mucus as his mouth dried out.

He thought of Copeland, floating around somewhere in the same sea, dead with his guts wrapped around his legs. He remembered the squadron leader's face at that morning's briefing, vital and alive, his eyes flashing with purpose. He thought of Ben aborting his take-off with engine trouble. Damn it! If Ben had been with him, he wouldn't have been bounced so easily and he wouldn't be bobbing around out here waiting for that bloody seaplane.

He opened his eyes again to search the southern horizon, but the sun had climbed to the top of its arc and he couldn't work out which way was south. Squinting upwards rucked furrows into his forehead and drew a dull pain from his scalp; the sun was starting to burn him. Scrabbling at the buttons under his life vest, he squirmed his way out of his shirt, cursing at the splashes of salt-water that stung his dry, swelling lips. Once he wrested the shirt free, he wrapped the sodden cotton cloth around his head, allowing it to drape over his face.

***

The sun curved westwards, but Bryan's eyes remained downcast behind his damp veil. His tongue grew leathery and his teeth roughened with dryness. As the light faded, a reluctant recognition crept upon him, nibbling away at his will to endure. With this insinuating acceptance came thoughts of Jacobella; the scent of her hair, the darkness of her eyes and the curve of her hips, and with the vision of her face came tears for the things that would never be. When the quiet tears were spent, exhaustion brought the warmth of sleep to Bryan's eyes, a sleep from which he had no desire to awaken.

***

Something woke him.

A slippery force pulled and pushed at Bryan's legs with fat grasping fingers. A fluid compulsion swirled around his body, stroking his belly and teasing at the fabric of his trousers. Alarm cut through the fog of slumber and he pulled the cloth from his face. In the meagre light of the crescent moon, the surface of the water shimmied with busy currents that chased and spiralled around themselves, fed by some force deep below the surface. Swallowing a surge of panic, Bryan paddled with his hands, pushing backwards, away from the turbulence, away from whatever was beneath him. As he moved, the currents quickened and pushed harder against his body, speeding his retreat. With the increasing turmoil, the water around him chilled, like the icy talons of death claiming his tribute. Then the surface bulged for an instant before cleaving away to disgorge a huge, dark, cylindrical shape.

Bryan spluttered as the displaced water splashed a wave over and past his head. Then, wiping the saltwater from his stinging eyes, he gawped in disbelief at the shimmering cobalt body of a British submarine, curtains of foaming water sliding down its curved flank as it settled into its enforced buoyancy.

The clang of metal on metal rang out from the top of the submarine's tower and a shadowy figure appeared to lean on the guardrail. He was joined moments later by another.

'I'm over here!' Bryan's attempt at a shout mustered little more than a gargling croak and he winced at the fresh cracks the effort opened on his lips. The submariners' demeanour remained unchanged.

'Damn it,' Bryan wheezed to himself. 'Over here,' he croaked again, flailing his arms at the water's surface with all the strength he had.

One of the men on the tower cocked his head, turned towards the new sound and leaned over the rail to discern its source.

'Strewth! There's someone flapping about down there.' The exclamation was followed by muffled exchanges that drew more figures from the craft's interior to crowd against the rail. Two men climbed down the tower's external ladder; one had a coil of rope slung over his shoulder.

'Ahoy!' One of the men called across as his companion knotted a wide loop into the rope's end.

'Yes.' Bryan forced his fractured voice to project. 'Hello!'

'He sounds British, sir. RAF, I reckon,' the seaman looked back to the tower's top and waited.

'Alright, then,' the reply floated back. 'You'd better bring him aboard.'

The second man braced himself, swung the looped rope around his head twice and cast it out towards the floating castaway. The rope splashed into the water next to Bryan. He pulled the loop over his body and gripped it under his armpits. The two submariners dragged him through the water and paused as he came to rest against the boat's side.

'Get ready, lad,' one called down as they braced to haul him aboard.

Bryan grabbed the rope with both hands as it tightened around his torso and lifted him free of the dark water. His back curved against the body of the submarine as he ascended its height in smooth jerks. Then hands grasped his arms and pulled him to a sitting position on the rough corrugated deck.

A face bobbed down level with his: 'Alright, now, chum. Can you stand?'

'I don't know,' Bryan said. 'I haven't tried for a while.'

'Let's give it a go, then.'

The hands tightened their grip and pulled him upright. The pain in his right foot stabbed afresh, but it was not beyond bearing. The men led him to the ladder. One ascended before him, the other waited behind him, coiling the wet rope with deft flicks of his wrist. It took Bryan a few minutes to make the climb; his swollen foot proving awkward to manage on the narrow metal rungs.

At the top, the seaman waited to help him off the ladder, guide him to the hatch and the obverse climb down into the boat. An officer by the hatch stood with binoculars to his eyes, scanning the horizon for lights or movement.

Bryan paused by the man: 'Thank you,' he mumbled.

The captain glanced at Bryan and nodded once before returning to his lookout.

The climb down was just as painful and awkward, and with each rung negotiated the temperature rose and the smell got worse. At the bottom, his guide led him through a bulkhead and along the boat's cramped interior.

'Mind your head,' the sailor said. 'Everywhere you go and whatever you're doing, mind your head.'

Bryan hobbled in the wake of his guide, squeezing past, and apologising to, bemused crewman along the way. Stepping through the last bulkhead, the seaman turned and waited for Bryan to join him.

'This is the where you'll be quartered,' he said. 'It's a good thing we've used all our torpedoes; it's a lot more spacious without them in here.'

Bryan glanced around cramped space, crowded with empty torpedo racks with hammocks strung between them.

'I'll go and get our medical officer,' the seaman said, making for the bulkhead.

'Water,' Bryan croaked. 'Please!'

The seaman raised a hand to acknowledge the request and wended his way back along the narrow gangway.

Bryan sank onto the floor, stretching his legs out and searching for a flat surface against which to lean his back. His foot settled into a robust and

11

rhythmic throb, pulsing pain up his leg in time with his heartbeat. He pulled the wet, twisted fabric of his shirt from around his neck and wiped away the sweat that was beading on his forehead. He closed his eyes against an upswell of emotion, breathing deeply to control the writhing reaction that clutched at his guts.

The minutes dragged by; clanks and rattles reverberated through the vessel and shouted orders drifted forwards from the heart of the submarine. A hissing sound inveigled its way into Bryan's ears, like the filling of a distant cistern, and the deck tilted slightly away from horizontal. The hissing was lost behind the thrumming of the motors and the air pressure increased slightly, like thumbs pressing gently against his temples. The submarine was underway.

'Ah, here you are. Welcome to *HMS Unheard*.' A man stepped through the bulkhead and handed Bryan a flask of water. 'Medical Officer, Lieutenant Rob Douglas,' he added by way of explanation. Bryan accepted the flask and took a swig, carefully licking the moisture onto his dry lips.

'Thank you.' Bryan took another draught, gulping greedily at the lukewarm liquid.

'And I brought you this.' Douglas handed Bryan a blanket as he kneeled down next to him. 'Any injuries?' he asked.

'My right foot took a rap when I bailed out,' Bryan answered.

Douglas undid the laces and eased Bryan's sodden desert boot off his foot. Bryan winced in response to the other man's speculative squeezing.

'It's bruised, not broken,' Douglas said. 'Leave the boot off until the swelling subsides.'

'What's this for?' Bryan held up the blanket.

'It's all I have spare, but if you roll it up it will serve as a pillow,' Douglas said. 'Not that you'll get much sleep; it always takes a new boy a few days to get used to the constant bloody noise.'

Bryan's brow creased under a frown: 'Why would I need to sleep?' he asked. 'We can't be more than a couple of hours from Malta.'

'That's almost certainly true' – the medical officer stood and wiped his hands on his shorts – 'but we're on our way to Alexandria.'

'What?' Bryan's frown deepened. 'But you were sent to pick me up, weren't you? You *must* take me back to Malta.'

'Er, no, actually. We've been out for a good week and a half hunting Italian shipping. The fact that we popped up for a breather right under you was a complete fluke.' He smiled at Bryan's expression of dismay. 'You're one lucky man. One very, *very* lucky man.'

# Chapter 2

**Saturday, 15 August 1942 – Ta'Qali airfield, Malta**

Ben stood and watched a flight of Spitfires curve through the heat-hazed air and flatten into their landing approach. The atmosphere on the airfield around him hummed with a relief spawned from redemption; the arrival of the surviving merchant ships in the convoy had averted imminent disaster. Together with supplies of food and oil, the battered boats had brought with them the intangible spirit of hope. Even these ragged aircraft, their chipped and worn paintwork begrimed with oil and dust, touched down today with the majesty of homecoming swans.

Ben wore sunglasses to hide his bloodshot eyes and to guard against a relapse into grief. The Spitfires taxied past to dispersal and, across the airfield, the engines of refuelled fighters barked into life, preparing to take their place over Grand Harbour to protect the labouring crews that worked to unload the wounded, listing cargo ships.

From the corner of his eye, Ben saw the squadron's adjutant come out of the radio tent and make towards him.

'Are you not flying today?' the adjutant asked.

Ben shook his head: 'My aircraft still isn't serviceable.'

'It's always best to get back into the saddle as soon as possible,' the adjutant said.

'I know,' Ben replied. 'I will.'

'Especially so' – the man held out the slip of paper he carried – 'as they want you to lead the squadron.'

Ben stared at the paper: 'No. Copeland is missing, I know that. But surely, he –' Ben stopped and gritted his teeth against resurging emotions. 'It should be Bryan's job. When Bryan gets back –'

The adjutant placed his hand on Ben's shoulder.

'It's been too long, Ben,' he said quietly. 'Missing at sea doesn't age very well.'

Ben took the slip of paper from the other man's hand.

'Acting squadron leader,' he said. 'Just until.'

The adjutant nodded, more in sympathy than affirmation.

'We should gather their things, ready to send them home,' he said. 'I can sort out Bryan's, if you'd like.'

'No' – Ben shook his head – 'I'll go back to Xara and do it now.'

Ben stood in the corridor, chewing his lip as he battled the last queasy tendrils of denial. Finally accepting a painful resolution, he grasped the handle and opened the door to Bryan's room. The air held a faint aroma of sweat and shaving soap, and Ben left the door open to allow the draught in the corridor to draw away these ethereal vestiges of his friend.

He retrieved the small, battered suitcase from the top of the wardrobe, set it on the unmade bed and flipped open its catches. Inside there lay a pair of brand-new socks and underwear, reserved against some future special occasion. Ben regarded them, smiling through the sadness at their pristine bleakness. He took the few items of clothing from their wardrobe hangers and, folding them carefully, placed them in the case. He wrapped the shaving razor and toothbrush in a hand towel and wedged it alongside the clothes. He cast around the room, but there was nothing else that could be classed as personal, nothing else that might remember a son to his parents. As he turned to close the case, his eyes fell on a small cane bedside table. Beneath its lip there lurked a drawer with a broken handle. Ben sat on the edge of the bed and prised the drawer open with his thumbnails. Inside lay an envelope with a lock of hair tied in red ribbon. Ben picked up the hair, noticing that it was a mixture of blond and auburn locks. The front of the envelope bore the handwritten words 'To Elizabeth and Robert'. Ben turned the envelope in his hands, noting it was sealed and resisting the momentary urge to open it. He placed both the letter and the be-ribboned hair into the case and turned back to close the drawer. There, previously hidden underneath the letter, was a picture postcard. Ben picked up the card and pushed the drawer closed. Flipping the card over he found the reverse unmarked by writing. Turning it back, he studied the picture on the front. The photo portrayed a solid, ornate building on the corner of a city crossroads. Its doors were topped with friezes, a statue of a saint wearing a mitre filled a niche on its wall and a belltower topped the roof. The legend in the lower corner of the card read: '*Saint Augustine – Bakery Street – Valletta*'.

Ben stared at the picture and echoes of a conversation with Bryan nibbled at his memory. His friend had been seeing a woman; pretending to be a Catholic so he could meet her on Sundays. Ben pressed his knuckles against his forehead. Her name… *What* was her name?

Jacobella! That was it.

### Sunday, 16 August 1942 – Valletta

Ben stepped off the bus at Grand Harbour. The city of Valletta exuded the same renewed vigour and confidence that had infected the airfield. Activity buzzed on the docksides around the moored cargo ships, and trucks rumbled along the access roads with resolute purpose. Ben's eyes were drawn upwards at the sound of Spitfires that curved over the harbour and banked north to patrol the approaches from Sicily. As the flight of fighters receded from view, he crossed the road and started his trek across the broken city.

Piles of shattered sandstone from bombed-out buildings punctuated the streets. The rubble was pushed to one side into precipitous heaps to allow a sometimes-tortuous access route along already narrow thoroughfares. Ben ambled slowly, not wanting to become sweaty and dishevelled in the summer's heat. He carried his cap in his hand, and used it to fan his face as he walked.

Ben turned onto Bakery Street just as the bells of St Augustine's began their strident call to worship. Bells from elsewhere in the city joined and echoed the solemn chorus to the faithful. Ben chose a spot outside the church's main entrance, set his cap back on his head and waited.

Within moments the stone of the city exhaled its inhabitants, family groups merged with their neighbours and the trickle became a stream. The tall wooden doors behind him creaked open and the churchgoers flowed around him to enter the dim interior. Ben looked around at their faces as they passed, searching for an unknown clue that might reveal the woman he was seeking.

The hair on his neck raised with the strange certainty he was being observed. He took off his cap and scratched at his skin to quell the tingling. Ben turned to seek the source of his premonition and met the eyes of a woman who stumbled to a halt at his turning. A flash of panicked fright played over the woman's features as Ben closed the short distance between them.

'Hello,' he said, 'are you Jacobella?'

The woman blinked once, holding Ben's gaze as her fears raced ahead of his words.

'Yes.' Jacobella breathed the answer through trembling lips.

'My name is Ben. I flew with Bryan.'

Jacobella shook her head slowly as the import of the past tense crystallised in her heart.

'I'm sorry.' Ben felt nascent tears gather in the corners of his eyes. 'He was posted as missing on Friday. I don't believe there's much hope.'

Jacobella's face tightened against the turmoil in her chest. She pushed past Ben, jostled through the bottlenecked crowd at the door and vanished from sight into the church.

Ben put his cap back on his head and wiped the tears from his cheeks. The flow of people lessened and the last few stragglers hurried past him to their worship. A black-robed man at the doorway cocked a quizzical eyebrow at him. Ben simply shook his head and the man closed the doors.

### HMS Unheard

Bryan perched on the edge of an empty torpedo rack, flexing his right ankle, coaxing it back to flexibility. His shoulders were wrapped in his blanket; an attempt to suppress the shivers induced by his still-damp clothes. He looked like a sick, dishevelled bird and he wore his disconsolation like a veil.

The medical officer stepped through the bulkhead and regarded him with professional detachment.

'How's the foot coming along?' he asked.

'It hurts,' Bryan said. 'You were right about the noise. Have you got anything to help me sleep?'

'Ah' – Douglas smiled – 'I have things that will keep you awake, and I have things that will *put* you to sleep. But nothing in between.'

'When do we arrive in Alexandria?' Bryan asked.

Douglas crouched down to examine Bryan's foot.

'Three days or so,' he said. 'As long as everything goes well.'

'Will you radio my squadron?' Bryan asked. 'Falcon Squadron in Ta'Qali. Let them know Flight Lieutenant Hale has been picked up.'

'We keep radio transmissions to an absolute minimum,' the medic replied. 'It stops people who might not like us very much from finding out where we are.' Douglas finished his examination and stood upright. 'Your foot's doing well. It should be close to normal by the time we make port.'

'They'll think I'm dead,' Bryan persisted.

'Them knowing otherwise would make no practical difference to anything. You can tell them yourself when we get to Alexandria.'

'You don't understand.' Bryan paused and levelled his tone. 'There's someone who'll be beside herself.'

'Well, at least she'll have herself for company,' Douglas said.

Bryan flashed a look at the man standing over him.

'It's not that I have no sympathy for you,' the officer's voice softened. 'I'm obviously not in the business of extending anyone's suffering. But it was blind chance that we found you in the first place. You mean nothing to our mission and, I assure you, the captain will not be persuaded to risk this boat and its crew just so your girlfriend gets to sleep easier. She'll hear the good news soon enough.'

Bryan slumped back into silence.

'Have you eaten?' Douglas asked.

Bryan shook his head.

'Come along' – the officer offered a supporting arm – 'I think I can smell what the label claims to be soup.'

### Wednesday, 19 August 1942

Bryan drifted in and out of what had become a perpetual doze. His watch had succumbed to cog-strangling rust and he now counted the time by the flush of fresh Mediterranean air that cleansed away the fug with every nocturnal surfacing. Four such nights had passed. Alexandria must be close, a supposition reinforced by the crew's lightening mood and a brightening in the voices that echoed along the metal hull.

Bryan retrieved his desert boots from the pipe over which they were slung. They had dried as far as submarine humidity allowed; the suede felt stiff under his fingers and was discoloured with streaks of crystallised salt. He pulled them onto his feet, leaving the right boot unlaced around his still-bruised ankle. Standing, he tested his weight on the injured foot; it still hurt, but the pain was bearably dull. He limped through the bulkhead and made careful progress along the boat's gangway.

Called orders and their answering shouts increased in frequency. The hiss of opening valves heralded the gentle tipping of the deck as *HMS Unheard* tilted her snout towards the surface and then levelled out into buoyancy on the surface. The vibrating thrum of the engines took on an airier resonance, free from the bass attenuation of encapsulating water pressure. A clang of metal announced the opening of the hatch which allowed the vessel to exhale the oily odour of closely-confined men and inhale the salt-crisp breeze of the Egyptian coast.

Half-a-dozen ratings not involved in navigation surged to the ladder to climb up to the fresh air and enjoy the approach into port. Bryan moved towards the captain.

'Sir?'

The bearded man turned at the sound of his voice.

'I wanted to say thank you,' Bryan said. 'Without this boat...' his voice trailed off.

'Don't thank me.' The captain split his beard with a grin. 'But perhaps you should thank your God. It seems He's given you a first-rate guardian angel. Come on, let's get topside.'

Bryan followed the captain up the ladder, gritting his teeth against the stabs of discomfort that the narrow metal rungs forced from his tender right foot. Looking up, the patch of blue sky framed by the opening above him made his eyes tingle, and the flow of clean air brushed his cheeks like a mother's thumbs. Blinking against the sunshine, Bryan emerged onto the top of the conning tower. Next to him on the cramped deck, a submariner ran up two flags on a cord; a white ensign and, below it, a smaller, hand stitched skull-and-crossbones.

Bryan scanned the port that opened up before the sleek cobalt bows of the submarine. Alexandria had the same dull yellow complexion as Malta, as if the city had been forged from the desert sands that formed its hinterland. But it also glowed with the secret life-giving force of the delta upon which it stood. A pilot boat ploughed its way out from behind the breakwaters to guide *HMS Unheard* to her moorings and a brief respite from the private dangers of submarine war.

'We've just radioed ahead,' the captain said. 'The RAF will be waiting for you dockside.'

***

Bryan limped along the gangplank and planted his boots on the dry and dusty stones of Alexandria's dock. He turned on slightly wobbly land-legs to regard the submarine and the men who now worked to make her sea-ready once more. Any euphoria at his escape from a lonely death was muffled under a fog of fatigue that pressed against his eyeballs.

'Are you the rescued pilot?'

Bryan turned to find an orderly officer squinting at him quizzically.

'Yes. Rescued,' Bryan said. 'Flight Lieutenant Hale. I just need to get transport back to Malta.'

'We have a car for you, sir,' the orderly said. 'You'll go to Cairo and they'll make your onward arrangements from there. Follow me, please, sir.'

Bryan trailed after the young man towards a battered blue car.

'Why do I need to go to Cairo?' he asked. 'I'm needed back in Malta.'

The orderly held open the rear door: 'Sir,' he prompted.

Bryan gave up and slid onto the seat. He rested his cheek on the rough, warm leather, closed his eyes and let sleep steal him away.'

*** 

The slam of the car door jolted Bryan into confused wakefulness. He blinked the sleep from his eyes and wiped the drool from his stubbled chin. His driver opened the rear door and stepped back expectantly. Bryan clambered out and looked around.

The car was parked against the pavement outside a terrace of three storey buildings, the sandstone of their flat facades glowed gold in the lowering sun. A sentry in RAF uniform stood on each side on the open door, both eyed the scruffy arrival with professional hostility.

'Let me show you in, sir,' the driver said, walking past the sentries and through the door. Bryan followed him in, squinting against the dimness of the interior. As his eyes adjusted, he saw the driver leaning over a desk, talking with a secretary. The woman turned her head to look at Bryan and a smile filled with warm sympathy softened her features. Bryan swallowed against a sudden swell of reactive emotion and lurched a few short steps to sit on one of the wooden chairs that stood against the wall next to the desk.

'I'll leave you to it, sir,' the driver called as he crossed to the door. 'Good luck.'

Bryan watched the man go, then turned to the secretary.

'Yes, sir. The rescued pilot.' She was speaking into the telephone handset pressed against her ear.

Bryan scanned her face as she listened to the responding voice on the line. After his involuntary internment with sweaty, bearded men he was particularly drawn by the soft line of her cheek.

'Yes, sir.' She concluded the call and replaced the handset on its cradle. She turned to Bryan: 'Wing Commander Millard will see you right away,' she said.

'Is this necessary?' Bryan asked. 'I just need transport back to Malta.'

The secretary emerged from behind the desk: 'Just follow me.'

She crossed the lobby to a corridor on the far side. Bryan hauled himself upright and limped after her. They walked past several doors, then she paused outside one and turned again to Bryan.

'Would you like me to bring you some tea?' she asked in a low voice.

'Tea?' Bryan said.

She nodded: 'Tea.'

'I suppose that would be nice.'

Her smile flashed again. She knocked, waited for the short response from within, and then swung the door open for him to enter.

Bryan stepped into the office and stiffened to attention in front of the large desk that stood squarely in the centre of the floor. The wing commander, sitting behind the desk, looked up.

'Relax and sit down' – he glanced at a note on his jotter – 'Hale, isn't it?'

'Yes, sir' – Bryan sank gratefully into the chair – 'Flight Lieutenant Bryan Hale, Falcon Squadron, stationed in Ta'Qali, Malta.'

'And quite the Houdini, I understand.' Millard's eyes crinkled at his own wit. 'Damned unlikely escape you've pulled off.'

'I'm very relieved and thankful to everyone,' Bryan said. 'But my main concern is to get back to my squadron on Malta.'

The office door opened and the secretary came in holding a tray with two cups on saucers. She put one on the desk and handed the other to Bryan. He grasped the edge of the saucer with both hands and nodded his thanks. The secretary left the room, and a tremor that he had not previously noticed began quietly rattling Bryan's cup against its saucer.

'I understand your compulsion, of course,' Millard said. 'But let me explain why that's not going to happen.'

'Sir?' Bryan lowered his tea to rest on his thighs so he could brace the crockery into silence.

'Our American friends have expressed some concerns' – the officer's face sagged to demonstrate the gravity of the situation – 'about the British Army, unfortunate as that may sound. You see, the Americans are running a thousand tons of equipment by rail every day out of an Iranian port north into southern Russia to support the Russian army's resistance against the Nazi invasion. The security of this supply route depends on us holding on in the desert.

'It's been back and forth across Libya for a while now. Recent intercepts suggest that the Germans will launch a big offensive at some point very soon. Regrettably, the Americans aren't confident the Eighth Army can stop it. I understand Whitehall have sent a new chap, Montgomery I think his name is, to put some stiffeners on the whole show. But it remains the American view that only air reinforcements can arrive in time, so it's only an overwhelming combined air force that can carry the day.'

'I can understand that, sir,' Bryan said. 'But with respect, my squadron is in Malta, and my loyalties lie with them.'

The wing commander pursed his lips and regarded Bryan with a solemnity that flirted with sadness. He picked up his teacup and took a sip.

'It's a well-known fact that in Malta there are generally more fit pilots than serviceable planes,' he said. 'The Americans are pouring planes into Egypt every day. This means *we* are far more likely to run out of pilots.'

Bryan inhaled to answer but was silenced by Millard's raised palm.

'Losing the Middle East' – he lowered his hand back to his jotter – 'would be as catastrophic as the fall of France. Losing that rail link to Russia would condemn us to re-fighting the Battle of Britain every summer for the next three years, with every consequence that would bring to British cities. And Malta would be lost to the Italians. I'm afraid you're staying where you're needed.'

Bryan shoulders sagged in weary defeat. He looked down at the crockery in his lap, the white saucer gleamed incongruously clean against his stained trousers. He lifted the cup to his lips, taking a sip of the lukewarm liquid to relieve the growing dryness of his mouth.

'You'll at least let my squadron know that I'm alive?' he asked.

'Of course.' The wing commander nodded and made a note. 'You'll have a few days in Cairo before we can send you up the line. RAF officers are considered honorary members of the Gezira Sporting Club. I highly recommend their swimming pool, exceptionally agreeable. But that will be after the hospital lets you go.'

'Hospital?'

'Yes' – the older man beamed a smile – 'for a general check-up, make sure you're not harbouring anything unsavoury, all absolutely routine. The car you came in is waiting to take you there.'

Bryan stood up, placed his cup and saucer on the edge of the desk and pulled himself to attention.

'Good luck, Hale,' the wing commander said as Bryan turned as smartly as his foot allowed and left the office.

Bryan retraced his steps to the lobby where the secretary beckoned him over to her desk.

'You'll need these,' she said, handing him a sheaf of passes and a copy of *The Services Guide to Cairo*. 'Pay particular attention to the maps' – she pulled a playful grimace – 'because the areas marked in red are out of bounds for good reasons.'

'Thank you.' Bryan clutched the papers to his chest and walked out to his waiting car.

***

The tepid water dribbling from the shower head felt like the fingers of a thousand lost lovers caressing his skin. The sweat and the salt that flushed from his pores yellowed the water as it circled the drain and gurgled away through its grille. With the relaxing of his muscles came a resurgence of the fatigue that penetrated down to his joints, making the simple business of remaining upright a conscious exercise of will. He dropped the lever that shut off the shower, sending a series of knocks and rattles through the pipes as the system settled to its new equilibrium. He dried himself on a rough, grey towel, pulled on the gown he'd been left and stepped from the shower room into the corridor.

'Ah, Mister Hale.' A nurse called him from a doorway. 'In here please.'

Bryan padded down the corridor, his damp feet leaving prints that quickly evaporated away into the dense evening air. The doorway led onto a large ward and Bryan followed the nurse down the row of beds, each containing a man swathed in varying quantities of bandaging.

'This is yours.' The nurse gestured at an empty bed.

Bryan slid between the clean sheets and dropped his head onto the pillow. Through hooded eyes, he watched the nurse hang a bag of clear fluid above his head. He felt the faint sting of a needle in his arm before the tide of his exhaustion washed him away to slumber.

### Thursday, 20 August 1942

A bustle of noise dragged Bryan from his dreamless torpor. The swish and clack of opening curtains progressed along the ward and he blinked against the shafts of dazzling sunlight that flooded the room. He pulled himself up to lean against the bedhead and rubbed the dregs of sleep from his eyes.

'Good morning, Bryan.'

He looked up at the nurse standing at the foot of his bed. Locks of blonde hair curled from under her white cap, a lop-sided grin crinkled her face and her blue eyes glinted with amusement.

'Good Lord,' Bryan breathed. 'Katie Starling. What are you doing here?'

'I'm a nurse, Bryan' – Katie struggled to straighten her face – 'and this is a hospital. It shouldn't be too much of a surprise.'

She came to sit on the edge of the bed and grasped his wrist between her fingers and thumb, lifting the watch from her apron with her other hand.

'Nurses go where we're needed,' she continued, gazing at the watch. 'And it seems they're expecting something to happen in Egypt that's going to need a lot of nurses.' She let his hand drop back onto the bed. 'Pulse normal' – she raised an eyebrow – 'which is a bit disappointing. Anyway, I understand you had a little adventure out at sea, involving a parachute and a submarine.' Her smile broadened again: 'How very Bryan.'

Her grin infected him and he reached out to squeeze her hand.

'They won't let me go back to Malta, Katie.' The smile faded from his face at his restated reality. 'In a few days I'll be sent to a new squadron in the desert.'

'A few days in Cairo, eh?' Katie said. 'It's a good job I've already discovered the places that serve the best Manhattans.'

# Chapter 3

## Friday, 21 August 1942 – Cairo

Bryan awoke again to the tapping of flat heels on the wooden floor as the nurses threw back the curtains to usher in another new dawn. He pulled himself up to a sitting position and looked around the ward, flushing with a moment's embarrassment at his comparative fitness. His eyes lingered on an empty bed opposite that he felt sure was occupied when he had gone to sleep.

'Flight Lieutenant Hale?' A nurse breezed up to the bed and began to peel off the dressing around the tube in his arm.

'Yes,' Bryan answered, wincing as the nurse pulled the needle from his forearm.

'The doctor has discharged you' – she raised her eyebrows – 'and it seems that Nurse Starling has decided to adopt you.'

The ward door opened and Katie came in, clutching a brown paper package under her arm. The nurse unhooked the saline bag, treated Bryan to another arch look, and left in the other direction. Bryan rubbed the life back into his forearm and smiled a greeting at Katie.

'They've set me free,' he said as Katie reached his bed. 'How do I get my clothes back?'

'You don't,' Katie answered. 'They were rank and I've thrown them away.' She dropped the package onto the bed. 'That's a new shirt, linen trousers and underwear.'

'Gosh, that's kind of you.' Bryan tore open the package, grabbed the underwear and wriggled into them under the covers. 'Are you not on duty?' he asked.

'No, Three days on and three days off.' She smiled. 'Your luck just seems to get better.'

Bryan swung his legs out of the bed and pulled on the trousers.

'You think so?' He buttoned up the shirt and pulled his grubby desert boots out from under the bed. 'I still need to find somewhere to stay.'

'Well, it seems Cairo Kate comes to the rescue again' – she gathered up the torn wrapping paper from the bed – 'I've booked you in at the Shepheard's Hotel, and I've let the RAF know that's where they can reach you. Make sure you've got all those chits and passes they gave you. We don't want you getting arrested.'

She brushed a stray cotton thread from his chest, her fingers lingering a second longer than necessary.

'Come on' – she looked down at his boots and grimaced – 'we need to go shoe shopping.'

'And cigarettes,' Bryan said. 'I'm dying for a smoke.'

\*\*\*

The taxi pulled up outside the hotel and Bryan and Katie clambered out.

'Crikey!' Bryan breathed.

One whole side of the street was filled by the Shepheard's Hotel, buffered from the road by meticulously manicured rectangular plots filled with clipped shrubs and small palms. At the centre of the imposing four-storey edifice was a grand entrance with a covered porch than ran out to the pavement, and the whole building enjoyed a commanding view west over the river.

'I remembered you were used to living in a palace on Malta,' Katie said. 'I didn't want to think of you slumming it in Cairo.'

'It looks like it might be expensive,' Bryan said.

'Ah-ha! One of the chits they gave you is for accommodation,' Katie answered. 'I told them at the front desk that you are very important. Hopefully they won't look too closely at the paperwork. Go' – she pushed him towards the entrance – 'get your room key. We've got a lot to do today.'

Bryan trotted up the steps and Katie turned to watch the traffic moving past. Her blonde hair stood out like a beacon in the strengthening sunshine, drawing long glances and lascivious grins from the passing drivers. She ignored them all.

After a few minutes, Bryan appeared at her side: 'All set,' he said. 'They seemed happy enough.'

'Good,' Katie said. 'Let's go shopping.'

\*\*\*

They sat at a small table deep in the cool interior of the café. A number of paper bags cluttered the floor around their feet. Their meal was finished and they sipped at glasses of acidic white wine, and smoked fragrant Egyptian cigarettes.

'Please keep a tally of what you've spent on me,' Bryan said. 'I'm sure my pay will catch up with me at some point. I will reimburse you, I promise.'

Katie waved a dismissive hand in the air between them: 'It's what friends are for.' She stubbed out her cigarette and looked up at Bryan. 'What happened to you exactly, out there?'

Bryan twisted his face into a rueful grimace: 'I was stupid enough to break the rules; it's as simple as that. I lost my temper and while I was busy seeing red, someone came up behind me and shot my engine to pieces,' Bryan said. 'I ended up bobbing about in the Med with a sore foot. You know the rest.'

'You're certainly playing by the rules now, Bryan,' Katie said.

'What do you mean?' Bryan flushed slightly at the change in direction.

'You've been a perfect gentleman all day,' Katie said. 'Which is a bit strange, considering we used to be lovers.'

Bryan's flush deepened: 'Things have moved on, Katie,' he said. 'We're different people.'

'Are we?' She leaned forward slightly, enjoying his discomfiture. 'Are you still in love with that woman?'

Bryan stayed quiet and Katie lit a fresh cigarette in the silence.

'Who *was* she?' Katie blew smoke across the table. 'Just out of interest.'

'She was an assistant journalist at the newspaper in Valletta,' Bryan said.

Katie leaned back in her chair: 'Was it the woman on the balcony?' Katie's hand flew to her mouth. 'So, *Habib* did mean darling, after all!'

'It didn't at that time.' Bryan's gaze dropped. 'But it was about to. And it would've, if I'd made it back to Malta.'

'Oh,' Katie breathed. 'You might not ever get back to Malta, now. And if things go badly in north Africa...' She let the thought languish in the space between them.

'Still' – she shared the last of the wine between their glasses – 'at least it shows that God has a sense of humour: Tearing you away from your sweetheart. Getting you rescued against all the odds, and then dumping you in a bed right in front of me!'

Bryan looked up into her face: 'You'd think he had more than enough to occupy him at the moment.'

'Listen, Bryan.' – Katie stubbed out her half-smoked cigarette, reached across and covered his hand with hers – 'The last week has been a real bruiser for you, and who knows how things will turn out when you get sent into the desert. But, cast your mind back. Do you remember when I left your room at Xara for the last time, I told you I knew that you were with

27

me only because you couldn't be with her? Well, it seems you still can't be with her.' She squeezed his hand with a gentle pressure. 'But take a look at who you're with.'

'I can see that very well.' Bryan smiled and withdrew his hand. 'May I see you tomorrow as well?'

***

Bryan followed the signs up the stairs to his floor, then sought out his room number along a corridor lined with shiny, panelled doors. He unlocked his door, elbowed his way in and dumped his shopping bags on the bed. He glanced around at the elegantly appointed room, with its fine cotton bedclothes, classical mouldings and hand-carved Egyptian writing desk. He stepped over to the window and moved the net curtains aside with a finger to better see the traffic drifting past in the gathering twilight between the hotel and the dark mass of the slow-moving Nile. The faint taste of powder and perfume lingered on his lips from the kiss he'd placed on Katie's cheek as they parted outside the café. The warmth of her breath lingered like a memory in his nostrils. He let the curtain slip back and resolved to go in search of a night cap.

He locked his door, retraced his steps to the lobby and followed a sign to the lounge bar. The oak-panelled room was large, but still managed to appear cluttered by the number of leather armchairs clustered in twos and threes around small, glass-topped tables. Many of the chairs supported staff officers of all stripes. Intermingled with them, earnest men in linen suits sat alone, smoking cigarettes and watching people pass with an air of practised disinterest. Their cigarette smoke mingled with that of cigars and pipes and drifted upwards to dissipate amongst the chandeliers that hung from the high ceiling.

Bryan headed to the bar and ordered a large whisky, charged it to his room and drifted through the forest of chairs to a long console table that bore sheafs of English newspapers. He picked up the newest copy of The Times he could find and weaved back to an empty chair. Sitting down, he nodded in greeting to a naval officer seated across the table. The man looked him up and down in appraisal.

'Good news about Malta,' he said. 'At least for now.'

Bryan let his paper drop into his lap: 'I've been a bit out of the loop. What's happened?'

'That tanker, *The Ohio*, made it into harbour.' The officer nodded slowly. 'It's put back their surrender date by a good few months.'

'Really? That is good news,' Bryan said. 'It didn't look like it would get that far.'

The other man narrowed his eyes: 'How do you know what it looked like?'

'Ah!' Bryan shook his head and lifted up his newspaper. 'That's a long story.'

### Saturday, 22 August 1942

Bryan walked down the last few stairs and paused in the lobby, casting his eyes around the wicker chairs and tables arranged around its walls. A flash of blonde hair across the room dragged his gaze to lock eye-to-eye with Katie. He smiled with a mixture of pleasure and relief, and crossed the lobby towards her.

'I wasn't sure you'd show up,' he said, brushing her cheek with a kiss.

'Neither was I,' she answered, stepping back to appraise his new clothes. 'Does this place serve breakfast?'

They walked through to an open courtyard arranged with tables covered by white tablecloths that gleamed in the morning sunshine. A waiter noted Bryan's room number and guided them to an empty table.

Katie studied Bryan's face as he read the menu.

'You seem brighter today,' she said.

'Things aren't as bad as I thought.' He dropped the menu onto the table. 'Parts of the supply convoy got through to Grand Harbour. What old Millard said is true: If we can win in Libya, then Malta will survive. My squadron have been told that I'm alive. So, this whole thing is nothing more than a temporary, if inconvenient, posting. If I keep asking, they'll send me back eventually.'

'So… What exactly has gone on with this woman?' Katie asked. 'Are you lovers?'

'No.' Bryan picked up the menu again and furrowed his brow in feigned interest.

'What, then?' Katie pressed.

'Friends,' Bryan said, still intent on his culinary options. 'Good friends.'

'I see.' Katie picked up her own menu. 'I see.'

\*\*\*

29

They walked the length of the covered porch and stepped on to the pavement and into the strengthening sun. A groundsman sprinkled water onto the beds in front of the building. He choked the end of his hose with his thumb to flatten the spray, causing rainbows to dance in the mist around his hands.

'I've been to Cairo before, you know,' Bryan said as they strolled north along the pavement, pacing themselves in the developing heat.

'As a tourist?' Katie asked.

'Hardly,' Bryan said. 'I was posted here with the RAF at the tail-end of '35. That was the last time the Italians decided to get shirty in Africa. But, in between everything else, I managed to absorb a little of the culture.'

They came to a bridge that carried the road west to the sinuous island of Gezira, that forced the river to split in two to flow around its mass. On either side of the roadway, as it crested onto the bridge, stood a huge statue of a lion. Each monolithic Panthera sat staring straight ahead with an impassive solemnity.

'For instance,' – Bryan paused and gestured up at the statues – 'legend has it that these chaps break into a smile when a virgin crosses the bridge.'

Katie frowned at the lions: 'I'm perfectly happy on this side of the river, thank you.' She crossed the road and continued north. Bryan hurried to catch up.

'I need to get a watch,' Bryan said as he drew level with her. 'Mine went rusty.' He wrung his face into an apologetic grimace: 'And a suitcase.'

Katie threw him a sidelong glance: 'You, Mr Hale, are shameless.'

They veered off the riverside road into a tangle of crowded streets that branched innumerable narrow alleyways that divided the dilapidated tenements. The doorways of these lumpen buildings sheltered patient artisans, squatting next to piles of their produce: woven baskets, hand-stitched rugs, earthenware pottery, fabrics, and trinkets in copper and bronze. Crowds milled through the constricted thoroughfares; Arab men in striped djellabas mingled with Sikhs wearing turbans of single, shockingly bright colours. These local men, keen to be about their business, dodged around sightseeing soldiers in British and Australian uniforms. Occasionally the press of bodies parted for a tradesman pushing a loaded handcart, or an old man riding a donkey-drawn trap. The heat stifled between the dusty walls and attenuated the scents of human sweat and warm animal skin.

'Sir, sir!' A young boy tugged at Bryan's shirt. 'You buy my amber grease.'

He held up an apple-sized chunk of what looked like grey wax loosely wrapped in a fragment of sacking. The scent from the object cut through the general fug, tingling with citric acidity in Bryan's nostrils.

'What's it for?' he asked.

'It make you into powerful lover.' The boy signed a chef's kiss in front of his lips. 'Make fair lady very happy. Very, very happy!'

'No, thank you!' Katie said. 'No sale. Go home, you rude boy!'

The lad dashed away in search of fresh prospects.

'That was a bit harsh,' Bryan said.

'If I thought you needed it' – Katie levelled her narrowed eyes at Bryan's face – 'I would've bought it for you.'

They drifted east and emerged onto a wider road. The sun lanced down on them as they stepped from the narrow lane's shade. Katie pulled a pair of sunglasses from her pocket and wiped a bead of perspiration from the side of her nose. She looked up and down the road.

'I recognise where we are,' she said. 'There's a bar just down here, Groppi's Garden I think it's called. Best whisky sours in Cairo.'

They found the bar and slid into its dim coolness with a shiver of pleasurable relief. They chose a table beneath a dust-caked ceiling fan and a waiter took their order and delivered their drinks.

'They hold a dance at The Shepheard's every Saturday night,' Katie said, taking a sip from her drink. 'I say 'dance', it's probably grand enough to be a ball. It might be fun if you wanted to let your hair down a bit.'

Bryan shrugged: 'I suppose…'

'We'll need to drop by the nurse's accommodation.' She wriggled her shoulders and pulled her sweat-dampened blouse away from her sternum. 'I'll need to change.'

'I don't know,' Bryan said. 'This all seems very strange… with everything that's happened…'

'You're still alive, Bryan' – she clinked her glass against his – 'Get used to it.'


## Xara Palace, Malta

Ben Stevens sat at a table in the dining room. A mug of weak tea grew tepid next to his elbow as he scanned the front page of the island's newspaper. The adjutant walked in and sat down opposite him. The man removed his cap and scratched briefly at his sweaty hairline.

'I have news,' he said.

Ben glanced up, then looked back to the paper: 'Uh-huh.'

'Flight Lieutenant Hale is alive!'

Ben dropped the paper: 'What? That's wonderful. Where is he? The hospital? I'll go-'

'Egypt,' the adjutant interrupted. 'We just heard from Cairo, AOC's office. A submarine stumbled across him and took him on to Alexandria. It seems they're hanging on to him there for a while.'

'Hanging on to him? That's not fair. His place is here, being our squadron leader. Still, it's by far the best news I've had in...' His voice trailed off and his face darkened: 'Oh, my days,' he muttered. 'I told his girlfriend he was dead.'

### Nurses' Accommodation, Cairo

Bryan stood on the pavement eyeing the spluttering tip of his Egyptian cigarette. He took one last draw, feeling the rough smoke dry the surface of his teeth and tossed the butt away into the gutter.

'Sorry it took me so long.' Bryan turned at the sound of Katie's voice to see her descending the steps of the residence hall.

'I thought you were going to change,' he said.

Katie held up a small suitcase: 'I'm not walking through Cairo in my party dress,' she said. 'You *do* have a bathroom at the hotel, don't you?'

***

Bryan unlocked the door and swung it open for Katie to enter.

'Oh,' Katie cooed. 'Nice room.'

She kicked off her shoes and padded across the rug to the bathroom.

Bryan dragged the chair from the writing desk across to the window, sat down and lit another cigarette. Behind him the gush of water into the bathtub underpinned Katie's soft humming. Bryan held his hand out in front of his face. The cigarette lodged between his fingers betrayed no sign of the cup-rattling tremor that had afflicted it just three days before.

The water stopped running and Bryan let Katie's aimless tune wash over him as he watched the passers-by stroll along the pavement next to the world's most famous river. Every one of them a stranger, passing into his vision and then out of his life.

'Damn!' The quiet curse came from the bathroom. 'Bryan!' This louder. 'I don't have a towel.'

Bryan stood and lifted the chair back to its place, stubbed out his cigarette in an ashtray and crossed the room to a white-painted wardrobe that stood against the wall. He pulled a soft cotton towel from the stack inside and opened the bathroom door.

A delicate tracery of steam rippled against the ceiling, and Katie reclined in the tub her arms crossed against her breasts for modesty. Bryan approached the tub and held out the towel in outstretched arms. Katie stood and Bryan wrapped the towel around her shoulders, squeezing her soft form to his chest. Katie looked into Bryan's eyes, their noses brushed for a moment, and then Bryan kissed her warm, wet lips, lifted her from the bath and carried her to his bed.

### Sunday, 23 August 1942

Bryan awoke early, roused by the light admitted by the undrawn curtains. He slipped carefully from the bed and gathered his clothes from the floor. Reflections of the rising sun flared back at him from windows across the river and he felt a sudden urge to be outside in the transient freshness of the Egyptian dawn. He went into the bathroom, splashed some water on his face and brushed the roughness from his teeth.

Bryan picked up *The Services Guide* from the writing desk and crossed to the door. He paused and looked back at Katie in the bed. Her breathing was steady and deep. The single cotton sheet that covered her moulded closely to her naked form beneath, and the memory of her singular passion brought a warm buzz of pleasure to his belly. He slipped out and closed the door quietly behind him.

Out on the street, the cool air from the river flowed over him like the breath of rejuvenation. He flipped through the guidebook and stumbled upon the section listing churches. Unbidden, his father's visage flashed into his mind's eye. He wondered what fire and admonishment the old man was steeling himself to deliver from his own pulpit in London this very morning to his cowering congregation of sinners and adulterers. An invasive memory of Katie's smooth skin slicked with the sweat of exertion banished the reverend's scowl from his head. Smiling at the dichotomy, Bryan checked the address of the English church and set off north along the river. He crossed the bridge under the uncaring gaze of the lion statues and continued north, enjoying the river breeze until he had to veer away from the bank in search of the Anglican church.

All Saints Cathedral was small for its title; it was certainly no bigger than his father's church in Hampstead. Its simple, pale edifice supported an elegant tower cloven by three vertical slits that allowed the piercing blue of the Cairo sky to alleviate the brutal blandness of the unadorned stone. Across the building's frontage, a tiled porch ran like a cloister, gifting its shade to the congregation that now streamed from the wide arched entrance, replete with the communion they had just received, happy and absolved.

Bryan hung around on the other side of the road, smoking a cigarette, until the last of the stragglers emerged. Then he crossed to the cathedral and slipped into its cool interior. The building's austere facade found its echo inside. Rows of simple wooden pews filled the floor in front of an altar covered in an embroidered silk cloth. Bryan took a seat on one of the nearest pews, closed his eyes and leaned his head back as the beads of sweat on his forehead chilled in the stone-cooled air.

'You've just missed communion' – the voice behind Bryan was accompanied by footsteps on the tiled floor – 'and morning prayer doesn't start until eleven o'clock.'

Bryan opened his eyes as a man sat down on the pew across from him.

'But I'll be happy to pray with you now, if it helps.'

The man wore a cotton surplice over an army uniform.

'I'm a volunteer helper,' he offered as clarification.

'That's very kind of you,' Bryan said. 'But my father is a vicar, so I've had the full tour of praying in all its forms.'

'Ah. Then forgive me for the intrusion.'

'You're not intruding.' Bryan smiled apologetically. 'The truth is, I don't really hold to a faith, so I don't really feel the need to pray.'

'Ah, I see.' The man nodded thoughtfully. 'Do you not think that might be an unnecessary risk to be taking, especially as there are hundreds of tanks and trucks not too far away to the west that are full of Germans whose intent is to send you on your way to meet your maker at their first opportunity?' The man swivelled to sit straight on the pew, directing his serene gaze towards the altar.

'I'm afraid I don't follow your argument,' Bryan said.

'You said you don't believe in God.' The man turned his head to regard Bryan. 'If the Germans do get to kill you, and you are right, and there is really no God, then nothing worse can happen to you. But' – the man pulled a sickly grin – 'if you're wrong… Suddenly, there you are, standing naked before God's Judgement with not one single plausible excuse as to why you denied His Glorious Divinity.'

The man turned his gaze back to the altar and a moment's silence coagulated in the cool air.

Bryan cleared his throat: 'Am I to understand that you do all this' – he gestured at the altar, the candles and the silver cross that stood upon it – 'as part of a gamble? You're hedging your bets because you're scared of being wrong, rather than being absolutely sure that you're right?'

A twitch flicked across the man's features but he did not answer.

Bryan stood up to leave, paused, and rested a hand on the man's shoulder: 'I'm not sure it's me that needs saving.'

### Valletta, Malta

Ben trudged the same route from the bus stop by the harbour, up over the gentle tumescence of the shattered city towards St Augustine's church on the northern flank of the capital. The bus had arrived late, so services were already underway and the streets of the city were mostly empty, the inhabitants having packed into any churches that had thus far escaped catastrophic bomb damage. Ben measured his pace to a stroll as the sun climbed to its strength-sapping zenith, narrowing the bands of shade cast by the buildings and broken walls past which he walked.

He arrived at St Augustine's and sat down on the stone steps. The leaden metre of voices joined together in hymnal singing oozed beneath the closed doors. Ben closed his eyes and let the soporific melody wash over him, drifting into a snooze under the blanket of the midday warmth.

The sharp clack of the door latch dragged him back to the present and he stood, brushing dust from the seat of his trousers, as the congregation spilled from the doorway and flowed around him. A thrill of expectation buzzed in his stomach at how his good news would erase the woman's unnecessary grieving as he searched the moving mass for Jacobella's fine-featured face and mane of dark hair.

The flow of worshippers slowed and guttered. Ben spun on his heel and scanned the retreating backs in case he'd missed her in the crush. But the elderly couples and bustling families were not harbouring Jacobella; her gracile stride did not step amongst them.

Ben climbed the steps and slipped into the church, pausing momentarily while his eyes adjusted to the gloom. The priest bustled around in front of the altar, clearing away the remains of the communion he'd just administered. Ben walked up the aisle towards him.

'Excuse me,' he called softly.

The priest paused in his work and turned to regard Ben. He remained silent, only his steady gaze indicated he was listening.

'I'm looking for someone,' Ben continued. 'I have some important news for her, and I know she comes to this church.'

The priest's eyebrow arched slightly, inviting more.

'I only know her Christian name,' Ben said. 'It's Jacobella.'

The priest's features darkened and he turned back to his task.

'She is no longer a part of this church,' the priest muttered. 'I'm sorry.'

'Do you know where I can find her?' Ben asked.

The priest placed the silver platter and goblet back onto the altar cloth and paused for moment with his back still turned, his head dropping slightly with his effort to contain his annoyance. Once composed, he turned again to face Ben.

'I do not know. I cannot say.' He held his hands out as if in supplication. 'Perhaps she has been killed. So many have been killed. Perhaps she is amongst their number.' He gestured to the now-empty pews. 'I have a congregation. They are my responsibility. The church must concern itself with ministration to the living. I'm sorry I cannot help you.' He turned back to the altar. 'Good day.'

'Is there anyone else that might know–'

'I said, I cannot help you. Good day!'

The priest picked up the platter and goblet, bowed to the altar and moved briskly across the stone floor and through the vestry door.

Ben retraced his steps to the church door and stepped out into the dispassionate glare of the sun, his previous excitement now doused with melancholy. He glanced up and down the road, but the congregation had fully dispersed; there was no-one left to ask. He hung his head and trudged back towards the bus stop.

# Chapter 4

## Monday, 24 August 1942 – Cairo

Bryan started awake at the knocking on the door. Next to him, the bed was empty. A note lay on the pillow. He picked it up and read it: *Back on shift this morning. See you tonight. K.*

The knocking repeated, louder and more insistent.

'Yes, yes, yes,' Bryan called. He swung out of the bed, pulled on the trousers that lay on the floor and went to open the door. A young porter stood outside holding a silver dish upon which a folded telegram rested. He thrust the dish forward and Bryan took the telegram. The boy did not retract the dish, but looked expectantly at Bryan.

'Um' – Bryan patted his trouser pockets in pantomime – 'I have no cash. I'm sorry.'

He closed the door on the porter and unfolded the telegram: *Report RAF HQ immediately. Do not delay.*

'Shit,' he muttered. 'Here we go again.'

***

Bryan sat on a chair against the wall of the lobby and watched the secretary typing a letter. The raucous ring of her telephone overpowered the clatter of the typewriter's strikers and both fell silent as she lifted the handset and listened for a moment.

'Yes, sir.' She replaced the handset and looked across to Bryan. 'Do you remember which office is the Wing Commander's?' she asked.

Bryan nodded, stood and walked across to the corridor. The staccato hammering of the typewriter recommenced behind him. He found the office door and knocked once before entering.

'Ah, Hale.' Millard looked up from behind his desk. 'I've got you a posting.'

Bryan approached the desk and stood awkwardly to attention.

'You're off to join the Special Maintenance Group at Aboukir, just outside Alexandria.'

'Maintenance?' Bryan's face dropped.

'They're doing some experimental work with Spitfires.' The officer tapped the side of his nose. 'Can't say anything more, but rest assured, it's bound to be important stuff. Your long experience flying Spits makes you perfect for the job.'

He pushed an envelope across the desk: 'That's a reissued paybook and a letter confirming your secondment. Draw new desert uniform from the quartermaster here, and once you're set, the secretary will arrange your transport.'

'Thank you, sir.' Bryan retrieved the paybook, saluted and went in search of the quartermaster.

\*\*\*

The RAF car swung off the main northerly road from Cairo and headed north-east into the bustling streets of Alexandria. The proximity of the sea reduced the temperature by a couple of degrees and Bryan dropped the window on his side to let the cool breeze penetrate. It brought with it a mix of human and animal scents, as had laced the air in Cairo, to lightly tingle in the depths of his sinus cavity.

Exiting the eastern edge of the city, they skirted the curve of a broad bay, dog-legged inland for a short distance and clanked to a halt at the gates of what appeared to be an airfield, just as the sun dipped towards the mellowness of early evening.

Bryan clambered out, retrieved his suitcase from the rear seat and thanked the driver. He walked up to the gate and handed the secondment letter to the airman in the guard hut. The man made a brief phone call and a few minutes later a man on a bicycle rode towards the gate, curling a plume of dust behind him.

'Flight Lieutenant Hale,' the man called as he approached. 'Welcome!'

Skidding to a halt, he dismounted and presented his hand to shake: 'I'm the technical lead here at Special Maintenance. My name's Desmond White, most people call me Snowy.'

The two men began walking back up the track into the station, Snowy pushing his dust-caked bicycle by his side.

'HQ gave me the heads-up over the telephone,' he said. 'I understand you have much experience on Spitfires. That's perfect for us.' He smiled broadly. 'We're working exclusively on Spitfires here.'

'Working on them?' Bryan asked. 'In what way?'

'Let's get you settled in your digs and I'll explain over supper.'

\*\*\*

The airfield had a solid air of permanence about it; wooden buildings outnumbered tented structures. Two small hangars dominated the skyline along the side of a wide, sand-coloured landing-strip. As the two men walked from the accommodation block to the mess hall, the sun was diving behind the ancient city a couple of miles to the west.

Inside they picked up plates of fried bully beef and reconstituted mashed potato, and found an empty table. Bryan chewed on the dry fibrous meat and pushed the potato mass around with his fork to extract the worst of the lumps.

'So,' he said around a mouthful of food. 'What's it all about?'

A steward placed a jug of water and glasses on the table, and Snowy poured himself a drink.

'Have you heard of the Junkers 86?' he asked.

Bryan shook his head.

'It was supposedly designed as a commercial passenger plane. But the Germans have modified it as a high-altitude bomber.'

Snowy took a forkful of the fried meat, chewed and grimaced.

'Then some bright Luftwaffe spark had an idea,' he continued. 'They realised that without a bomb load it could claw its way to an even greater altitude and, hey presto, you've got yourself an untouchable reconnaissance aircraft, way beyond the ceiling of any standard fighter.

'Our best intelligence is that they have two, perhaps three, of these aircraft in Tunisia. They're sending one across every day, and like clockwork, accurate bombing raids and artillery strikes follow later that evening. Our work is focussed on getting a Spitfire tuned to the point that it can get up to their altitude, or at least close enough to scare them off.'

'What altitude are we talking about?' Bryan asked.

'Over forty thousand feet,' the other man replied. 'We suspect it could be up to forty-six thousand feet under perfect conditions.'

Bryan laid down his fork and poured himself a glass of water.

'A Spitfire will choke out at thirty-eight thousand tops,' Bryan said.

'Yes,' Snowy said. 'So, you see our problem.'

### Cairo

Katie trotted up the steps and hurried through the lobby of the Shepheard's Hotel. She climbed the stairs two-at-a-time and scampered along the corridor. Stopping, slightly breathless, she knocked on Bryan's door.

'Who is it?' A man's voice she didn't recognise.

'I'm visiting Bryan' – Katie frowned in confusion at the number on the door – 'isn't this his room.'

'No-one here by that name,' the voice replied.

'Oh,' Katie said softly. 'I'm sorry. Forgive me.' She walked slowly back along the corridor to the staircase.

### Tuesday, 25 August 1942 – Aboukir Airfield

Despite the sluggish coastal breeze that stirred up little swirls of dust across the landing strip, the temperature was already building as the sun climbed higher into the cloudless eastern sky. Bryan was glad of the cool shade as he and Snowy walked into the hangar. In the middle of the large space stood a Spitfire. The engine and propeller were missing, and panels lay detached on trestles, but even in this disfigured condition the aircraft caused a frisson of electricity to tingle along Bryan's forearms.

'So, how far have you got?' Bryan asked as they walked across to the disarrayed fighter.

'The engine is in the workshop.' Snowy indicated a large cabin structure at the other end of the hangar. 'They're working on the cylinder heads to get the best possible compression ratio. We've acquired four-bladed propellers, and manufactured our own wing-tip extensions.'

Bryan walked to the wing's end and ran his fingers along the sharpened profile of the wing-tip, waggling the attachment between thumb and fingers to test its sturdiness.

'We've taken out the armour-plating from the cockpit, and we've removed the two cannons, leaving her with four machine guns.' Snowy pulled a mock grimace. 'Hopefully that's enough to take them down, if we can ever get close enough.'

'How high have you taken her?' Bryan asked.

'It's difficult to be sure,' Snowy answered. 'Certainly over thirty-eight thousand, possibly even a tad past thirty-nine. They're putting this one back together this afternoon, so you'll be able to take her up yourself for a test flight tomorrow.'

\*\*\*

Bryan sauntered out through the airfield gates and walked north along the road. The evening breeze that caressed his face lured him on and, after a while, the wide sweep of the bay came into view. He crossed the coast road and found a space to sit overlooking the dirty sand of the beach.

The impassive waters of the Mediterranean lapped small waves onto the shore, shifting and rearranging the flotsam landed there. He gazed westwards across the water to where, a thousand miles away over the horizon, the rocky island of Malta sat defiant and vulnerable under the German bombers. Jacobella rushed into his mind and the thought of his betrayal pricked his heart with guilt. Then Katie, sweet, kind Katie, soft and warm under his grasping, greedy hands. She deserved more than he gave and, as always, she gave more than he deserved. He dropped his head back to stare into the fathomless blue depths above him and wondered idly about the men he would soon be seeking to kill nearly eight miles up in the cold, clear sky, and how in heaven's name was he going to reach them.

### Wednesday, 26 August 1942

Bryan and Snowy walked across the airfield in the fresh dawn air. Ahead of them a group of fitters manhandled the Spitfire out of the hangar, leaning against the stabilisers and pushing the fighter backwards into the nascent daylight.

'You can take her up in a standard climb for most of the way,' Snowy said. 'When you get over thirty-six thousand, you'll need to be a bit gentler with the climb slope and, in the end, she'll make it plain when she's going no higher.'

They arrived at the Spitfire as a fitter deposited a parachute on the port wing and draped a pair of white canvas overalls and a leather flying helmet across it.

'There's cockpit heating vented in from the engine, but you'll still be grateful of these.' Snowy handed Bryan the overalls. 'Check your oxygen is on and working before you open up the heating tube.'

Bryan stepped into the overalls, pulled the helmet onto his head and swung his parachute onto his back.

'We suspect our German friends have installed pressurised cabins in the JU86,' Snowy continued. 'We have no such home comforts. So, if it gets too unpleasant, bring her down gently and keep your oxygen on until you land.'

Snowy shook Bryan's hand: 'Good luck' – he beamed a smile – 'and enjoy yourself!'

Bryan climbed into the cockpit and a fitter waited on the other wing to help him settle. Once strapped in, he closed the canopy against the dust and

41

fired up the engine. Wary that this Merlin had recently been in pieces in the workshop, he watched the gauges carefully for signs of trouble. Satisfied all was well, he snaked the short distance to the hard-packed runway, swivelled into the negligible breeze and pushed the throttles forward.

The pointed wingtips curved slightly upwards as if eager with anticipation, and the body of the craft lifted a moment later. The landing gear clonked into place and Bryan eased the throttle forward, pulling the nose up into a steady climb.

On his port side, the city of Alexandria extended away along the coast, its jumbled sandstone structures lending it the appearance of a massive crenelated beach. Beyond it, stretching out under his nose, the Mediterranean sparkled a million reflections of the strengthening sunlight. At ten thousand feet Bryan clipped his mask across his face and flipped on the oxygen feed. He watched the altimeter tick up steadily towards twenty thousand feet as he flew further out to sea.

'Halfway,' he murmured to himself.

He opened the heating vent and tilted the Spitfire into a wide bank to starboard. The seascape rotated slowly beneath him, shuffling the coastline back across his windscreen. On his port side, the verdant Nile delta smudged into an expanse of dark green. On his starboard side, the bleached-out yellow of the desert, too far away to enjoy the river's magical kiss, marched away into distant, dry haze.

The altimeter ticked on and the omnipresent roar of the engine dulled against Bryan's bulging eardrums. He squeezed his nose closed through the mask and swallowed hard until a painful pop restored the noise around him. The needle slowed its progress around the dial until it stopped, vibrating in resonance with the engine's distress, on the cusp of forty thousand feet.

Bryan waggled the control column and got very little response. The fighter hung at its extreme limit, motionless, for all practical purposes, in the meagre air. Bryan looked out at the earth. He could see the whole Nile delta laid out below him like a giant stingray, edged at its extreme horizons by its pale, arid hinterlands. He looked for a minute at this abstracted green shape into which his saved life had been thrust and where his sordid worldly concerns had recently revolved, then he eased the throttle back, allowing the stall to dip the Spitfire's nose and begin the long descent to Aboukir.

\*\*\*

Bryan peeled off the overalls and wiped the sweat from his brow with the rough white garment before throwing it onto the wing. Snowy was walking out to join him and while Bryan waited, he jiggled his jaw left and right to un-bunch the aching muscles in his cheeks and temples.

'How high did she manage?' Snowy asked.

'The altimeter was reading forty, or very close to it,' Bryan said. 'But, considering the altimeter has never been that high before, I'd sprinkle that with a pinch of salt. Although' – Bryan waggled his jaw again – 'it certainly felt like it might've been that high.'

'That's the minimum we need if we're to be in with any chance of reaching them,' Snowy said. 'Do you fancy having a go at them tomorrow?'

'No.' Bryan turned to regard the aircraft. 'I don't think so. If they see that we're getting close, they'll lose their lovely sense of security. At the moment, they believe they're untouchable. If we start wallowing about just below them, they'll get spooked and change their game.'

Bryan began to pace in a slow circle around the Spitfire, his sharp gaze flitting over its form, looking for something extra to whittle away. Snowy walked with him.

'Reconnaissance doesn't happen at night,' Bryan said. 'So, we can lose all navigation lights together with their wiring, fuses and switches.'

Snowy took a notepad and pencil from his top pocket and started scribbling.

'I reckon the Junkers is unarmed,' Bryan continued. 'They'll be escorted on their climb until the fighters can go no higher. At that point, they know they're safe. So, why bother carrying guns?'

Snowy nodded to hide his lack of comprehension at Bryan's line of thinking.

Bryan turned to him: 'So, we can remove the bullet-proof windshield and replace it with standard Perspex.'

'Ah!' Snowy's pencil scratched its way across the narrow page of his notebook.

Bryan walked around to the front of the wing. Three patches of red tape punctuated the leading edge, two over the unfired machine-guns and a larger one over the empty cannon port.

'Do we have any fifty-calibre guns?' Bryan asked.

'If not, I'm sure we could get them from the Americans,' Snowy replied.

'If they fit in the cannon bays we can lose the other guns,' Bryan said. 'Two 50s will make a bigger mess than four 303s, and they'll probably weigh a bit less. Mix ball and armour-piercing in the belts, and let's try starting with half the usual belt-length.' Bryan's eyes narrowed as he gazed down the fuselage. 'Are the tanks topped off every time she lands?'

'I suppose they must be,' Snowy said. 'It's standard procedure.'

Bryan leaned against the fuselage and lit a cigarette.

'We know approximately how far we're flying and how high we're going,' he said. 'So, we can work out how much fuel we need for the round trip. I'm sure it will be a lot less than a full tank.'

Snowy licked the end of his pencil and flipped to a fresh page. Bryan waited for Snowy to finish writing and look up, then he pointed to the radio mast behind the cockpit.

'Get rid of the wireless set,' he said. 'That also allows for a smaller battery to be installed for everything else.'

A frown creased Snowy's brow: 'If you've got no wireless, you can't receive vectors,' he said.

'Ah!' a broad smile split Bryan's face. 'We need to make my Spitfire as skinny as we can.' He stroked his palm possessively across the fuselage. 'When we're scrambled to intercept, we take off as a pair. You get the vectors and I simply follow you. Once we get visual contact, I'll climb to engage. You'll stooge about ready to have your pop when I've forced him down.'

'Crikey,' Snowy said as he scanned his notes. 'Is that everything?'

Bryan turned and placed both palms on the Spitfire's body: 'Sand off the paint.'

'Paint...' Snowy echoed as he wrote.

'I shall fly with only a reserve parachute, and' – Bryan turned back to face Snowy – 'I shall be sure to have a shit before reporting for duty.' He waggled his jaw again and pressed his fingers into the sides of his neck, grimacing at the pain that still throbbed there. 'How long will all that take?'

'Two days at least, I would think,' Snowy replied.

'Excellent,' Bryan said. 'Let's go and see if the mess has any beer.'


**Thursday, 27 August 1942**

Bryan and Snowy looked on at the bustle of airmen working on and around the Spitfire. Panels lay about on the hard-packed floor as men dismounted the machine guns and wrapped them in oiled rags. A man leaned into the cockpit, examining loops of cables to find those that ran to redundant switches before he snipped them through and stripped them out. All this was backdropped by the dull scratching of glasspaper against metal as two men rubbed away the brown and sand camouflage paintwork.

'Everything seems to be ticking along here,' Snowy said. 'Do you fancy a jaunt into Alex'?'

'Yes,' Bryan said. 'Watching all this hard work has made me a bit thirsty.'

The two men left the hangar and walked across the airfield to the mess. An old staff car that served as the station runabout was parked there, keys dangling in the ignition. Hot air belched from the interior as they climbed in. They dropped the windows and Snowy hastened to start the engine and get rolling.

An airman emerged from the guard-hut and lifted the barrier. Snowy turned north and headed towards the coast road.

As they motored, Bryan ran through a sketchy summary of his RAF career. As he spoke, his mood flattened slightly under the weight of what he'd been through. He paused often, sidestepping a memory or dodging the need to voice a name.

The car entered the city and Snowy cruised along the elegant seafront. Bryan lapsed into silence and lit a cigarette, staring with detachment at the sand-coloured buildings punctuated by the grey-trunked palm trees that lined the road. Snowy turned left off the coast road into the body of the elongated city. Drawing to a halt in a side-road, he killed the engine and extracted the keys.

'Still thirsty?' he asked.

Bryan cracked a half-smile: 'Yes. Always.'

The two men clambered out of the car and Snowy led the way, pausing often to peer around junctions to get his bearings. Within a few minutes they arrived at the steps of the Cecil Hotel.

'When searching for entertainments in Alexandria, the more discerning gentleman' – Snowy gestured up the steps – 'generally starts here.'

Inside, the bar was not yet busy. The air circulated like warm soup, driven by large wood-framed wickerwork ceiling fans that rotated with a leisurely restraint befitting the large opulent space. The room was oak-panelled, carpeted in blood-red, and populated almost exclusively with buttoned leather armchairs. Waiters in white jellabas and red felt fezzes hovered in expectation around the walls, but the two men chose to order and drink at the bar. Snowy perched himself on a barstool while Bryan remained standing, hunched with his elbows on the copper bar-top, watching the beads of condensation trickling down the side of his ice-cold beer.

'I'll admit' – Bryan did not look up from his glass – 'that right from my very first solo flight I just wanted to get into a scrap with other people in planes. I'm not like that on the ground.' He paused for reflection. 'Well, I did have a punch up with a sailor once, but he very definitely started it. No, for me, combat is the purest form of competitive flying. So, I was really quite stoked when old Chamberlain came on the radio and announced we were at war' – Bryan took a swig of his beer and turned to look at Snowy – 'but I really didn't think it would go on this long.'

'It can't last forever,' Snowy said. 'The Americans are chucking in tons of equipment now, and the Russians are soaking up the German army at a hell of a pace. I suspect we'd have to try quite hard to lose it now.'

'It's all got a lot bigger than I expected it to,' Bryan returned his gaze to his beaded glass. 'I used to feel like I had some level of control over things, but that's all gone to pot. If it weren't for an outrageous dollop of luck, right now there'd be a little shoal of Mediterranean bottom-feeders picking the last bits of dear ol' Bryan off his bones. And I can't work out whether that means I have *every* right to be alive, or none at all.'

'Perhaps you need to ask a priest,' Snowy suggested.

Bryan tapped the base of his empty glass on the bar: 'Perhaps I just need another drink.'

***

Bryan and Snowy emerged onto the steps of the hotel as the sun reddened towards western horizon. Snowy had acquired a slight sway.

'I need something to eat,' Snowy said. 'Soak up the booze a bit.' He slapped a hand on Bryan's shoulder. 'Come on, I'll take you to Mary's House, buy us some dinner.'

'Why does that sound like a brothel?' Bryan asked.

'Nah' – Snowy waved a hand in dismissal – 'it's much more than a brothel.'

They doglegged their way across the city. Snowy smiled and nodded to every local they passed. Most ignored him outright, none responded in kind. After a five-minute walk, the two men arrived outside what looked like a large residential building on the corner of a crossroads.

'It doesn't have a sign,' Bryan observed.

'It doesn't need one.' Snowy straightened his jacket, climbed the steps and knocked on the door.

Bryan followed him up as a small panel opened in the door and a pair of deep brown eyes flitted between their faces in appraisal. The panel closed and the door opened releasing a soft wave of music into the street.

Snowy and Bryan went in, walked down a short corridor and entered into a large panelled room with a staircase at the far end that led up to a balcony. A bar filled one side and along the opposite wall a low stage supported a quartet who delivered slightly tawdry music to the couples who swayed in overly close clinches on the dancefloor abutting the footlights. The rest of the room was filled with tables, and the two pilots skirted the dance floor in search of one that was free.

They sat down and Bryan picked up the menu. Snowy hooked his finger over the leather-bound card and pushed it back to the table.

'Strange as it may seem, given where we are, they do a really good liver and sausages.'

They ordered their meals and the waitress returned quickly with a label-less bottle of white wine. Bryan sipped the acidic, oily liquid and surveyed the room. The girls had an air of used elegance that belonged to an earlier age. They all wore evening dresses of varying vintage and many wielded cigarette holders. The majority were Egyptian, but some looked Turkish and a few appeared to be European, most likely French. The few that weren't dancing sat alone at tables closest to the dancefloor or circulated the occupied tables looking for an opening.

'Why were you acting like some mad uncle on the way here, provoking the natives?' Bryan asked.

'I've been out here a while,' Snowy said. 'Like any decent sort of chap, I started off being genuinely friendly. It all worked reasonably well for a while. They went on with their business and we looked after defence and foreign affairs for them. Then, when the Italians declared war, looking after their defence quickly turned into us sticking our noses into almost everything.'

The waitress brought their food and the woody smell of roasted garlic wafted into their faces.

'I can understand them being a bit put out,' Snowy continued. 'Under the circumstances, I even expected a little bit of anti-British truculence.' He chomped on a chunk of the liver and closed his eyes as the spicy offal melted in his mouth. 'But they went a bit too far.' He sawed off a piece of sausage and paused again, chewing in slow appreciation. 'At the end of last year there were pro-Hitler demonstrations' – his eyes bulged slightly at the remembered outrage – 'pro-Hitler, can you believe?'

'I can't imagine that ended well,' Bryan said as Snowy chewed in reflection on another mouthful.

'It *had* to end, whether it ended well or otherwise.' Snowy levered a shred of gristle out of his teeth with his thumbnail. 'So, in February we sent a few tanks to the palace to deliver some nicely-drafted abdication papers for King Farouk to sign.' Snowy pulled a wan grin. 'Farouk saw sense, appointed a prime minister that met Whitehall specifications and on we carry as if nothing had ever happened.'

As they came close to the end of their meal a circulating girl drifted closer to their table.

'So, I reckon' – Snowy scraped the last of the sauce from his plate with his knife and scooped it onto his tongue – 'a good half of those people I greeted in the street would be happy to see us both dangling from the nearest lamppost. So, to answer your original question: it's just a bit of a laugh, really.'

Snowy laid his knife and fork across his plate and swivelled in his chair to regard the dancefloor: 'They dance with you for the price of a drink,' he said over his shoulder.

His change of posture marked him out as free, and a girl arrived almost instantly at his shoulder. Snowy winked at Bryan, stood up and allowed the girl to lead him to the dancefloor. Two or three of the ladies made passes to the table, but Bryan diverted them with a polite shake of the head. He lit a cigarette and relaxed to watch the swaying dancers, wryly observing the liberties taken by most of the men with their wandering hands.

Snowy's meal had obviously settled his stomach and he was in the running for the best dancer on the floor. He ducked his head and spoke into his partner's ear. A few moments later she nodded, they stopped dancing and the girl led Snowy towards the staircase. She paused at a large dresser, pulled a towel from a small pile and picked a bar of soap from a wicker basket, then she trotted up the stairs with Snowy in her wake.

Bryan caught the eye of a waitress and ordered another bottle of wine.

# Chapter 5

## Saturday, 29 August 1942 – Aboukir Airfield

Snowy drifted in and out of a snooze. The engineering reports on his desk blurred and sharpened as he struggled to focus on annotations and calculations in the heat of his stifling tent-office. An orderly came into the tent and Snowy snapped awake, his attention roused by the man's eager features.

'Forward spotters are reporting a single high-flying aircraft making an incursion, it appears to be following the coastline. I've instructed the hangar crew to haul out the Spitfires ready for scramble, sir.'

'Excellent' – he picked up the reports and dumped them back into his in-tray – 'find Hale and let him know.'

The man jogged off across the landing ground and Snowy changed from his grubby shorts and desert boots to heavier canvas trousers and flying boots. He grabbed his flying helmet from a drawer in his desk and slung his jacket over his shoulder. With prickles of sweat already tickling his thighs, he walked quickly across the dusty aerodrome to where the two Spitfires stood, side by side on the wide, hard-packed runway.

Snowy's aircraft stood in its familiar brown and sand desert camouflage, the borders of the two colours blurred together by dust from the real desert borne in on the hot breeze. Beside it, the second Spitfire glinted dully, bouncing sullen reflections of the climbing sun from its bare, hazed metal skin. Stripped of all paint except its roundels and identification letters, it looked like it had reared from the nearby sea, a piscine sister, lighter and lither than its earthy sibling, ready to thrash that tiny bit higher into the sky.

Snowy pulled his jacket on and buckled his parachute straps. He climbed into the cockpit and an airmen leaned in to help with his straps.

'Where is Flight Lieutenant Hale?' Snowy asked the man.

'In the latrine, sir.' The airman twisted his head towards the wooden hut on the edge of the airfield. 'Here he comes now.'

Bryan trotted up to his fighter; the sheen of the stripped aluminium skin radiated heat onto his already sweating forehead as he clipped the small reserve parachute onto his harness. He climbed up into the cockpit and looked across at Snowy. The other man gave him a brief thumbs-up and then fired up his engine. Moments later Bryan's engine joined the racket and the two Spitfires raced together across the airfield and into the air, curling a wide spiral of dust in their wake.

They climbed hard, heading inland to achieve half the altitude they strove for before wheeling in a wide bank to continue clawing higher in their ascent to the coast. Bryan eased into position behind and below Snowy's port wing so the other's craft filled his windscreen. With no means of communicating, he could only follow along behind, trusting the other to navigate him towards his moving target.

The climb remained steep and Snowy adjusted the bearing with little nudges to starboard as he received corrections to their vector, curving them into almost an easterly course with the sea glittering on their left. After a minute of steady climbing, Snowy waggled his wings repeatedly. Using Snowy's nose as a pointer, Bryan drifted out from behind him to scan the hazy vault ahead. There, cruising serenely at the tip of a short condensation trail, he saw his target.

Bryan, still climbing, nudged his fighter onto the exact same course as his prey and studied the aircraft as he edged closer. The elongated wings, tapering evenly to end in a blunt point, were overlong for the fuselage size, reminiscent of a glider. A black cross sat on the pale-blue underside close to each wing-tip and the entire trailing edge of both wings carried a pronounced control surface. The engines sat well inboard on the widest part of the wing, as close to the fuselage as their propellers allowed. Protruding in front of the propellers the fuselage ended in a bulbous, rounded cockpit, shaped like the fat end of an egg, with a multi-paned windshield covering much of its forward curve.

Bryan grunted in satisfaction at the lack of nacelles or turrets for defensive guns and continued his stalk. The enemy crew, unaware of the approaching danger, continued to fly straight and level as Bryan drew closer.

The German plane had no vertical stabiliser. Instead, each horizontal stabiliser was abutted with a vertical panel, giving an H-shaped profile to the tail. So, as Bryan climbed into the turbulent wake of the enemy's twin engines, he had an unhindered view along the spine of the intruder. He eased up a little to clear the turbulence, lined up on the multi-faceted nose and opened fire.

Bullet strikes danced along the fuselage between the engines and walked into the Perspex of the cockpit. Shards of glittering windshield exploded like an ice-bomb, pluming backwards to patter through Bryan's propeller. An arm violently protruded through a broken pane, as if pulled by some unseen force to wedge its owner's shoulder into the narrow opening. The arm flailed for a second, then fell limp in the buffeting slipstream, either broken or lifeless.

Bryan's guns clanked into silence, his reduced ammunition load expended, and he throttled back a shade, allowing the stricken aircraft to wallow in front of him, like a wounded behemoth confused by its sudden injury. The port wing dipped for a moment, turning the craft towards the coast, then it straightened and continued in a shallow dive.

Bryan shadowed it as it descended. Snowy joined him as the altitude dropped, but made no move to attack the drifting enemy. Instead, the two Spitfires followed their beaten adversary down, escorted it beyond the coastline and circled to watch it plough into the sea, tip its tail into the air and sink beneath the waves.

*** 

The girls in Mary's House drifted past the two men, serenely detached but watchful, waiting for their good customer to finish his meal.

'It came down easier than I thought,' Snowy said.

'It's basically a defenceless cargo plane,' Bryan answered. 'A few rounds into the cockpit and the job was done.'

'Pressurised cabin.' Snowy grimaced. 'I bet that made their eyeballs bulge.' He swirled his wine around its glass watching the oily legs sinuating down the inside. 'We'll see next week if they add any guns.'

'Next week?' Bryan frowned.

'Yes, that's their normal schedule.' Snowy sipped at his wine and winked at a passing girl.

'They'll be back tomorrow,' Bryan said. 'They didn't get the intelligence they were after today, so they'll be back tomorrow.'

'What?' Snowy's eyes widened in realisation: 'Good Lord, yes, you're right. Better go easy on the vino, I suppose.'

The band drifted to the end of a slow waltz and dived into the livelier tempo of a foxtrot.

'Are you going to try one of the girls tonight?' Snowy nodded towards the dancefloor. 'It only costs a pound and they're all very clean.'

'Er, no' – Bryan pushed his plate away and lit a cigarette – 'I'll give it a miss, I think.'

Snowy paused his laden fork halfway to his mouth and regarded Bryan from under raised eyebrows: 'You're not...?'

'No,' Bryan said. 'I'm not. It's a bit more complicated than that.'

Snowy's fork completed its journey and he nodded in encouragement for Bryan to expand on the subject.

'Well, I bumped into a nurse in Cairo,' Bryan continued. 'I knew her for a time on Malta, and she's always been' – he searched for a gallant turn of phrase – 'very kind to me.'

An Egyptian girl, with her black hair pinned high, meandered past their table, the dark-blue silk of her embroidered dress reflecting the chandeliers' light like sinuating caresses across her torso. Bryan's eyes followed her passing.

'As lovely as they are' – Bryan's gaze turned back to his friend – 'they won't come close to Katie.'

Chewing on the last of his dinner, Snowy nodded sagely.

'On top of that, there's a Maltese woman that I have' – again he paused to select his words – 'feelings for.' He stubbed out his cigarette and lit a fresh one. 'I'll do all I can to get back to Malta; I need to see what she might mean to me, to my future.'

'Ah! Love,' Snowy said, casting his eyes across the dancers on the floor. 'Love and kindness.'

'I'm not judging you, Snowy,' Bryan said. 'Any red-blooded bachelor would-'

'Widower,' Snowy interrupted, his eyes still flitting between the dancing girls.

A moment of awkward silence hung between the men. Snowy turned back and took a sip from his wine.

'I'm sorry,' Snowy said. 'That wasn't fair. I should've let it pass.' He drained his glass and stood up. Two girls converged on him and he walked between them towards the dancefloor.

Bryan poured himself some more wine and settled back in his chair to wait.

## Sunday, 30 August 1942

The two Spitfires climbed south; Bryan tucked in behind Snowy's wing. The reconnaissance aircraft had indeed come. It had set off a couple of hours earlier than before, but it was now approaching along the same flight path as its ill-fated predecessor. Snowy led the tiny formation in a long slow turn and they continued their climb northwards, towards the coast and their quarry. Below them, the coastline sparkled with a border of small waves, their crests echoing the early morning sunshine like a belt studded with diamonds.

Bryan scanned the azure arch ahead of Snowy's fighter and caught the brief twinkle of sunlight on Perspex. Snowy waggled his wings but Bryan was already making his move, lofting over his leader and squeezing the throttle forward to better grip the rarefied air.

The German spy plane continued east for several minutes as he stalked closer. But today they flew without their previous presumption of invincibility, and wary eyes quickly spotted their hunter. The long, gracile port wing of the Junkers dipped and the big craft banked around to the north, heading out to sea.

Bryan curved in a slightly wider bank, hoping to preserve his rate of climb as he turned. He settled onto a parallel course out to the starboard flank of his target. He glanced down to his left to see Snowy running a parallel, but much lower, course on the intruder's port side. Bryan aimed his nose at a point ahead of the German plane, like a sportsman leading a pigeon, calculating where they would converge when he'd matched their altitude, and the chase ground on.

Bryan's Spitfire eased into range on an enemy that lacked the agility or traction to evade him. The other's pointed wingtip crept into Bryan's gunsight and he waited as the wing traversed his windscreen. As the engine slunk into his target rings, Bryan flipped off the safety and pressed the fire button. His two machine-guns juddered the Spitfire's airframe for the six seconds it took to empty his ammunition belts. Black smoke streamed from the engine and Bryan edged wide to avoid any debris that might shed from the damaged plane. As he drew level, he saw a face half-covered with an oxygen mask. The man surveyed the engine, then shifted his gaze to look at Bryan. His eyes held neither fear nor defeat, and after a moment he turned back to his controls.

Bryan blinked, then started. He looked down at his own control panel.

'Shit!'

The chase had been longer than he'd realised and his fuel gauge was creeping low. Bryan eased back on the throttle to let the big reconnaissance plane pull away from him, then dipped his nose and swooped into a shallow dive back towards the coast.

Pulling the throttle back to idle, Bryan traded his great altitude for airspeed. He kept the climbing sun on his left shoulder, his eyes flitting between his fuel gauge and the watery southern horizon. He craned his neck to look behind, hoping to see Snowy shadowing his progress, but the blue dome stood empty and cloudless.

Sweat beaded in Bryan's eyebrows and trickled down to sting his eyes. He shut off the heating tube and wiped away the perspiration with the back of his hand. A loosening of tension on the controls presaged a stall and Bryan eased the throttle forward to counter it. He swallowed down a flutter of panic and squinted at the horizon, searching for its edge to harden into the suggestion of land. He tweaked back on the throttle, using the increasing air density to counter the reduction in power, all the time scanning the furthest edge of the sea for the beach he knew was there somewhere.

A darkening in colour, a suggestion of solidity, drew a thin line between the sea and the lighter blue of the sky. Bryan gasped in relief behind his mask, letting his eyes linger as the coastline strengthened from a mere suggestion to a tenuous reality. Breathing deeply of his oxygen, he checked the fuel gauge and the altimeter. On gut feeling, he tweaked the throttle forward to reduce his rate of descent, balancing his assets as best he could. The profile of the coastline fattened with agonising lethargy as the feet dropped away below him with clockwork consistency.

Bryan shut off the oxygen, pulled off his mask and helmet, and wiped the sweat from his face. He watched the altimeter tick below comfortable bail-out height, and the fuel gauge settle at next-to-nothing, its needle bouncing delicately on the end-stop in resonance with the engine's vibration. He raised his gaze to the approaching landfall and weighed up the merits of ditching in the sea against seeking a suitable landing site on solid ground.

The engine coughed twice and sputtered to a halt. Decision made.

Bryan slid the canopy open, and eased his flaps down. Glancing from his airspeed indicator to the sea and back again, he lost height and speed in balance, just as if the gently swelling Mediterranean water was a friendly

Kentish airstrip. At the last moment he pulled back on the stick and braced himself against the instrument panel.

The silver Spitfire dipped its tailwheel into the clear water, carving a brief and narrow wake before the wings and fuselage pancaked onto the surface, surging the last of its momentum into a plume of water that cascaded out in front of the ditched craft. Bryan unhooked his seat strap and clambered out onto the port wing. Seawater gurgled with malicious glee as it forced ingress, steaming and spitting as it swilled onto the hot engine. Bryan shrugged out of his parachute harness, tossed it back into the cockpit and dived into the sea. He pulled a dozen strong strokes, then turned to tread water. The Spitfire's tail lifted as the aircraft succumbed to the inflowing water. With a final, explosive hiss of steam, the fuselage followed the mass of its engine in one last descent, the tail slicing a terminal swirl into the iridescent oil patch that marked its passing.

Bryan inflated his Mae West, checked his bearings against the sun, then settled into a steady backstroke towards the beach he knew to be somewhere in that direction.

*** 

Snowy sat behind his trestle desk absently watching the tent flap undulate in sympathy the evening breeze. Before him, loaded into his battered typewriter, the combat report remained unfinished as he mused on the words he was about to commit to paper.

From the road the sound of a heavy truck engine rumbled at the edge of his consciousness as he gazed in unfocussed ambivalence at the billowing fabric. The noise swelled briefly as the truck accelerated away into the twilight, breaking his reverie. He turned back to the typewriter and poised his hands over the keys.

'I'd say there's a fair argument for increasing the fuel load on the striker aircraft.'

Snowy jumped at the unexpected voice and looked up to see Bryan stooping through the tent flaps, his clothes laced with salt stains and his face and lips reddened with sunburn.

'Good Lord, man! I thought we'd lost you,' Snowy exclaimed. 'Where the bloody hell have you been?'

'For a bit of a swim.' Bryan slumped into the chair in front of the desk and flexed his shoulders. 'Somewhere in the region of two miles, I suspect.'

He looked imploringly at Snowy. 'Do you have any cigarettes? Mine got damp.'

'Yes, of course' – Snowy tossed his cigarettes and matches onto the desk – 'and something better.' He pulled open a filing cabinet drawer and fished out a half-bottle of whisky and a glass.

Bryan lit a cigarette and watched Snowy pour a measure of the amber liquid.

'What happened after I left?' Bryan asked.

Snowy handed him the spirits. Bryan took a sip, wincing as the liquid burned its way into his tender lips.

'I carried on tracking them,' Snowy said. 'They kept straight and level for quite a while. But when the damaged engine finally stopped, they couldn't stay above me for long.' He shrugged. 'It didn't take much to finish them off.'

A blurred memory of a face across the void intruded into Bryan's mind: 'Any parachutes?' he asked.

Snowy shook his head: 'They nose-dived straight into the sea,' he said. 'Ker-plunk and kaput.'

'So that's it,' Bryan said, leaning back in his chair. 'Job done.'

'Intelligence suggests they had three of those buses,' Snowy said. 'Why would they stop coming now?'

'Come on, Snowy. You know what sand and dust does to engines.' Bryan drained his glass and held it out for a refill. 'I'll warrant that third plane has been cannibalised for spares already. We've solved the problem. Unless and until they ship in replacements, *modified* replacements *with* gunners, we're redundant.'

'I suppose you're right.' Snowy took a slug of whisky straight from the bottle. 'Happy days!'

'Listen to me.' Bryan leaned forward in his chair. 'I was kept from going back to Malta because something big is supposed to be kicking off here. I am not going to hang about at the arse-end of Alexandria twiddling my thumbs while that happens. I want to request a transfer to a frontline airfield here on the mainland, or a passage back to Malta.'

Snowy looked into the steely eyes that shone from Bryan's puffy face: 'Yes,' he said, screwing the cap back onto the bottle. 'I'll call them first thing tomorrow.'

## Monday, 31 August 1942

Bryan pushed his empty plate away and looked in exasperation at Snowy's half-finished breakfast.

'Come on, man,' he implored. 'The sooner you make the call, the sooner I can get moving out of here.'

Snowy looked up from under a mild frown: 'Do you really think the office-dwellers in Cairo are going to answer a telephone before nine o'clock?' He shook his head and took another forkful of scrambled egg. 'You need to learn the art of relaxation,' he mumbled around his mouthful of food.

Bryan subsided into his chair and fell to picking the peeling skin from his sunburned nose.

'I'm serious, Bryan,' Snowy said. 'You've got a glittering record. I could get you lined up for a seat on the mail plane bound for the west coast, and from there a nice cruise back to Southampton. I'm sure the ministry would love to put you on the after-dinner circuit, and then send you off to run a training school somewhere in Scotland.'

'You *could*.' Bryan pinched a flake of shed skin between his fingertip and thumb, holding it in front of his face and treating it to an intense scrutiny. 'And I *would* murder you in your bed before I go.'

'Ha!' Snowy laughed, pushing away his unfinished food. 'Come on, then. Let's go and make the call.'

The two men walked out of the mess into the growing heat.

'Incidentally, why did you ask about parachutes last night?' Snowy asked.

'What you said about bulging eyes,' Bryan said. 'It struck me as a particularly nasty way to go.'

'Particularly,' Snowy agreed.

They reached the tent-office and Snowy sat down, lifted the handset and waited for the operator to connect him.

Bryan remained standing, smoking a cigarette and gazing absently out of the tent-flaps as he listened to Snowy explain the situation to headquarters. Snowy dropped into silence and the tinny vibrations of the telephone voice leaked from earpiece like the buzzing of a distant mosquito.

Then: 'I do understand you're busy, but Hale is an asset; he should be placed where he can be best used...

'A bottleneck, you say...

'No, I've heard nothing...

'Good, Lord…

'Alright. I'll wait to hear from you…'

Bryan turned to see Snowy hang up the handset, the other's face drawn with concern.

'Heard nothing about what?' Bryan asked.

Snowy looked up and blinked: 'Rommel started his advance at dawn today. They're in action at Alam el Halfa.'

'Where's that?'

'Ninety miles west from here,' Snowy said. 'It can't be *more* than ninety.'

'Then what are we waiting for?' Bryan urged.

'Orders,' Snowy said. 'Someone at HQ has to agree with your theory that there'll be no more high-level reconnaissance flights to deal with. Then someone else will have to agree to your posting, and then-'

'The bloody battle is happening now!' Bryan interrupted. 'They're on the move, coming this way, as we speak.'

'There's a defensive line with infantry, tanks and minefields.' Snowy stood up from his chair. 'We have several airfields full of far more planes than Rommel has to play with.' Snowy walked to the tent entrance. 'It's not an emergency yet. But' – he clapped his hand on Bryan's shoulder – 'I'll get the fighters we have fuelled and armed in case we have to repel boarders.'

Bryan watched Snowy walk across to the hangar. Knowing Snowy was right didn't dispel the jitters of tension that trembled up and down his legs. With a baleful glance at the silent telephone, he set off to walk out his frustration, heading towards the western edge of the airfield.

His suddenly heightened sense of being on the periphery, with no immediate sense of purpose, tipped him into introspection. His heart was lassoed from three directions as if by elastic ropes: Jacobella and her city of Valletta pulled from the north-west, Katie in Cairo pulled from the south-east, but the harshest tug was from the unseen battlefield out there somewhere in the desert to the west. Bryan sat down on the dusty earth and scanned the hard blue sky that shimmered with the building heat and considered the unusual concept of air superiority with professional relish.

The sun climbed towards midday, laying a soporific blanket of lethargy across the airfield. Bryan stood up, gingerly stretched his stiffening shoulder muscles and walked back towards the mess in search of tea and shade.

\*\*\*

'Wake up, man!'

Bryan started awake and winced against the instant stab of cramp in his neck. He peeled his cheek away from the leather back of the armchair and looked blearily into Snowy's face.

'I just got the phone call. It's been approved.' Snowy beamed at him. 'We're being posted to Landing Ground 97 to join a Spitfire squadron there.'

Bryan clacked his dry tongue against the roof of his mouth: 'We?'

'Yes, we,' Snowy said. 'I made another call to HQ when I got back from the hangar. I requested the same transfer.'

Bryan pulled his protesting spine upright in the chair, blinking the sleep from his eyes.

'So, when you're packed' – Snowy crouched down to put his face level with Bryan's – 'we can be off.'

*** 

The two pilots walked towards the old staff car, each carrying their world in a small suitcase.

'So, we're taking the car?' Bryan asked.

'Unless you want to wait for official transport,' Snowy replied. 'Which will roll up tomorrow, or the next day.'

'But it's not yours,' Bryan said.

'It's nobody's, which sort of means it's everybody's' – Snowy grinned at his companion – 'which means it's at least a little bit mine.'

They climbed into the battered old car and Snowy turned the ignition. He scanned the dash, checking the fuel gauge.

'Clear for take-off,' he muttered and pulled away.

The car exited the airfield gate and rattled along the now-familiar road towards Alexandria.

'What made you request a transfer as well?' Bryan asked.

'I realised it was time to stop running away,' Snowy replied.

Bryan looked sideways at the other man as he lit a cigarette: 'Running away from what?'

Snowy remained silent for long moments, seeking a way to begin his answer.

'My wife's name was Judith,' he began. 'Judith was pregnant with our first child when she died. Our house is in Ealing; a place not immune from the air raids, but certainly far enough away from the worst of things. It was January last year, the 8th. Judith had travelled into the city for the afternoon'

— Snowy blinked against the moisture gathering in his eyes — 'on a shopping trip for baby clothes.

'It seems, when the warning sounded, she jumped onto a westbound bus rather than get stuck in a shelter for the night. The bus was just underway, about halfway down Liverpool Street, when it took a near-as-damn-it direct hit. The bus ended up on its arse-end, leaning against a building, perforated with shrapnel. No-one survived.' Snowy cleared his throat and his features tightened against his rising emotion. 'They wouldn't let me see her,' he added quietly.

The car entered the eastern outskirts of Alexandria. Bryan watched the parade of seafront palms march past his dropped window and held his tongue, waiting for Snowy to master himself.

'Ah!' Snowy expelled a tight sigh of resurgent grief. 'I blamed myself for all of it,' he continued. 'Judith wanted to wait on starting a family. She was worried about the war, scared to bring a child into such an uncertain world. But I persuaded her it would be alright. I realise now I was keen to leave a child behind while I still could, in case something bad happened to me later. So, there she was, buying baby clothes in the centre of London.

'And I happened to be at home waiting for her; it was the second day of a three-day leave. Ordinarily, Judith would've gone to a shelter as soon as the air-raid warning sounded; she was a sensible, careful woman, especially since she'd become pregnant. I'm convinced she risked the bus-ride to avoid wasting a night of my leave.

'I've spent a year-and-a-half blaming myself, Bryan. I volunteered for a posting to Egypt because everything in England reminded me of Judith. I go to Mary's House and paw the girls in the hope that I can distance myself from what real love feels like. I've been running away as hard as I can run, because I blamed myself for the worst thing that's ever happened to me.

'But that all changed on Saturday. When we got close to that reconnaissance plane, flying over our territory, unarmed because they believed they were invincible, because they believed we are weak, I realised *they* were to blame for Judith's death. Because the men flying over London who dropped the bomb that ripped my wife and baby to shreds believed the exact same thing. They think they can do whatever they choose, take whatever they want. Well, it's time I stood in their bloody way.'

Bryan lit two cigarettes and passed one to his friend.

'I know from my own recent experience that revenge can be a very dangerous motivation,' Bryan said quietly.

Snowy took a draw on the cigarette and pulled the smoke deep into his lungs: 'It's not revenge, Bryan; it's justice.'

The western suburbs of Alexandria thinned in density and petered out as the car barrelled along the coast road into open territory. The temperature crept up and dust infiltrated the dropped windows, settling on the dashboard in the lee of the windscreen. The barren landscape shimmered in the heat haze, flat and forbidding. Yet every few miles its homogenous hostility was disturbed by a cluster of huts huddled around a well sunk amongst a stand of palm trees. Between these tiny settlements, young boys tended herds of goats, small upright figures that waxed and waned in solidity through the distorting radiance of the baking sand.

The location of Landing Ground 97 became apparent several miles before they reached it; a ridge of dust climbed away in the prevailing breeze, straddling the desert like an ethereal headland. As they drew closer, Bryan picked out the tiny shapes of aircraft climbing eastwards while others circled, spiralling downwards, seeking to land. The road carried them level with the now-visibly bustling airstrip, but continued west with no discernible turn-off. Snowy dropped a couple of gears and steered onto the rough sandy expanse dotted with small boulders that stood between the pilots and their frontline posting.

As they crawled closer, it became evident there was no fence and therefore no entrance gate. Bryan pointed out a small tent, the closest thing to the road, and the man in a tin helmet, holding a rifle at the ready, who was watching their progress. Snowy veered towards the tent and slowed his progress so as not to spook the armed man.

Snowy pulled up outside the tent and both men got out. While Snowy was explaining their purpose to the guard, Bryan leaned on the car roof and surveyed the airstrip. Aircraft were dispersed over the vast area of the unfenced facility, many of them were unfamiliar fighter types, many of them were exotic twin-engine bombers. As he squinted through the haze, engines began firing, one after the other. Bryan brought his cupped hands up to his forehead to better shield his eyes from the glare and spotted a squadron of Spitfires standing in line abreast. He watched entranced as the whole line of fighters surged forward as one and climbed into the air together. The dust cloud they kicked up billowed and roiled, drifting off to smudge the coastal skies away to the north.

'Jump in!' Snowy's voice punctured Bryan reverie. 'We're to report to the intelligence officer, over there.' Snowy pointed to a grouping of large tents at the eastern edge of the landing ground.

Snowy drove a slow, curved route to the tents based on where he thought the perimeter road might be had there been a fence. As they drew close, a man ducked out of a tent that was pitched directly next to a truck that had a long whip-like aerial extending behind the cabin. The man wore a baggy pair of shorts and an open-necked shirt with the sleeves rolled up high. He stood hands on hips, watching their approach.

Snowy pulled up next to the truck and the two pilots climbed out. The man had no discernible marking of rank outside of the implications involved in being older than them, so the pair stood awkwardly before him, confused at the mild protocol vacuum.

The man thrust out his hand, breaking the impasse: 'Welcome.' He beamed a smile. 'My name's Dixon, Noel Dixon.'

Bryan and Snowy each shook his hand and introduced themselves, then the group retreated into the shade of the tent.

'Sit down, lads,' Dixon said and parked himself behind his trestle desk. He studied his pad for a moment and read out his notes. 'Two experienced combat pilots, proficient on Spitfires, to go on-strength as required.' He looked up, glancing between the two men. 'That's all they've told me. I trust it's correct?'

Both men nodded.

'Right.' Dixon arched his hands in front of his nose. 'The squadron flies the Spitfire Mark V under the call-sign of Firebird. We're mostly engaged in escort missions for medium bombers and for Hurricane fighter-bombers. Once the escort responsibilities are discharged, free-lancing ground attack is allowed, especially against supply columns.' His gaze flitted between the two pilots. 'Do you have any ground-attack experience?'

'Yes,' Bryan answered. 'I once stitched up a 109 that had landed in a park in Dartford.'

Dixon regarded him through narrowed eyelids.

Bryan shrugged: 'Well, it's true. I did.'

Dixon cleared his throat: 'Moving on, we're lucky enough to be fighting with something like a four-to-one numerical superiority. Balanced against that, the German anti-aircraft crews are very good, and as they use the same guns against tanks, you should assume the desert is full of them.

'Draw a tent from supplies and find a place to pitch it with the others. I'll introduce you to the squadron leader tonight in the mess, which is' – he pointed outside beyond the truck – 'that trestle table and that marquee. It's mixed officers and men; no time for niceties out here when you're likely to be on the move at a moment's notice. East or west, who knows? Although it's mostly been east lately, to be honest. It's all a bit like France in '40, except without all the champagne.'

Dixon lapsed into a distracted silence for a moment, then: 'Any questions?' he asked. 'No? Off you go, then.'

***

By late afternoon the two pilots had pitched their tent alongside a dozen or so more, set at a safe distance from the bustle of activity that thrummed across Landing Ground 97. As the sun reddened into its westerly descent, they followed the general drift towards the mess tent and joined the queue that formed by the trestle table outside it.

The men they encountered were outwardly pleasant enough, but far from genial. The sparsity of their living conditions together with the shock and stress of defeats and retreats had hardened their outlook. Hard work and defiance were redolent in their demeanour, but sentimentality had been callously scrubbed away by the abrasive desert over which they'd fought.

Bryan and Snowy shuffled along the line, each collecting a plate from a tottering pile, onto which two men in greasy aprons spooned slices of an indeterminate fried meat and pallid boiled potatoes. A third man dispensed dark, lukewarm tea into tin mugs from a flame-blackened metal urn. The pair took their meals into the shade of the marquee and sat at one of the long trestles set up there.

'There's a difference,' Snowy said.

'Between what?' Bryan asked, slicing off an experimental morsel of meat.

'Dixon said it was like France in 1940,' Snowy answered. 'But in France, we had somewhere to retreat to.' Snowy scooped up a mouthful of watery potato. 'Right now, our backs are well and truly against the shit-house wall, and there's nothing beyond the shit-house.'

'It's not ideal,' Bryan said. 'But Dunkirk was just a three-minute newsreel to most Americans. Now there are planes out there on the landing ground that I've never seen before; American planes. That's the vital difference.'

63

'That's probably why Rommel's on the move,' Snowy said. 'And Rommel is nobody's fool. I reckon this is the killer blow.'

'We have an army out there,' Bryan said. 'You said yourself, that has to count for something.'

'Well, thinking about it, the army didn't count for so very much in France, did it?' Snowy countered. 'The Panzers that slashed through our lines then are sitting out there now.' He leaned forward, warming to his theme. 'You know how long it took us to drive from Alex. Their armour can't be more than twice that distance away from us *at this very moment*,' he hissed. 'Once they get to Alexandria, they'll take all the fuel they need. Cairo is practically defenceless, so the whole delta will be overrun by-'

'Shush!' Bryan interrupted, jerking his head towards the marquee entrance.

The intelligence officer strode into the tent towards them accompanied by another man, taller, of slender build, with sharp features set in easy resolution over a thin-lipped mouth.

'Gents,' Dixon flashed a brief smile of greeting. 'This is Squadron Leader Wallace Barnard.'

No-one in the marquee had stood up when the officers entered, so Bryan and Snowy stuck to their seats.

Dixon pointed at them in turn: 'Hale and White.'

Barnard sat down opposite the pair and the intelligence officer drifted out of the marquee.

'Sorry to interrupt your dinner,' the squadron leader said. 'I wanted to get you up to speed. It's been a busy day. We've lost a few, so it's good to welcome you on board.'

Bryan and Snowy continued to pick at their meals.

'The enemy started a big push in the early hours of this morning. It's fairly clear the intention was to break our lines before dawn. That has not happened.'

Snowy glanced sheepishly at Bryan and returned his gaze to his plate.

Barnard continued: 'They've been under constant bomber attack all day, with one brief respite as a sandstorm blew through. Pathfinders will be marking enemy concentrations for our bombers throughout the night. At first light we'll be on escort runs followed by freelancing against ground targets where the opportunity arises.

'We need to hang on here, chaps. If we can fend them off one more time, I'm sure good things are going to start happening quite soon. As you've flown together already, I suggest one of you flies wingman for the other. There's less opposition up there than you might have faced before, but the 109s do still turn up and they're every bit as nasty as they always have been.' His stern features split into a brief smile: 'Welcome to Firebird.'

# Chapter 6

## Tuesday, 1 September 1942 – Landing Ground 97

The orderly leaned in through the tent-flap and played the beam of his torch onto Bryan's face. Bryan blinked into wakefulness and held up a hand to protect his eyes.

'Hoi,' he gasped. 'Fuck off!'

'Now, now' – the torch clicked off – 'that's no way to speak to your mother.'

The flap dropped back into place as the orderly moved on to his next victim.

'What's up?' Snowy's querulous voice penetrated the darkness.

'I think we're supposed to be,' Bryan said.

He swung his legs off his cot and sat for a moment, waiting for the flares and flashes layered on his corneas by the torch beam to subside and the dim interior of the tent to become discernible. He grabbed his shirt and shorts from his case next to his bunk and hooked his desert boots from under the cot. The socks bundled inside the boots rewarded this disturbance with a robust waft of odour.

Bryan dressed and ducked out of the tent. Two waxed canvas wash-basins suspended on wooden cradles stood in a small clear area in amongst the tents. The movement of bodies in the dark and the soft splashing of water drew him towards them. He waited for a basin to become free, then splashed the tepid water onto his face, slicking his sodden locks flat against his head.

'Strewth!' The voice in the darkness was hushed with wonder. 'Someone's getting a proper pasting.'

Bryan looked out towards the west. The black, star-filled vault descended to a horizon that rippled with light, vivid white and yellow flashes mingled into the background glow of green and red flares; the junction of earth and sky coruscated with bomb-bursts, rippling out an eerily gentle rumbling across the flat desert sands. Snowy appeared next to Bryan, water from his own perfunctory wash dripping from his nose.

'That looks a lot livelier than chasing reconnaissance planes,' he said.

Bryan turned to scrutinise his friend's face through the pre-dawn gloom.

'Do *not* tell me the only combat you've seen is shooting down that crippled, unarmed Junkers.' Bryan kept his voice low as other pilots were watching the lightshow close by.

'Erm, yes.' Snowy's eyes remained fixed on the glistening horizon. 'I've always been more a research and development type. You know, a spot of test-piloting here and there. Always very much behind-the-lines sort of stuff.'

'You bloody fool!' Bryan's whisper hissed with incredulity. 'Why in hell's name did you request a transfer to this?' He gestured towards the tumultuous bombardment out to the west.

Snowy turned to look him straight in the eye: 'I've already told you why,' he said, his voice was flat and calm.

Bryan exhaled heavily; his indignation punctured by Snowy's sanguine determination. He regarded the lights of the distant battle for a moment, then turned back to his companion.

'Alright,' he said. 'You're flying as my wingman, and we'll keep an eye out for each other. Fly tight and listen for my voice on the wireless and do what I say. If you have time to shoot at the same thing as me, do so, if not, don't fret about it. If I go down, get low and head home as fast as you can.'

Snowy smiled: 'Piece of cake,' he said.

They went back to their tent, picked up their flying helmets and walked across the landing ground to the mess, joining the queue with the rest of Firebird Squadron. Breakfast looked suspiciously similar to last night's dinner, but the over-brewed tea cut a welcome swathe across their sleep-slimed tongues. Conversation was low and sparce, and as they finished their meal Squadron Leader Barnard strode in and stood at the end of their trestle table.

'Good morning, gentlemen,' he said. 'First job this morning is to escort a couple of squadrons of A-20 Boston bombers to their targets.' He nodded towards the marquee entrance at the flashing lights that stabbed relentlessly at the still-dark sky. 'As those targets are not so very far away, we'll take off and climb over the landing ground, attain and maintain angels fourteen and wait for the bombers to pass beneath us.

'Then it's a simple, keep-your-eyes-peeled, top-cover mission. If enemy fighters make an appearance, we'll escort them back after the drop. If no opposition is met, we'll let the bombers come home alone and seek out suitable ground targets to strafe. When I say suitable, I mean isolated. Gun placements and soft-sided vehicles are especially useful to knock out. Don't bother with the tanks; it's unlikely you can hurt them enough for the risk involved.

'There are revolvers for anyone who hasn't already got one.' He pointed to a wooden crate at the back-end of the marquee. 'And remember, if there's one good thing about this God-forsaken desert, it's that you can belly-land an aeroplane almost anywhere. So, if you get hit, the further eastwards you can coax the thing to go, the easier you'll be to find and rescue. Any questions?'

The answering silence crackled with the fresh tension of impending action.

'Alright then. We fly in pairs, organise that yourselves. Good luck everybody.

*** 

The dark sky began its slow surrender to daylight as Snowy walked out to the Spitfires dispersed at the edge of the landing ground. His gait felt lop-sided and awkward, thrown out of kilter by the leaden weight of the revolver suspended on his belt. He pulled the gun from its holster and checked the safety catch was engaged. The metal was dulled with a layer of grease that left a smear on his thumb.

'Six bullets,' he mused to himself: whatever battle he may be required to fight with this gun, it was evidently expected to be a short one. He slid the weapon back into its holster and buttoned the flap.

He arrived at his fighter and turned to check where Bryan might be. He spotted his friend approaching the next Spitfire a few dozen yards away and returned his thumbs-up. One of the two airmen waiting by his aircraft helped Snowy into his parachute and boosted him onto the port wing, the other vaulted onto the starboard wing and helped settle Snowy into the cockpit.

Engines burst into life all along dispersal, crackling their intent into the brittle dawn air. The airmen sat one on each wing, their faces swathed with grubby bandanas and old flying goggles pulled down over their eyes, to guide Snowy on his way, in Bryan's wake, towards the take-off strip. Keeping the revs as low as possible to mitigate the dust kicked up around him, Snowy trundled blindly in a straight line, glancing from left to right to get navigation signals from his wiry pair of grease-monkeys. After several minutes they both made throat-slashing motions, and when Snowy eased off the throttle and squeezed the brakes, they slid down the wings, dropped off the trailing edge and vanished into the billowing dust behind him.

Snowy flipped on the wireless and looked out down the ragged line of fighters extending away from his starboard wing-tip. The sun completed its escape from the eastern horizon, shooting horizontal rays into his rear-view mirror and beginning the upward ratchet of the morning's temperature.

The crackling static in his earphones compressed to a squashed silence, then: *'Firebird Squadron, you are clear for take-off.'*

Snowy eased the throttle forward and rumbled across the hard ground, a quick glance to his right showed the wavering line of dust-smirched Spitfires racing along beside him. The tail lifted and with it came the relief of forward visibility. Another few moments and the bone-vibrating rumble ceased as the wheels lifted from the ground. Snowy retracted the gear and looked out again along the line of fighters, all now airborne. The furthest of them banked into a wide starboard turn and the next followed its lead. Snowy waited for the manoeuvre to travel down the line and followed Bryan into the squadron's spiralling climb. The formation turned through the dust plume, truncating it with their backwash, then they were out into the crystal blue dawn, clawing for altitude.

As they wheeled around, the western horizon swept across Snowy's windshield. Funnel-shaped columns of thick black smoke rose in their dozens, diagonally, like leaning towers, to merge in a dark band that rolled its greasy way towards the coast. Snowy shifted his gaze back to Bryan's tail and the sparkling, clear sky above it.

Barnard led the squadron to slightly over fourteen thousand feet and levelled into a lazy circle. After a few minutes, twenty aircraft cruised in through eastern haze. They flew in five diamond-shaped formations strung across the sky; each group stepped up from front to back. Snowy watched with a keen professional interest as the strange formation flew beneath the circling Spitfires. The squat bombers carried a large engine on each of their deep wings. The rounded noses were fully glazed and glinted in the strengthening sunshine. Cockpits sat in line with the propellers, and the cockpit roof extended backwards forming a ridge that ended in a semi-glazed open nacelle where a lone gunner toted a single mounted machine-gun. The aircraft's over-sized tailfins gave the formation the air of hunting orcas. Their topsides were painted with dark green and brown camouflage.

They carried British roundels, but the strange mix of confidence and naivety in their design marked them out as American-made aircraft.

The Spitfires completed their final turn and levelled out heading west, above and slightly behind the bombers. Their heading edged the two formations towards the coast and the fires and smoke of the battlefield swung slowly out to the left, traversing from the nose of Snowy's fighter towards its port wingtip. A thrill of surprise tickled Snowy's skin at how quickly they arrived at the frontline; how close their iron enemies had become.

Below, the bomber formation banked ponderously to port and steadied onto a southerly course that would take them over the German advance. Barnard took the escorts on a gentler turn, placing them on the western side of their charges.

The wireless crackled a tinny voice into Snowy's ears: '*Firebird Leader to Firebird Squadron. Eyes peeled, lads. Call out anything you see.*'

Snowy scanned the sky on his starboard side; it was full of Spitfires. Curiosity dragged his gaze back to the chubby bombers ploughing ahead below him. The drifting smoke of previous attacks hazed the air around them and small bursts of dirty grey smoke began appearing ahead of their noses. Committed to their run, the bombers flew straight and level into the thickening field of exploding shells. Snowy gasped as one bomber bucked with impact and flames streamed from its mid-section, roared along its fuselage and licked tongues of fire into its slipstream. Snowy watched in chilled fascination as the bomber continued in steady flight for a few moments before its starboard wing snapped upwards and the fuselage rolled into a dive, scorching an arc of fire towards the ground.

Seconds later, small objects cascaded from the open bomb doors of the other aircraft, at least a dozen from each. Snowy watched them fall until he lost them to distance. Below, on the desert floor, unidentifiable vehicles trailed plumes of dust as they manoeuvred to gain an advantage, strove to steal another half-mile of sand. Sudden bomb-bursts peppered larger plumes amongst them, advancing in a rippling wave to engulf and thwart their tiny purpose.

The bombers banked eastwards for home, one trailing a thin streamer of white smoke from a damaged engine.

'*Alright, Firebird.*' Barnard's voice chimed in metallic tones in Snowy's earphones. '*Jerry's a no-show; do what damage you can and I'll see you all back at base.*'

The squadron' patrol formation flattened and bulged as pairs of fighters disconnected into shallow dives towards the battlefield.

'*Stay close, Snowy.*' The voice snapped Snowy's attention back in time for him to see Bryan's Spitfire roll out to starboard and pitch into a dive. Snowy lurched into the same manoeuvre and pushed on the throttle to catch up. He glanced nervously into his rear-view mirror to see other Spitfires of the squadron descending towards the battle-line etched on the desert with bomb-craters and dust clouds, then checked his compass; Bryan was taking them due west. He swallowed hard and focussed on Bryan's tail as the altitude dropped away and the orange-yellow of the desert floor swung closer, peppered with isolated rocks, their size exaggerated by the long shadows cast by the low dawn sun.

Bryan flattened out no more than two-hundred feet above the sand and rushing rocks, seemingly settled into his westward cruise. Sweat pricked out across Snowy's forehead and cheeks; he was inside enemy territory and too low to bail out. The realisation shocked him back to his responsibilities and he hurriedly checked his mirror and quickly scanned the dome above for danger; all was clear. He gripped the control column a little tighter and strove to slow his breathing.

'*There's something*' – Bryan's voice was calm, like a cricket commentator – '*at two o'clock. Let's take a look.*'

Snowy gazed out across his starboard wing to find a smudge of dirt tainting the solid blue sky. Something about the dust cloud suggested that its source was heading towards the frontline. He tilted into the slow bank that Bryan had adopted to get behind the target. As they curved closer the amorphous cloud developed several legs, each leading down to the vehicle that was creating it.

'*Bingo!*' Bryan's voice remained calm. '*Let's have a pop!*'

Bryan pulled into a steeper bank as they rounded the end of the convoy and streaked into attack the half-dozen vehicles stretched in an oblique line across the hard ground. Snowy followed, instinctively drifting wide to avoid hitting his partner.

Spiralling wisps of gun-smoke tore into Bryan's slipstream and one of the trucks blossomed in the soundless, billowing explosion of burning petrol;

barrels ejected by the force curved a brief arc of flame above the conflagration before bouncing their fire into the sand.

Snowy stabbed at the firing button; nothing happened. The trucks flashed below him.

'Shit!'

He saw the bulk of Bryan's Spitfire break left to make another attack. Snowy carried on straight. He fumbled at the firing button; the safety was still engaged.

'Damn it to hell!'

Snowy pushed the safety to *fire* and hauled his fighter around to the right. The desert reeled across his windscreen and the convoy reappeared. Three trucks now belched thick black smoke into the hot air and Bryan's Spitfire flashed across them dousing another into a roiling fireball.

Off to the side, one truck had made an attempt to escape the carnage, but bogged itself in softer sand. Snowy veered his approach towards it, suddenly aware of a figure running from the stationary vehicle, shirtless and flailing through the sand.

Snowy squared the truck in his sights and thumbed the firing button. Shells thundered into the soft-skinned vehicle and an immediate catastrophe of burgeoning orange flame erased its outline. Snowy held the button down and twitched the control column to the right. Shell strikes careened away from the wrecked truck across the desert floor, snaking after, catching and engulfing the fleeing driver in a shredding maelstrom of metal.

Snowy roared over the man, the last of his ammunition detaching from the sand and curving to whip harmlessly through the empty air as he pulled up and away.

'*All done.*' Bryan's voice betrayed a breathless edge. '*Let's get off home before this smoke attracts some unfriendly attention.*'

The pair headed north, gaining altitude towards the coast and skirted the northern end of the battlefield. They circled Landing Ground 97 as a squadron of Hurricanes lifted off, and, once the dust had cleared, they landed and taxied to dispersal where the other Spitfires of Firebird Squadron were being refuelled and rearmed.

Snowy swung out of his cockpit, his crotch and armpits still damp with sweat. He unhooked his parachute, threw it onto the wing and walked away from dispersal towards the mess tent. Bryan walked a converging path, pausing momentarily to light a cigarette.

'You scared me bloody rigid,' Snowy called at his friend. 'I thought you'd gone bonkers, haring off into the west like that.'

Bryan arrived at his shoulder and matched his pace.

'Absolutely the safest thing to do,' Bryan said. 'Seek out a soft target for the green pilot.'

'Safest?' Snowy scoffed. 'Flying a few bloody yards above the ground behind the front line?'

Bryan cast him a sideways glance: 'Did anyone shoot at you?' he asked.

'I suppose not,' Snowy mumbled.

'Well, there you have it,' Bryan said. 'It was a good job, nicely done,' he added. 'With less petrol they can't advance so quickly, and, come to that, they can't run away as fast either.'

They walked quietly for a minute before Snowy broke the silence.

'I killed a man back there,' he said.

Bryan shot him another glance but remained silent.

'I mean, I killed him *deliberately*. He was running; trying to get away. I moved the control column a fraction of an inch' – Snowy mimicked the action in front of his chest – 'and killed him. I could've chosen not to do that.' He looked down at his hand, the wrist twisted a few degrees to the right, and let it drop back to his side. 'I'm fairly sure he had no choice about driving that truck.'

'That's as may be,' Bryan said. 'But, on the drive to this airfield, you told me about a bomber that flew to London one night. Someone delivered the fuel that went into its tanks that afternoon. Hell, a whole factory full of someones had a hand in making the bombs it dropped.' He put his arm around the other's shoulders. 'None of them are innocent in this, Snowy, old son. Not a single one of them.'

They paused to watch a squadron of Hurricanes fighter-bombers straggle back to the landing ground. One trailed a line of delicate white vapour, descending with its wheels still retracted. It belly-flopped onto the packed earth, thrown into a lazy spin by its empty bomb-racks. The pilot clambered out and trotted clear as the escaping vapour graduated to thick black smoke.

'I have to tell you' – Bryan started off towards the mess-tent again – 'it's a real pleasure to be doing good business again.'

\*\*\*

Darkness fastened its final buttons along the western horizon and the air exhaled its warmth away to the cloudless void as Bryan pushed back the

73

surface scum on the canvas basin and splashed the half-rancid water onto his face, twisting his fingertips into the corners of his eyes to dislodge the tiny nuggets of dust and grime that clung there. His stomach groaned and squeaked as it worked on the greasy meat stew he'd eaten too quickly and too late in the day. Reminders of its taste bubbled into his throat every few minutes. His fatigue was complete, but it brought its own satisfaction.

With the darkness nearly complete, the twinkling of explosions reasserted its rippling presence away to the west. An occasional detonation was large enough to rumble its anger across the miles of desert, its fury too large to be defeated by the distance. Bryan burped loudly into the gloom and walked back to the tent.

Snowy was already supine on his cot, staring at the canvas ceiling. Bryan sat on the edge of his, lit a cigarette and leaned forward to tug at his bootlaces.

'What do you reckon?' Snowy asked.

Bryan levered his boots off and swung his legs up onto his mattress.

'The German army wins battles when it can move quickly in straight lines,' Bryan answered. 'I think they've been stopped this time.'

Snowy pulled himself up onto his elbow and frowned at Bryan through the darkness: 'What if they've got a surprise up their sleeve?'

'As I understand it' – Bryan took a long draw on his cigarette, lighting his face with its orange glow – 'Rommel is the kind of man who uses all his surprises upfront.' He leaned over and stubbed his cigarette out on the sandy floor. 'We'll see, I expect, tomorrow.'

### Wednesday, 2 September 1942

Firebird Squadron circled the landing ground waiting for two squadrons of fighter bombers to take off. The twenty-odd Hurricanes sprinted in line abreast then clawed their way into the air. They had no use for too much altitude, so they set their shallow climb to westward even before their wheels had fully retracted. The Spitfires above matched their course, stepping up in pairs to form a defensive umbrella.

Bryan contemplated the horizon they approached; it was draped with a seemingly permanent black curtain of roiling smoke rising from yesterday's smouldering hulks and today's freshly blazing wreckage, each ascending finger co-mingling with its neighbours to form a solid hazy bar across the desert that degraded back to smutty blue as it rose. A movement pricked at his eye and his muscles tensed; a distant formation at a higher altitude dotted the sky ahead. They continued straight and level, resolving into the now-familiar shape of twin-engine American-built bombers. Bryan relaxed, gazing up at the corpulent shapes as they passed by in silent serenity, cruising back to their base.

Bryan checked his rear-view mirror; Snowy's white-painted spinner bobbed in his slipstream, tucked nice and close on his port side. Bryan shifted his gaze to the aircraft below his port wing. The Hurricane formation became unstuck, disassembling into groups of two or three that swooped towards the battlefield in search of targets on the ground.

'*Bandits at two o'clock*,' Barnard's voice rasped across the wireless. '*Let's get into them.*'

Bryan swivelled his head to look ahead of his starboard wing and caught the gaggle of fighters approaching fast from the northwest, aiming to cut a diagonal across his nose in pursuit of the Hurricanes. Their squat outline, snub nose and squared-off canopy marked the intruders as Messerschmitt 109s.

Firebird Squadron collectively dipped their noses to intercept and a few pilots jabbed a burst of fire at the enemy fighters as they scissored across in front. Bryan flew through the ragged tail of the formation, wincing as two aircraft flashed dangerously close over his canopy. He stabbed a glance into his mirror, pleased to see his wingman still there: 'Stick with me, Snowy,' he barked. 'Breaking right.'

Mindful of his partner's inexperience, Bryan pulled into a bank that took the pair away from the complex dangers now swirling over the battle line, hoping one or more of the attacking Germans had thrown a left turn and started a run for home.

As they wheeled around, Bryan spotted a thin line of white vapour, and at its head a 109 barrelling back the way it had come: 'Bingo,' he muttered to himself, checked Snowy was still in place, and set a course to intercept the fleeing fighter. The German pilot, his senses heightened to menace after taking damage, veered away in a northerly direction and accelerated sharply, causing the vapour that streamed from his engine to gush thicker and darker.

Bryan pressed transmit: 'Snowy, why don't you take a shot at this one?'

Bryan checked his mirror for threats as Snowy eased up alongside. The sky was clear and Bryan returned his attention to the chase. They slipped in directly behind their quarry, dispersing his smoke trail into their thrashing slipstreams, gaining steadily as the seconds ticked away.

Snowy squeezed a one-second burst; tracers flashed glowing fingers across the gap, flailing away above the Messerschmitt and dropping impotently in front of its nose. The German fighter wobbled slightly, then the canopy flopped open and a dark bundle slid from the cockpit, cartwheeling past the tail and falling away beneath the Spitfires. The 109 rolled lazily, turning its sea-green underbelly to the blue sky, and curved into a vertical dive towards the desert.

'*Look at that!*' Snowy's voice bounced with enthusiasm. '*I bloody well got him!*'

Bryan dipped his wing, looking back at the off-white parachute that blossomed like a sickly flower against the sienna landscape: 'I'm not sure that will count,' he said.

'*Why not?*' Snowy's elation deflated.

'You're generally expected to have hit them with something,' Bryan said.

'*Well, perhaps I did,*' Snowy reasoned. '*It'll count if you confirm it.*'

'Are you watching my tail?' Bryan asked.

'*Er, yes.*': Snowy's Spitfire dropped back to echelon on Bryan's port side and they flew on.

The horizon gained a thin blue edging of Mediterranean water as they continued north. Bryan reasoned that Firebird would be on its way home by now and resolved to do the same. Then a shape passed through the blue line into the lighter backdrop of the cloudless sky. Another one followed it, both previously invisible against the landscape.

'There's a couple of aircraft heading east,' Bryan transmitted. 'Not sure what they are. Probably ours, but let's take a look.'

Bryan curved into a long starboard bank, jockeying to come round below and behind the unknown aircraft. As the distance slowly closed, he searched for some feature that might identify the pair. Glimpses of yellow paint on their noses sparked a creeping suspicion.

His earphones clicked: '*American?*' Snowy suggested. '*Kittyhawks I think they call them. On their way home, no doubt.*'

As the Spitfire's drew closer below the other aircraft, the angle widened. The pale grey underside of the wings yielded a view of their insignia: three vertical bars enclosed in a black circle.

'They're Italians!' Bryan blurted.

At that moment, the two Italian aircraft surged forward and split, one breaking hard left, the other breaking hard right. Bryan flung his Spitfire into a precipitous right turn after the second enemy fighter, pulling hard to keep the Italian's tail in view above his canopy. Tears blurred his vision and a pain like an old throbbing bruise crept across his forehead. He gritted his teeth against the force that pushed down on his spine and held the turn.

The Italian pilot cracked first; he lurched back into an instant of level flight and splayed out into a wider left bank. As Bryan rolled to follow, two shapes flashed over his canopy; a Spitfire closely followed by the other Italian.

'Shit!' Bryan gasped. He pulled hard to drag the fuselage of the fighter he pursued into his sights and stabbed out a short burst of fire. The tracer curved away from the turn, but a clatter of hits peppered his enemy's starboard wingtip. The Italian fighter flipped into a spin and fell away in a precipitous dive, feigning more serious damage to affect an escape.

Bryan let him go, slammed into an opposite turn and checked his mirror for threats, the hot buzz of adrenaline tingling in his muscles. He scanned the sky and found Snowy jinking from side to side in front of the remaining Italian fighter. Tight puffs of gun smoke spurted behind the aggressor's wings as he fired snapshots at his wallowing would-be victim. Bryan pushed his throttle forward and swooped in a wide arc onto the Italian's tail.

He pressed transmit: 'Snowy! Listen!' His shout reverberated in the narrow cockpit. 'Break right as hard as you can! Do it… Now!'

Snowy's Spitfire jerked violently to the right, as if whisked away from its tormentor by the strings of a celestial puppeteer. At the same instant, Bryan rammed his thumb onto the fire button cascading fire into the tail of the Italian aircraft. Debris whipped back around Bryan's cockpit and, as his guns clanked to empty, he pulled up over the battered enemy fighter. Bryan dropped his wing a touch to watch as the Italian machine settled into a slow dive, flames sputtering from its wing-roots.

Bryan scanned again for danger, but the sky held only Snowy, circling nearby.

'Let's go home, Snowy,' Bryan called. 'Enough fun for one day.'

\*\*\*

They circled the landing ground once to make sure it was clear, and then landed line abreast. Bryan slid his canopy back and looked across at his friend as they taxied towards dispersal. Snowy's drawn face didn't return his gaze, fixating instead on fishtailing away from the runway.

Once at dispersal, Bryan shut down quickly and climbed out of the cockpit. He shucked off his parachute and trotted across to Snowy's Spitfire just as its engine juddered to a halt. The wings and fuselage of Snowy's fighter were smattered with holes and rents. Bryan's heart lurched. He jumped up onto the wing and rapped his knuckles on the canopy. Snowy turned to look at him and pulled the canopy open.

'Have you been hit?' Bryan demanded.

Snowy blinked: 'I don't think so. I didn't feel anything.'

'What happened to you?' Bryan asked. 'You were supposed to stick with me.'

'I thought they were American planes and we were all on our way back to base,' Snowy said. 'I looked down to check my fuel gauge' – he dipped his head, looked at his control panel and gave his head a little shake – 'then you said something I didn't catch, and when I looked back' – he turned his head back to Bryan – 'everyone had vanished. The next thing I know someone's bloody shooting at me from behind.'

'Get yourself out of there,' Bryan said. 'Let's go for a brew.'

Bryan jumped down onto the ground and waited for Snowy to haul himself out of the cockpit. Snowy stood for a moment gazing at the perforated skin of the wing, and then dropped to the ground next to Bryan.

'You smell funny,' Bryan said.

'Yes.' Snowy grimaced. 'I think I've pissed myself.'

Snowy walked with the stiff-legged gait of the mildly concussed. Bryan matched his slow pace and remained silent, allowing his friend to process his thoughts.

They arrived at the mess tent and Bryan guided Snowy to a seat away from the men that milled around inside. Bryan pressed a hand onto Snowy's shoulder to settle him into his seat, then crossed to the serving table. He poured two mugs from the tea-urn and leaned across the trestle towards one of catering crew.

'Pssst!'

The sweating man turned to regard him.

'You've got some sugar.'

'No.' The man said and returned to his work.

'My friend very nearly had his arse shot off twenty minutes ago,' Bryan's voice bristled with quiet menace. 'He's on the edge of shock, and I'd like him to have some sugar in this sludge that you pretend is tea, and I strongly suspect you've got some fucking sugar.' He pushed one of the mugs forward.

The man looked into Bryan's face, then flitted a glance over at Snowy: 'I'll take a look,' he said.

He ducked behind a canvas partition and returned a moment later with an open tin and a spoon. He put a spoonful of sugar into the mug.

'There,' he said.

Bryan's semi-malevolent gaze continued to bore into the other's eyes. The man ladled another spoonful into the mug and retreated in haste behind the canvas wall.

Bryan took the teas back to Snowy, sat carefully across from him and placed the sweetened brew between his friend's hands.

'Thank you,' Snowy said.

'Ah, it's just the same old shit tea,' Bryan said.

'No' – Snowy looked up, the colour was slowly returning to his blood-drained face – 'I mean thank you for saving my bacon.'

'It's why we fly in pairs,' Bryan said.

'Damn it!' Snowy's face creased with emotion. 'I thought you'd abandoned me.' His voice was low, but tight with feeling. 'I was cursing you to hell at the top of my voice. That was the last thing I was going to do on this earth; curse you, despite everything, curse *you* to hell. And then you saved me.'

Over Snowy's shoulder, Bryan spotted the squadron leader entering the marquee. Bryan caught his eye, pulled a silent expression of dark concern, and inclined his head slightly towards Snowy. Barnard sidled across slowly, appraising Snowy as he approached. He stopped at the end of the table, glanced once more at Bryan, reading the unspoken request in his eyes.

'Listen lads,' he said. 'We've got a few damaged aircraft, and we've lost a couple today. So, I need to rota pilots until we can get back to strength. You two can stand down for now and report for flying tomorrow at midday. Things should be resolved by then.' He turned to leave, then paused: 'Well done today,' he said. 'I think we might have stopped them in their tracks.'

Bryan watched Barnard's retreating back with quiet gratitude.

'How about that, Snowy?' he said. 'We get to have a lie-in.'

Snowy lowered his chin towards his chest in an attempt to hide the tears that cut tracks through the dust on his cheeks.

### Thursday, 3 September 1942

Bryan stared at the canvas slope of the tent's roof with eyes that itched with fatigue. Snowy's fitful mutterings had finally subsided into a settled slumber and the sleeping man's deep breathing now laid a rhythmic undercurrent to the continuing rumble of the bombardment in the west. The soft sound of footfall on the sandy ground and the flashing sweep of torchlight across the canvas wall caught Bryan's attention. He rolled off his cot and ducked out of the tent flaps. An orderly was doing his rounds of the little tent village, rousing its inhabitants to another day of hot and unpleasant war. The curses and pithy advice of those so awakened punctuated the deep desert darkness.

Bryan lit a cigarette as the orderly approached: 'We're already awake here, mother, thanks for calling.'

The airman flashed his beam into Bryan's face anyway, flitting it maliciously from eye to eye before passing to the next group of tents, chuckling quietly to himself.

Bryan blinked away the dazzle and stuck his head back into the tent. Snowy slept soundly on. Bryan grabbed his shirt and set off past the canvas troughs and their first congregations of washing pilots, across the field in search of authority.

He headed towards the group of tents near the mess where he and Snowy had met the intelligence officer upon arrival. When Bryan reached that man's tent, he was absent, but luck had placed the squadron leader at the desk leafing through some documents.

'Ah, good morning.' Barnard paused, frowning.

'Hale,' Bryan prompted.

'Yes, Hale.' His gaze dropped back to the papers. 'How is your friend getting on?'

'I think he's sweated out the worst of his terrors, sir,' Bryan said. 'But I wanted to talk about me, actually.'

'Yes?' Barnard continued studying the papers on the desk.

'I'd like to request a transfer to Malta as soon as possible, sir.' Bryan said. 'My proper squadron is there. I'm only here by accident.'

'Well.' Barnard dropped the papers and regarded Bryan for a moment. 'I'm sorry you don't regard Firebird as a *proper* squadron.'

'That's not what I—'

Barnard held up his hand to silence Bryan: 'We've got a battle to win right here. You're a good pilot, Hale, and I need as many of those as I can get. If the situation changes, perhaps we can talk again.'

'May I just—'

'No, Hale, you may not. I'll see you at dispersal at midday. Dismissed.'

Bryan regarded his commander in silence for a moment, then turned and left. He walked around the southern perimeter of the landing ground as the dawn cracked the dark horizon behind him. The sea sucked the night-chilled air northwards, so he was comfortably upwind of the dust storm lashed up behind the fighters lining up to take-off on the first mission of the day. Their engines peaked to a sudden crescendo and they raced like stampeding horses until they lifted away from the dun earth. As they rose in concert, one of their number flattened out as its propeller staggered to a halt. It dipped back to earth, landed heavily and ground-looped to a grinding standstill. The pilot clambered free and loped away as flames flickered from beneath the engine cowling.

Bryan turned from the tiny drama and walked back towards the mess. As he approached, he noticed Snowy was seated at a table, eating his breakfast. Bryan collected a plate for himself and joined his friend.

'You're looking brighter,' he said as he sat down.

'There's not much a good night's sleep can't put right,' Snowy said. 'At least that's what my mother used to say.'

'Well, if it helps, I think you've learnt the last thing about fighter combat that you needed to know.' Bryan smiled: 'Stay behind the other bloke's guns if at all possible.'

Snowy mirrored the smile for a moment, then a cloud flattened his features: 'I'm sorry I went a bit flaky when we got back. It's just that churning in my guts... the dread... it was exactly like the moment they told me about Judith. The impossible... the unthinkable... becoming the cold reality. I suppose it uncorked a few things I'd bottled up.'

'None of us are immune, Snowy. Believe me.' Bryan tipped the dregs of his tea onto the floor. 'Now, we've got three or four hours before you're expected to get back on the horse. What say we try to find enough water to have a half-decent wash?'

81

***

Bryan and Snowy sat in the mess tent's shade listlessly flicking flies away from the beads of sweat that trickled down their freshly-shaven cheeks. The buzz of returning engines reverberated through the languorous heat and Bryan checked his watch.

'We're on rota in twenty minutes, mate.' Bryan levelled a look at Snowy.

'I'm raring to go,' Snowy said, shifting his weight on the bench and peering through the tent's entrance. 'Looks like something's up,' he added.

Bryan turned to follow his gaze. A subtle change in demeanour travelled through the airmen that milled about their business on the field; one passed a word to another who went on his way to pass the news. Whatever had sparked it, the momentum of the change invigorated the movements and quickened the step of those that had heard the news. The feeling tickled the senses of the other pilots gathered under the canvas and within moments all of them had turned to the sunlit entrance of the mess in expectation of something as yet unknown.

Squadron Leader Barnard and a half-dozen pilots of Firebird walked from the haloed glare of sunlight into the humid interior of the marquee. Barnard dropped his flying helmet onto a table and scratched his sweaty scalp.

'It would appear that the Afrika Korps are retreating,' he said.

Low exclamations of relief and muttered epithets met his announcement.

'Firebird pilots' – he squinted around the faces at the tables – 'be ready to fly in fifteen minutes.'

***

Firebird Squadron lofted across the flight-path of their charges; a gaggle of Hurricane fighter-bombers cutting a direct route westward. Bryan scanned the empty blue dome for threats, then dropped his eyes to the desert below.

The Hurricanes overflew the frontline that they'd been bombing and strafing for the past three days. The golden desert landscape was defiled with dozens upon dozens of wrecked vehicles, crumpled and blasted, surrounded by the black stains of their immolation. Dotted amongst them, solitary or in small groups, broken tanks languished, their barrels dipped towards the sand in defeat and destruction. Beyond this graveyard of rent metal and crisped flesh, billowing dust clouds marked the progress of the fleeing survivors, their vehicles drawing together, like ants on a hunting spree, into a ragged column heading back towards the narrow gaps in their own minefields. The Hurricanes fanned out and dropped towards their chosen targets.

'*Eyes peeled, Firebird.*' Barnard's measured reminder crackled in Bryan's earphones as the squadron leader nudged the loose formation of Spitfires into a sweeping circle over the retreating enemy.

Bryan swept the sky, lingering for long moments on the western quadrant, checked his mirror where Snowy bobbed in his slipstream, then looked down again to the desert below.

The Hurricanes ran in criss-crossing lines, in and out of the streamers of dust, leaving brief, smattering explosions in their wake. Tracer lashed up from open backed trucks, curling and twisting into the space through which the fighters barrelled. Hurricanes relieved of their bombload banked to attack once more, gunfire flashing from their wings to lick indiscriminate devastation along the lines of naked vehicles and the soldiers that rode them.

One by one the Hurricanes peeled away from the snaking column, bursting out into the clear air and heading east.

'*Alright, Firebird*' – Barnard's voice again – '*let's follow them home.*'

'What?' Bryan murmured to himself. He looked down again at the column of vulnerable vehicles crawling away beneath them to safety. He shook his head in disbelief, but tilted his nose east to follow his leader.

# Chapter 7

## Friday, 4 September 1942 – Landing Ground 97

Bryan lay awake, waiting for the footfall of the morning torch-bearer. Dawn broke and still he did not come. Bryan swung his legs off his cot and pulled on his socks and boots. He lit a cigarette and pushed his way through the tent flaps. Only the quiet snoring from a close-by tent resonated gently through the chill air. Bryan glanced back towards his bunk, but realised sleep would not easily return; fatigue pressed on his shoulders, but the visceral need for action buzzed in his blood and goaded his muscles to restlessness. He meandered between the tents, surrendering to his urge for movement. He paused by the canvas basin and rubbed some water into his eyes, expunging any lingering vestige of drowsiness, then wandered off towards dispersal.

The muted sounds of tools on metal drifted across the hard-packed earth, the universal constant of men working on machines that populated the periphery of every airfield. The dim light of blinkered lanterns glowed next to the dark bulk of the fighters that rested under draped camouflage, the netting adorned with a thousand strips of sand-coloured fabric that rippled in the developing early-morning breeze. The scent of oil and aviation fuel rolled with the moving air, bringing a familiar sizzle to Bryan's nostrils. Men moved with deliberate care beneath the netting, engrossed in the routine tasks that kept sand-worn engines airworthy.

Bryan drifted away from dispersal back towards the mess tent. A different clink and clatter of activity leaked from beneath the canvas here, underwritten with a different perfume. Bryan poured a mug of warm tea from the barely steaming urn and gulped down the bitter liquid, glad at least to wash the tobacco-flavoured film of slime from his tongue. Footsteps drew his attention and he saw Squadron Leader Barnard striding towards the administration tent.

'Sir,' Bryan called softly. 'May I speak with you?'

Barnard nodded and beckoned for Bryan to follow him as he walked into the tent. Bryan hurried after his commander and waited while the man sat down behind his trestle desk.

'You're going to ask why we're not pursuing the enemy, aren't you, Hale?' Barnard asked.

'Yes, sir, I was,' Bryan said.

'We've been told to conserve our forces,' Barnard said. 'There will be routine patrols, of course, but beyond that we're very much on stand-by.'

'But, couldn't we be hurting them, making them weaker,' Bryan said, unable to suppress the twitch in his muscles.

'Well, intelligence suggests their re-supply lines across the Med are being disrupted sufficiently for us to pause and re-group with minimal risk.' Barnard reached for the wedge of papers in his in-tray.

Sensing imminent dismissal Bryan squeezed in his last shot: 'If the situation has changed that much, sir, may I request–'

'We're not conserving forces for the fun of it, Hale,' Barnard interrupted. 'You *know* I can't tell you everything, but I'm certain you're clever enough to work most of it out for yourself.'

'Yes, sir.' Bryan turned to leave.

'And, Hale.' Barnard's words caused him to pause. 'When I believe we no longer need you, I *will* let you go.'

Outside the rising sun painted the dark sky blue. Bryan trailed back across the landing ground, arriving at his tent just as Snowy poked his head outside.

'What's happening?' Snowy asked.

'Nothing much for the foreseeable future, apparently,' Bryan muttered.

## Monday, 14 September 1942

The ball bounced high and the batsman swung wildly at shoulder level, spinning his body in a full circle with his effort. Miraculously he made a glancing contact and the ball skittered wide of the wicket-keeper on its way towards the boundary.

'Single!' The shout came from the batsman's partner, already pounding his way down the pitch. The batsman recovered smartly from his spin and scampered in the other direction. The two running men crossed mid-way, their respective dust clouds mingling and rising together into the evening air. Easily safe, the runners stumbled to a halt as the retrieved ball curved back through the air from the boundary towards the wicket. The bowler caught the throw, glared briefly at each batsman in turn, then turned to walk back to his mark for the next ball of the over.

Snowy and Bryan sat amongst a small group of spectators next to the blackboard that had been pressed into service as a scoreboard. The chalk squeaked across the surface as the new run was added to the score.

'Why' – Snowy nodded towards the nearest of the twenty or so stones that marked out the boundary – 'does the RAF feel the need to paint rocks white?'

'It's something to do' – Bryan flicked his cigarette butt at the stone – 'when there's nothing to do.' He grimaced at his internal ache of frustration.

The bowler loped in measured strides to the wicket, his arm swinging in a graceful arc to unleash a viciously spinning delivery. The batsman lunged into a defensive stroke, but the bounce evaded his bat, curved the ball inwards and glanced it off his knee.

'Howzat!' The bowler turned his imploring face to the umpire, arms outstretched in supplication. The umpire, an airman with his mouth and nose covered by a grubby neckerchief and his eyes shaded behind sunglasses, took a moment to appraise this development in circumstances, then solemnly shook his head. The bowler turned to receive the throw from his wicket-keeper allowing himself a disbelieving shake of the head, glared with renewed determination at the facing batsman, then started the journey back to his mark, examining the pocked and battered ball as he walked.

'What on earth are we up to?' Bryan's exasperation burst into his words. 'We should have Rommel's head on a stake by now.'

'To be fair' – Snowy shaded his eyes to better see the next delivery – 'I heard the army did chase him for a little while before they came back.'

The batsman connected with a full-bodied swing and the ball sailed into a graceful parabola. A fielder skittered around underneath its descent with his hands upstretched. The plummeting ball slid through his grasp, hit his shoulder and plopped to the ground. The batsmen skidded to the end of their first run and sprinted into a second.

'But the desert war has been like that for a while,' Snowy continued. 'Back and forth, to and fro.'

An airman jogged across from the direction of the mess. He stopped by the scoreboard and watched intently as the bowler released another delivery. The batsman swung, missed, and the ball thudded into the wicket-keeper's glove.

'Listen up!' the newcomer called. 'Firebird Squadron to report to the mess.'

The players pulled stumps and they and their spectators drifted towards the mess. When they arrived at the marquee, the squadron leader and intelligence officer were waiting for them.

Barnard watched the men shuffle in and settle in their seats before he spoke.

'We've received the plans for the next stage of the campaign,' he announced. 'Montgomery is adamant: there must be no more retreating. He's also aware that we need to be of a sufficient strength to assure victory before we can risk an advance. So, there will be a lull in operations for rest and re-training. This is largely for the sake of the army, of course, but I'll be taking the opportunity to rotate Firebird pilots onto periods of leave over the next four weeks.'

'Four weeks,' Bryan groaned to himself.

'This is, of course contingent upon events,' Barnard continued. 'But we're confident that the Germans lack the resources to risk another attack, and their supply lacks the volume to change that situation in the short term. I cannot stress enough, the plans we've received today are for a major offensive operation, and elsewhere even bigger things are afoot. The rota' – he indicated a sheet of paper pinned to the central tent-pole – 'is there. Enjoy your leave.'

Men bustled towards the notice, crowding round and elbowing each other to get the first look. Bryan and Snowy remained seated, waiting for the crush to ease. Bryan glanced across at his friend: Snowy's features belied a wisp of dark tension.

'Are you alright?' Bryan asked.

The spell snapped and Snowy pulled a wan smile: 'Doesn't it feel a bit strange to you?' he asked quietly. 'Announcing there's going to be a socking great battle, but before that comes along, you can pop off on your holidays for a bit.'

The knot of men around the rota drifted out of the marquee, heading back to continue the cricket match. Bryan stepped across the tent to scan the names and dates on the paper. He came back and sat next to Snowy.

'We're both in the first batch,' Bryan reported. 'We get to go on our holidays the day after tomorrow.'

## Wednesday, 16 September 1942

The smell of evaporating petrol from the sides of the freshly filled jerry-can dissipated as the sun burned it away. The *gloink, gloink* of its contents slopping about inside ran a counterpoint to the men's footsteps as they crossed from the supply dumps beyond dispersal towards the administration tents and the communications truck next to which Snowy had abandoned the old staff car.

'What are your plans?' Bryan asked.

'I'll take the car back to the airfield to start with,' Snowy answered. 'And if they don't put me on a charge for misappropriating the King's property, I'll slip down to Mary's House for a bite to eat, a bit of dancing and… well, you know.'

The car, in the lee of the high-sided truck, lay under a layer of sandy dust thick enough to soften its outline. Snowy unscrewed the filler-cap and Bryan glugged the fuel into the tank.

'It's a shame you're not coming with me,' Snowy said. 'There's a lot more to Alexandria than sausages and tarts at Mary's. We could see a lot in five days.'

Bryan eyed the passenger seat for long moment, wavering.

'I had to leave Cairo without saying goodbye,' Bryan said. 'I don't know if Katie will be free, or even if she wants to see me again. But the one thing I know for sure about Katie is that she's always worth the risk.'

The pair shook hands and Snowy climbed into the vehicle, throwing his kitbag onto the passenger seat. The starter kicked on the third attempt and the car bumped away towards the distant road, divesting its accreted dust like a swirling cloak behind it.

Bryan went back to the tent, picked up his case, tied the tent-flaps closed and headed to the mess. Outside the marquee a canvas-sided truck sat squat and solid. Half-a-dozen men stood waiting to embark; Bryan joined them. Two men approached from the admin tents. One climbed into the driver's seat and the other, an orderly, handed each of the assembled men a copy of *The Services Guide to Cairo* and a handful of chits and passes.

Bryan climbed into the truck with the others and the orderly secured the tail-gate. The truck rumbled slowly across the landing ground towards the coast road, swaying gently back and forth over the uneven, rock-strewn ground. Bryan gazed out through the truck's open back at the sprawling airstrip behind them; the sleek shapes of dozens upon dozens of combat aircraft dotted the ochre expanse, silent and still, like sleeping raptors.

\*\*\*

Bryan shifted his weight, hoping to get some blood flow into his aching buttocks as the truck ground its way into Cairo city. His head throbbed from the constant gunning of the truck's engine that, over the last six hours, had failed to produce anything faster than sedate progress along the interminable dusty road that dragged out of the desert and into the delta.

The big vehicle nudged its way along increasingly busy roads until it clonked to a halt outside RAF Headquarters. Bryan hung back, staying on his seat and feigning a search of his pockets for something important, while the other airman piled out of the truck and entered the building. Bryan then dropped off the truck, crossed the road and walked quickly around the corner and away; for what he had planned, the last thing he needed was a group of braying airmen queering his pitch.

Dusk was wiggling its way down over the rooftops as he finally arrived at the steps of the Shepheard's Hotel. Bryan pushed his greasy hair back with a sweep of his fingers, pushed the door open and strode across the lobby to the desk.

'Hale,' he announced in a quiet but firm tone. 'I was here a little under a month ago.'

The man at the desk looked up, his face impassive.

'And I'm back,' Bryan continued, pushing his accommodation chit across the polished wood.

The man looked at the chit and a frown crept across his brow.

'It was sufficient last time,' Bryan said. 'Wing Commander Millard recommended the hotel personally.'

The receptionist pulled the register closer to him and flipped back through its pages.

'Hale?' he asked.

'That's correct,' Bryan said.

'We have the same room available, sir.'

'That'll do nicely.'

\*\*\*

Darkness rolled over the city and the river's sinuous flow mirrored the hotel's lights. The building's rows of regimented rectangular windows became free through reflection to dance with fluidity borrowed from the water, shattering and reforming time and again in the wakes of passing craft. Bryan pulled the curtains closed and walked through to the bathroom where the taps gurgled steaming water into the bath.

He undressed, shut of the flow, and lowered himself into the tub, gasping with pleasurable relief as the hot water tingled against his grimy skin and massaged the knots from his muscles. He dipped his head backwards under the surface and scratched at his itching scalp with dirty fingernails.

After a few minutes of surrender to the sensual delights that hot water can bring to a desert-weary soldier, Bryan's eyes opened and he stared at the ceiling in thoughtful contemplation. Coming to rest here, no matter how pleasant the moment, was a perplexing paradox for a man compelled to complete his journey. Waiting on the pleasure of military planners irked him. The lost opportunity to chase down a fleeing enemy stuck in his craw. But his prize still awaited him, he knew, if he could survive to claim it. The fulcrum of the war in Africa, once tipped in the right direction, would set his feet back on the path he desired; Barnard had promised him that.

Bryan's eyes dropped closed and the restorative warmth of the water nudged his mind to wandering. The image of Katie rising from this very bath invaded his mind, the water draining from her body giving her smooth skin a vibrant sheen, the soft crush of her breasts against him as he surrendered to his urge and embraced her frame to his chest.

'Meanwhile...' he mumbled to himself.

### Thursday, 17 September 1942

Bryan stepped through the hospital entrance into the large lobby. He stood and looked around, allowing the bustle of activity to flow around him. Everyone had something to do, and a lost-looking airman was outside of their concerns. Just as he resolved to approach the reception desk, a nurse crossed his path, halted and turned on her heel, regarding him with narrowing eyes.

'I know you, don't I?' she said. Her face brightened as the penny dropped: 'You're Nurse Starling's friend!'

'Yes!' Bryan jumped at the chance. 'Would you be able to tell her I'm here to see her?'

'Sit down.' The nurse indicated the chairs against the far wall. 'I'll see if I can find her.'

Bryan took a seat and watched the passage of people crossing the lobby; each one intent on reaching their destination, pressed by the importance of their task. Then, at the edge of this eddying tide of medics and orderlies, at the foot of a staircase that let onto the lobby, Katie appeared. She and Bryan were the only still souls amongst the gentile clamour and their eyes met for a long moment. Something flickered across Katie's features, something that subtly altered the face he knew. Then she dropped her gaze and wended her way across the lobby towards him. By the time she arrived at his chair, her mouth held its characteristic upturn and her eyes sparkled with welcome.

'Well, well,' she said. 'Look what the cat's dragged in!'

Bryan stood up: 'They sent me a telegram,' he said. 'Do not delay, written in block capitals. They practically dragged me away.' He became aware he was resisting a strong urge to touch her. 'I'm sorry Katie, there was nothing I could do.'

Katie took a small step back, sensing the frisson: 'I went to work; I left a note,' she said.

'Ah.' Bryan's shoulders sagged. 'I came here to say sorry; I'm here. I'm sorry.'

Katie's eyes narrowed with mischief: 'That's not why you're here,' she said. 'Look, we're very busy. My shift finishes at seven this evening; meet me outside.' Her smile broadened: 'I'm glad you're safe, Bryan. Now scarper!'

Bryan sank back into the chair and watched her cross the lobby and climb the stairs.

***

Bryan blew cigarette smoke into the cooling evening air, smiling and nodding to the trickle of nurses that the shift-change expelled from the hospital doors. Presently his eyes alighted upon Katie. He dropped his cigarette and crushed it under his foot.

'Hello, Bryan,' she said reaching up on tiptoe to place a kiss on his lips. She dropped back on her heels, gazed for a moment into his eyes, then wrapped her arms around him, burrowing her head against his chest: 'You're safe.' Her voice was muffled against his shirt. 'Come on.' She disentangled herself. 'I need to change out of this uniform.'

They followed the flow of nurses down the road towards the accommodation building. Katie put her arm through his, pulling him close to her.

'I assume you were involved?' Katie asked.

'I was up near Alexandria when it kicked off,' Bryan said. 'But I managed to get a transfer right away.'

Katie shot him a glance, lips pursed to still a rising rebuke.

Bryan noticed the look: 'It's why I'm here,' he said. 'Simple as that.'

Katie nodded slowly, looking away to hide her face: 'We've been very busy with it,' she said. 'Lots of them have gone, either discharged or died. But there were so many with burns, terrible burns. It's dangerous to move them, so they stay with us. It's such a slow process and there's so much pain.'

'Well, if there's any luck involved, they're lucky to have you looking after them,' Bryan said.

'Speaking of luck' – she turned back to him, her cheek streaked with the echo of an errant tear – 'yours isn't so good this time. This was my first day on rota. I don't have a day off until Sunday.'

'I don't go back until Monday,' Bryan said. 'And the even better news is' – he tapped his breast pocket – 'I've been paid, so I hope you'll allow me to buy you dinner.'

***

Bryan shared the last of the wine between their glasses. The warm buzz of spiced mutton sat comfortably in his belly. He took a sip of the wine, letting its harsh astringency cut through the last of the meat juices in his mouth. He watched Katie nibbling contemplatively on the last of the flatbread, enjoying the light pressure of her un-shoed foot on the top of his boot.

'They've issued plans for an offensive,' he murmured.

'I'd heard rumours,' she said.

'It's not for a while, as I understand it. But when it starts, it will be bloody ferocious,' Bryan said.

'Needs must, after all,' Katie said through a wan smile. She clasped her hands together under her chin, fingers intertwined. 'I trust your luck will return.'

'May I walk you back to the residence?' Bryan asked.

Katie smiled and shook her head: 'Do you enjoy creating this awkwardness?' she asked. 'Is it so you don't have to ask?'

'I'm just trying to be polite,' Bryan said.

'You don't need to be polite, Bryan,' Katie said. 'I didn't expect to ever see you again. But you're here.' She reached down to pull on her shoe. 'Where are you staying?'

'The Shepheard's,' Bryan said. 'The exact same room, as it happens.'

'Oh. With that lovely bathroom?' Katie's smile broadened: 'I would love a nice hot bath.'

## Friday, 18 September 1942

Bryan washed and shaved in the bathroom that still wafted with a memory of Katie's perfume. A nugget of contentment nestled in his chest, grown from the recent memory of her soft touch and tender administrations, and nurtured by the knowledge that she would be beside him again tonight. But the moment he paused to ponder it, quiescent emotions rose and the acid tang of creeping guilt made his gut writhe like a jealous cat.

He dressed and descended to the restaurant. Eschewing food, he ordered a pot of coffee, sipping the dark and bitter liquid and grimacing as it exacerbated his unquiet stomach. If there was no escape, at least he could explore the limits of his prison: he lit a cigarette and headed out of the hotel. The simple salve of movement quietened his bubbling unease and he emerged into the mid-morning sunshine and hailed a passing cab. The old sedan swerved in to park by the pavement and the driver waited for Bryan to clamber into the back, grinning at him in expectation in the rear-view mirror.

'Gezira Sporting Club, please,' he said and slumped back onto the stained and worn leather of the seat. The old car's rattling engine precluded any conversation from the driver and Bryan began to relax. The taxi turned onto the lion-guarded bridge and crossed to the huge riverine island beyond. A few minutes later, the taxi paused in the gateway of what looked like a transplanted country estate. The driver leaned out of the window, called something across to the gatehouse and then proceeded up the curving drive and drew to a halt at the edge of a tree-dotted lawn. Bryan climbed out, placed the fare in the driver's outstretched palm, leaned in to stuff an extra note into the man's top pocket and stepped back onto the grass as the big car rattled into a U-turn and clanked off down the drive.

Bryan stumbled slightly as the turf gave way a fraction under his feet. He looked down in surprise at the short, tightly-packed blades, still damp from the morning watering. He resisted the urge to squat and press his palm into its incongruent verdancy. Instead, he walked with purposefully slow strides across its springy surface to a signpost in the lawn's centre. Several hand-lettered signs pointed towards facilities in a variety of directions: *Cricket Pitch*; *Bowling Green*; *Polo Field*; *Race Track*; *Tennis Courts*; *Lido*.

The Lido stood on the other side of the lawn. Its entrance sat in the centre of a squat two-storey building that carried a tiled rotunda in the middle of its flat roof, giving the whole edifice the demeanour of a small temple. Each end of the first floor carried a large covered balcony where couples and small groups chatted in the shade, sipping from crystal tumblers. Bryan headed towards the Lido.

The entrance led into a marbled atrium. Bryan closed his eyes for a moment to enjoy the stone-chilled air on his face before ordering a drink at the small bar that ran along the side wall. The entrance was mirrored by another double-door that stood open on the opposite side of the atrium. Bryan sipped his gin and tonic, purring in pleasure at the clink of the ice-cubes, and stepped through the door onto a canopied veranda. The shaded area was crammed with wickerwork chairs and tables around which people in bathing suits thronged, sipping at long drinks and watching their friends splash in the large pool that flanked the veranda. On the other side of the pool, more wicker furniture dotted a wide paved area. Bryan weaved his way through the crush of people, around the end of the pool and onto the paving on the other side. He found an empty table, settled into a chair and closed his eyes against the sunshine.

A shadow fell across his eyelids: 'How's the foot?'

Bryan opened his eyes to see the medical officer from *HMS Unheard* standing before him.

'Ah, Lieutenant Douglas,' Bryan said. 'Good as new, thank you.'

'May I?' Douglas sat down on the other side of the small wicker table.

'When I last saw you, I rather had the impression that you were putting to sea again almost immediately,' Bryan said.

'That's what we thought too.' Douglas took a sip from his drink and swilled it around his front teeth. 'But we got orders to stand by instead.'

'To conserve forces, for the big push?' Bryan asked. 'That's why they won't let me go back to Malta.'

Douglas shot him a quizzical glance: 'Why would the operations of a submarine be affected by the army's plans for an advance in the desert?' Douglas asked. 'Surely, we should be going about our business regardless, sinking enemy supply ships that are heading for the African coast. There has to be another reason for them to order a delay.'

Bryan squinted across the table at the other man: 'Is there a "Because" coming?' he asked.

'Because' – Douglas nodded slowly – 'there is something bigger and more dangerous about to happen in the Med.'

'Such as?' Bryan prompted.

'Invasion?' Douglas murmured.

Bryan's gut convulsed with a lurch of dread that straightened his back in the chair.

'What?' he hissed. 'You're suggesting that the Germans are planning to invade Malta?'

'No' – Douglas levelled his gaze across the table – 'I think the Americans are planning to invade Algeria.'

Bryan slumped back into his chair, his mind racing through the possibilities.

'If the Americans have the forces for a seaborne invasion, why not marshal in England and cross into France or Belgium?' he asked.

'Think about it,' Douglas said. 'Who would you rather have defending the beaches you're trying to land on? The Germans in their concrete bunkers, or the Vichy French in their Algerian fox-holes? There's even a decent chance the French garrisons will consider the Americans as liberators.'

'Alright, that makes a lot of sense,' Bryan said. 'And you'd probably bet that an American army with a secure bridgehead could defeat Rommel, given the time. But after that, isn't Africa a bit of a cul-de-sac?'

'Well, it saves the Suez Canal and the oilfields, so it is an important end in itself,' Douglas said. 'Beyond that, we have to assume - barring a revolution - the Wehrmacht isn't going to surrender until we get allied soldiers into the city streets of Berlin. As you said, everyone expects those soldiers to take the obvious route across France to get there. But, from Tunisia it's a little over one hundred miles across the Med to Sicily. From Sicily you step into mainland Italy. Fight your way north through the length of Italy and you're straight into southern Germany.'

Bryan downed the rest of his gin and crunched his way through what was left of the ice cubes as the implications sank in.

'May I get you a drink?' he asked.

'You may,' Douglas replied.

***

The bulb in the bedside lamp flickered in rhythm with the churnings of a distant generator. Bryan lay on his back, feeling his heartbeat and breathing slowing back to normal. Katie lay next to him, propped up on her elbow, twiddling a finger in the hairs on his chest.

'Remember I told you about our burns patients?' she said. 'I was chatting to one of them today, he's a tank commander. I mentioned you and the things you got up to back home before you were shipped out to Malta.'

'Up to?' Bryan grunted.

'Bluebird Squadron, Kenley, Biggin Hill and all that,' she said. 'He was very interested, but I could only tell him the few little bits that you've told me.'

Bryan reached out an arm and scrabbled blindly on the bedside table for his cigarettes.

'So…' she continued. 'He asked if you might drop in and visit him, and perhaps tell him some more.'

Bryan found the pack and pulled out a cigarette. Katie reached over him to retrieve the matches, brushing her breast against his cheek.

'Would you do that?' she asked. 'For me?'

### Saturday, 19 September 1942

Bryan stepped once again into the lobby of the hospital, this time with Katie by his side.

'Let's get you signed in.' Katie put a solicitous hand on Bryan's elbow and guided him to the reception desk.

Bryan signed the visitors book and followed Katie up the same stairs he'd watched her descend two days before. They led to a wide corridor with a polished wooden floor, the walls punctuated with double doors that were propped open to reveal wards of equally spaced beds and their pyjamaed and bandaged occupants. Towards the end of the corridor the open double doors gave way to single doors that stood closed. Katie came to a halt in front of one.

'His name's Dennis, but he likes to be called Denny.' Katie knocked gently then pushed the door open.

The motion wafted some air out of the room and the scent it carried stopped Bryan in his tracks. In an instant, he was back in a hospital room in Haywards Heath looking into the burnt and blinded eyes of George Anders. Bryan swallowed hard, dismissed the ghost from his mind's eye and followed Katie into the room.

'Good morning, Sergeant,' Katie cooed. 'I've brought that visitor you requested.'

Denny was propped up in his bed. His face appeared uninjured apart from where a dressing was taped under his jawline. His arms, laying atop the bedsheets, bore only minor abrasions, but both his hands and wrists were heavily bandaged. Thick dressings wrapped his torso from the armpits down, and a cage held the sheets away from his hips and legs.

'Hello, Mr Hale,' he said. 'It's good of you to come.'

Katie slipped from the room and Bryan moved a chair closer to the bed and sat down.

'It's my pleasure,' Bryan said, wincing inwardly at the awkwardness of the phrase. 'Are you comfortable? Do you need anything?'

Denny nodded towards a tube taped into his arm: 'The medicine takes the edge off things, thank you for asking.' His face brightened as he changed the subject: 'Katie tells me you've been a fighter pilot since before the war. She said you might even have been flying over El Halfa during the battle.'

'I was,' Bryan said. 'Escorting bombers mostly, three or four times a day. It looked very messy from up there.'

Denny nodded: 'I've never known a battle like it, Mr Hale.' His features hardened slightly. 'We were told to dig our tanks in and we weren't to move for anything.' His eyes narrowed. 'What kind of order is that? You wouldn't tell the navy to drop their anchors and fight where they sat.' He looked up into Bryan's eyes: 'Tanks battles are very much like naval battles,' he said. 'Especially in a desert.

'Anyway, there we sat, waiting. Us and three other tanks behind this short ridge,' he continued. 'I saw something moving about a bit in the distance and one of the other commanders reckoned it was the German advance. So, we decided to drop a few shells in amongst them to slow 'em down a bit. Well, the next thing we know they've punted some smoke shells in between us and them, and we can't see a bloody thing. I wriggle halfway out of the turret hatch with my binoculars so I can keep a better eye on things. Then, as the smoke clears away, I sees it.

'They'd brought up one of their 88s.' Denny's eyes again latched onto Bryan's. 'They tell me they're actually anti-aircraft guns. All very well if you're at twenty thousand feet running at full pelt; not so good when you're looking straight down the bloody barrel at three hundred yards.

'There was no muzzle flash, just a wee puff of white smoke, and I saw the shell coming, snaking towards me like a thin green line close above the ground, cutting a little furrow in the sand as it came towards us. There was an almighty clang, hot liquid spattered my legs, and then there was silence.'

Denny regarded the cage that spared his legs from bearing the weight of two cotton sheets and nodded, marshalling himself in the face of the memory.

'Then... she brewed,' he continued. 'There was fire everywhere, blasting like a blowtorch up around me in the hatch. I levered myself out with my arms and fell off the tank. I'd dragged myself away for a good few yards before I realised my legs were on fire. I tried to put it out myself' – he held up his bandaged hands in testament – 'but then a soldier ran up and shovelled sand over me, God bless him.'

Moisture squeezed into the corners of Denny's eyes: 'Of course, I lost my crew. Good mates, all of them. Not a single one even had the chance to get out of their seats.'

Silence sank between the two men and Denny seemed to deflate, sinking back into his pillow. He turned to regard Bryan with hooded eyes.

'Enough of that,' he said quietly. 'You came to tell me *your* stories.'

'Yes. Yes, of course.' Bryan cleared his throat. 'Well, I joined up before the war, as you know. We were still flying around in biplanes back then...'

As Bryan's tale progressed, Denny's eyes drooped shut and his breathing slowed. Bryan watched the small movement of the other's clavicles become ever slighter. He stopped talking and reached out to touch Denny's pale, motionless forearm.

Bryan rose carefully and placed the chair back in its place against the wall. He opened the door and stepped into the corridor.

'Nurse.' Bryan swallowed against the catch in his voice and tried again: 'Nurse!'

***

Bryan wandered back towards the hospital, the dull glow of several whiskies heated his empty stomach and buzzed in his blood. He arrived just as the shift-change exodus started to flow. Katie appeared through the doors and navigated the milling crowd to reach him. She looked up into his eyes and leaned in to hug him to her.

'He's dead, isn't he? Bryan asked.

Katie released her grip, put her arm through his, and the pair walked slowly away from the hospital steps.

'Yes,' she said. 'Denny died about half-an-hour after you left. It was peaceful. He looked content.' She squeezed Bryan's forearm with her free hand. 'Thank you for visiting him,' she said. 'I'm sure that meant something special to him.'

'It didn't mean what you think it did,' Bryan said.

Katie cocked a quizzical look at him: 'Oh?'

'He didn't want to hear about me. That was just a gentle ruse,' Bryan said. 'He wanted to tell someone about what had happened to *him*. I suppose he felt he couldn't tell it to a nurse or a doctor. I'm sure the staff would've made time to listen, but he wanted to tell it to someone that 'smelled right', someone who'd been in action, someone who knew. He would've preferred another soldier, no doubt. But his time was getting close, and I was the best he could get.'

Bryan felt Katie's grip tighten on his arm.

'He told me his story like he would've told it down the pub, had he got home,' Bryan continued. 'I suspect he even had someone else in his mind, and he was talking to them, not me.'

'His dad, maybe.' Katie sniffed against a swell of emotion. 'Perhaps his dad was a soldier in the last war.'

'I suppose he'll be buried here?' Bryan asked.

'Yes,' Katie answered. 'And I don't suppose his dad will ever get to visit him.'

They walked in slow silence for several moments.

'What shall we do tonight?' Katie asked.

'Why don't we have a little wake, just you and me,' Bryan said. 'Let's keep Denny alive for one more night.'

# Chapter 8

## Sunday, 20 September 1942 – Cairo

Katie roused to the splashing of bath taps wheezing out water in the bathroom. Their noise mingled with the dull throbbing that tightened the skin on her forehead and pulsed in her temples. Bryan emerged from the bathroom with a towel wrapped around his waist and shaving soap lathered around his jaw. He paused the stroke of his razor and grinned widely.

'You look terrible,' he said.

'I'm hungover.' Katie sat up in bed and squeezed her eyes closed against the pounding swell of pain the movement brought to her skull.

'I let you sleep as long as I could,' Bryan said. 'But we're in danger of missing breakfast if you don't get a move on.'

'Ooooh, breakfast.'

Katie climbed carefully out of the bed and padded across to the bathroom, keeping her head as steady as possible. She shut off the taps, dabbled her hand to test the temperature then climbed into the tub, lowering herself gently into its warm embrace. She scooped a double handful of the clear water and splashed it onto her face, washing the sleep from the corners of her eyes. She blinked away the water and regarded Bryan standing at the wash basin. He'd followed her into the bathroom to finish his shave; now he rinsed his razor and whipped the towel from around his waist to dab his face dry. He picked up a bar of soap from the washstand and passed it to Katie with a smile. He dropped the towel by the bath and walked into the bedroom to get dressed.

Katie lathered the soap between her hands and rubbed away the smudged vestiges of last night's makeup, all the while pressing her knees together and willing the buzzing in her abdomen to subside.

\*\*\*

Katie eyed her plate of scrambled eggs with deflated enthusiasm as her stomach squeaked and bubbled at her neglectful treatment. She grasped the nettle and took a swig from her coffee, following it with a forkful of her breakfast. She swallowed purposefully and closed her eyes briefly, waiting for a revolt. The bubbling settled and the strong, hot coffee began to spread its magic into her blood. She added another mouthful of scrambled egg to reinforce the effect.

'I thought it might be nice to go to church,' she said.

Bryan levelled a look across the table: 'I was thinking cocktails by the pool at the Gezira Club.'

'Church first, then cocktails,' Katie said.

Bryan stayed silent.

'There are difficult times ahead, Bryan,' Katie said. 'It might do us both a bit of good to pause the party for an hour or so and settle our minds on something else.'

'Alright, Sweetheart,' Bryan said. 'Let's see if it does that.'

***

The taxi dropped them off on the road outside All Saints Cathedral on Gezira Island. A trickle of people flowed towards its doors from both directions, some were civilians, but most wore uniform. Katie regarded the squat building sat within its own dusty little square.

'How lovely,' she said. 'How did you know this was here?'

'It's in the guidebook,' Bryan said.

Katie linked her arm through Bryan's and they crossed the pavement to the church doors. As they entered, the cooler air pulled a shiver out of Katie's muscles. Bryan gently nudged her towards one of the rear pews. She sat and slid along the polished wooden seat to make room for him. As the pews ahead of them filled, Katie rubbed her palms up and down her arms to quell the sudden goosebumps rising there.

'It's a cathedral,' Bryan whispered, his eyebrows raised in mock excitement. 'Probably means we'll get a bishop.'

Katie continued rubbing at the stubborn goosebumps on her arms and looked around the church. The looming space made her feel smaller than she was, as if she was retreating into her own diminutive frame. She'd hoped for the relief of relaxation, but the closeness of this congregation of unknown people sapped a part of her identity, diluted whatever purpose she thought she'd brought. The strain of recent weeks, Bryan's departure and unexpected return, and yesterday's death of Denny, a patient amongst hundreds who suddenly came to mean so much, pressed down on what she already carried in her heart.

'Can we leave-'

Her whisper was bludgeoned away by the reverberating squall of the organ's first chord and the wooden clonking of the congregation coming to their feet. Bryan stood, and Katie, trapped by the music, stood with him. Bustling movement behind her caught her attention and she looked over

101

her shoulder to see an open wooden door disgorge a procession of robed choirboys led by a man carrying a large silver cross atop a polished wooden staff.

Katie cranked her head around to face forwards and sidled a bit closer to Bryan's side. She watched from the corner of her eye as the procession passed down the aisle. Behind the dozen-or-so choirboys there plodded a portly man in resplendent robes and a bejewelled mitre. Bryan glanced at her and smiled impishly, but he missed the message in her eyes.

The congregation droned through the first hymn and were at last instructed to sit. Katie craned over her shoulder to see the doorway was closed and two surpliced vergers stood, one either side of the heavy wooden doors, like wardens of moral rectitude. She turned back, accepting that she was stuck for the duration, half listening to the lilting words of the reading that echoed softly around the nave. The reading finished and the organ once more mustered the crowd to shamble upright and sing. Katie followed the words in her hymn book as they crawled through the verses to the end. The final chord echoed away to silence, everyone sat once more, and the bishop hauled his bulk into the pulpit to deliver his sermon.

'There was a soldier in my congregation last week, and we chatted after the service,' he began. 'This young man told me about the fiancée he'd left at home and he admitted he had been puzzled by a gift she had sent him. It was a harmonica, and it came with a letter saying she was looking forward to hearing the tunes he'd learned when he went home on leave. He was baffled. "She doesn't know I'm tone-deaf," he told me. "What am I to do?". I simply advised him to always try his best to make her happy and sent him on his way.

'But, in reality, it was his fiancée who was tone-deaf. She sent the instrument to be a distraction. She wanted her future husband to sit alone practising to play that harmonica in the hope that this would prevent him from seeking out other distractions in the street and alleys of Cairo. She was tone-deaf to the truth that, when love is strong, fidelity sings along in beautiful descant harmony.

'Fidelity is like a precious stone, as real and lasting as the diamond in a wedding ring. Fidelity is unconditional. When you voice your wedding vows, you are promising; if your spouse changes, *you* will be faithful; if there are hard times, *you* will be faithful; if you are parted for days, months or years, you *will* be faithful. May God grant you through your prayers the strength and commitment to be faithful until the end in both your worldly love, and your spiritual love for The Lord. Let us pray.'

***

The congregation shuffled through the door past the smiling clergyman and into the dazzling sunlight. Bryan hailed one of the taxis that were sidling past in search of business, and they clambered into the back.

Katie stayed silent, glaring out of the window with unfocussed eyes, tussling with a surge of icy indignation that eventually melted into the warm background glow of guilt. As the taxi swept through the gates of the Sporting Club, the contradictions untangled and she clenched her jaw in resolution.

The taxi pulled up close to the lido and they climbed out. Bryan paid the driver and the car pulled away.

'The bar is in the lido,' Bryan said, starting towards the entrance.

'Can we go for a stroll first?' Katie asked.

Bryan looked into her eyes for a moment, and she looked away down the pathway to escape his scrutiny: 'I can see tennis courts down this way,' she said. 'Let's take a look.'

'Alright,' Bryan said. He returned to her side and they started to walk down the path. Bryan lit a cigarette, took a couple of deep draws, and then broke the uncomfortable silence: 'Going to church obviously wasn't the greatest of ideas.'

Katie took a steadying breath, exhaling slowly through her nose: 'A letter arrived a couple of weeks ago,' she said. 'It had been chasing me around the Mediterranean for a while. It was from my husband.' Katie stopped walking. 'May I have a cigarette?' she asked.

Bryan opened his pack and she drew one out, holding it to her mouth between her fingers as Bryan struck a match to light it. She avoided catching his eye, fearing it would derail her. She started walking again and Bryan matched her pace.

'The letter was full of things about home, about how he was coping with his injured leg, how he'd stopped needing crutches and now coped with just a walking stick, how his scar looked like rasher of streaky bacon.' She inhaled deeply of the tobacco smoke. 'He went on to say how much he loved me and missed me, and how he couldn't wait for me to come home.'

'Katie, I–' Bryan began.

'Please be quiet,' Katie cut him short. 'Just listen to me.' She took another pull on the cigarette and continued: 'My husband is exactly the kind of man that I always thought I would marry. I was happy when we got married, and had the world carried on the way it was, we would've had a blissfully happy life together. But the world didn't carry on; the war came along and the world conspired with it to show me many, many things. One of those things was you, Bryan.

'When you vanished from The Shepheard, I thought it was unlikely I'd ever see you again. Having you turn up in my hospital ward in the first place was just a happy accident, just another jolly little distraction.' She frowned slightly at the echo of the word. 'So, when the letter turned up, I had to think about a lot of things that had slipped my mind. I decided to straighten out, go back to being the Katie I used to be. Because then, I'd be able to go home one day and everything would go back to normal. But then you came back. Sitting there in the hospital lobby with a few days leave to while away.'

They reached the wire fence that enclosed tennis courts. A sedate game was underway, the players suppressed by the weight of the early afternoon heat, their whites dazzling in the sunshine. Katie dropped her cigarette onto the path and crushed it under her sole.

'Do you remember when our paths crossed in Gibraltar? I said that I might've fallen in love with you at another time, in another place. Well, it turns out, that other place is Cairo.'

'Is this because of that sermon?' Bryan asked.

'No!' Katie turned away to hide the moisture brimming in her eyes. 'Yes!' She turned back, heedless of the tears that now tracked her face. 'I was going to watch you leave tomorrow and let that be an end to it. But now' – she raised her hands in hopeless supplication – 'I'm the one that has to leave. Goodbye, Bryan.'

Katie turned and walked away. Her shoulder muscles bunched in expectation of the voice that would call her back, but it was silence that followed her down the pathway to the taxi rank.

### Monday, 21 September 1942

Bryan stepped out from the covered porch of The Shepheard's Hotel onto the pavement, carrying his case into the chill dawn air, looking and feeling like an aimless itinerant. He paused and looked back at the hotel's grand façade for the last time. It had to be the last time; he didn't have the resolve to resist Katie, and he didn't have the space in his heart to treat her the way she deserved.

He walked through streets that were beginning to flex with the awakening population. Traders were setting out their wares and donkey-carts delivered or collected the goods needed to satisfy the wave of Egyptians that the morning would wash into the lanes. As he walked, the musical babbling of their salutations, squabbling and gossip washed over him like a salve. With each step his regret slipped away, replaced by the glacial creep of a familiar, mechanical resolve for the battle ahead.

He arrived at RAF headquarters and entered between the bleary-eyed guards on its doorstep. He reported his arrival, handed in unused chits and joined the other waiting airmen on the chairs that lined the wall. The minutes ticked by, filled with overheard tales of drinking and conquest, peppered with the exotic names of sweet, yielding women; the made-up names that had filled the boasts of a thousand men, and whose weary bearers would wait today in the sultry, sticky heat for the next boastful man, and then the next.

An orderly stepped into the room: 'Landing ground ninety-seven,' he called. 'Transport is outside.'

*** 

Bryan leaned his elbow on the tailgate and idly scanned the landscape as it passed. The road snaked down to run alongside the airfield and Bryan noticed groups of airmen dotted about the flat expanse, each group centred around a wheelbarrow into which they hefted rocks lifted from the sandy ground. It seemed LG97 was expanding.

The truck lurched off the road and lumbered onto the landing ground, wheezing to a halt outside the mess tent. The adjutant checked the returnees off his clipboard list as they disembarked, and the men drifted away towards their tents. Bryan dallied at the mess tent; he poured a mug of tea to wash the aftertaste of exhaust fumes from his throat and eavesdropped the murmured conversation of the men sitting at the tables around him. An undercurrent of lethargy ran through the gathering, interrupted briefly by the animated chatter of airmen boarding the truck outside to begin their leave in Cairo.

Bryan watched the truck grind away, finished his tea, then walked across the airfield to his tent. He ducked inside and laid his case on his cot. He

105

noticed a kitbag on the other bed. Snowy hadn't been in the mess, there were no cricket matches on the go, and neither of them would be flying until tomorrow at the earliest. Bryan left the tent, resolved to find his friend.

Once clear of the clustered tents, Bryan shaded his eyes and scanned the landing ground. Out at the edge of the wide runway there was a rock where no rock should be. Bryan squinted against the interfering shimmer of the heat haze and the rock resolved into a figure sitting cross-legged on the hard ground. He lit a cigarette and walked towards the figure.

Engines crackled into life and a pair of Spitfires taxied away from dispersal, paused briefly to let the airmen dismount from their wings and get clear, then accelerated along the strip. Bryan reached the figure as the fighters ripped past, just fifty yards away. The seated man's head inclined to watch them climb away, retracting their wheels like birds tucking their legs into their feathered bellies.

Bryan paused, squeezing his eyes and mouth shut while the swirl of dust kicked up by the fighters rolled over him, then he spoke: 'Hello, Snowy,' he said. 'How was your leave?'

The man's head swivelled, his face covered by a neckerchief and dust-rimmed sunglasses.

'Not bad,' Snowy said, turning his gaze back to the runway. 'The chaps at Aboukir airfield let me use a bunk in their mess for the duration. But they wouldn't let me keep the car.'

'That's not unreasonable, I suppose,' Bryan said.

'Maybe not,' Snowy replied. 'But I can tell you that hitch-hiking from Alexandra to the middle of the desert is *not* the best fun I've ever had.' He shook his head to himself: 'The army can be so rude. You wouldn't believe what was shouted at me from the back of passing trucks.'

Bryan crouched down next to his friend.

'What are you doing sitting out here?' he asked.

'Oh, I don't know,' Snowy answered. 'Maybe I'm hoping some of it will rub off on me.'

Another pair of Spitfires roared past, left the ground and banked away, blasting their propwash over the two men. Bryan spluttered against the churning dust, holding his palms to his face like a mask.

'Can we get away from the runway, please?' he shouted against the engine noise.

Snowy stood up, dislodging runnels of fine sand from the creases in his clothing, and the pair walked along the edge of the runway towards the aircraft dotted about in dispersal.

'What are you hoping will rub off on you?' Bryan asked.

'Resolve, I suppose,' Snowy answered. 'Boldness?' he ventured. 'Aplomb? Poise? Swashbuckle?' He swept the horizon and its assembled warplanes as if searching for another word to obfuscate his plight. His head and shoulders drooped in defeat and he pulled the neckerchief down from his face. 'Courage,' he admitted at last. 'I think I lack the courage to do this.'

Bryan glanced across at the hunched, unhappy figure walking next to him.

'I reckon there's two or three weeks before things start to happen again around here,' Bryan said. He nodded towards two more Spitfires taxiing towards the runway: 'It looks like they're running standing patrols in pairs. We can use those to run through some of the things you need to practise.' He slapped Snowy on the back. 'It's alright to be uneasy. But never forget; running away at just the right time is a major part of being a successful fighter pilot.'

Bryan glanced across to see a smile turn the edges of Snowy's mouth.

'So, tell me about Alexandria.' Bryan strove to maintain some levity: 'How are the girls at Mary's House?'

'Mary's House now has a lot of American visitors,' Snowy answered. 'They don't treat the girls so well.'

Snowy turned his head towards Bryan and pulled off his sunglasses. His left eye was heavily bloodshot and the socket was darkened with purple bruising.

'Good Lord,' Bryan said. 'How'd you come by that little beauty?'

'I informed one of the Americans that he might consider being a bit more courteous to his dancing partner.' Snowy replaced his sunglasses and pushed them gingerly up his nose. 'Luckily the fellow's friends prevented him from explaining in any further detail why he thought I was mistaken, and I took their kind advice about finding somewhere else to drink.'

'Snowy!' Bryan shook his head in mock dismay. 'Now is not the time to be fomenting an international incident with our allies.'

'Seriously, Bryan, it made me think,' Snowy said. 'Why did I believe that I was treating them any better than he was?'

'From what I've seen, you are always kind to them,' Bryan answered. 'I think they all genuinely like you for that.'

Snowy shrugged: 'Being kind to a woman shouldn't go hand-in-hand with expecting her to fuck you later.'

Bryan turned his face away for a moment to hide the flush that rose on his cheeks: 'Sometimes you have to take your kindness where you can find it, Snowy.'

## Tuesday, 22 September 1942

Bryan sat across from Snowy in the mess tent. Slow curls of steam ascended from the mugs set on the trestle between them. A notebook laid open next to Snowy's mug.

'The most important thing' – Bryan lit a cigarette and pushed the pack across to Snowy – 'is to look like you know what you're doing.'

'Even if you don't?' Snowy lit his smoke, adjusted his sunglasses and hunched down on his elbows to listen.

'Especially then,' Bryan answered. 'Our opposition is expecting to be outnumbered. If he can get an easy kill, he will happily take it and run for home. Sticking close to my tail as long as you can protects us both.'

'That's where it went wrong last time.' Snowy pursed his lips at the memory.

'It will happen again,' Bryan said. 'We *will* get split up. When that happens, there is nothing, believe me, nothing on that control panel that requires your attention. Least of all your fuel gauge.'

Snowy flushed at the mild rebuke.

'Never stop looking around,' Bryan continued. 'Especially check behind you. Even when you're attacking something, check in your mirror, over and over.' Bryan sucked in a lungful of tobacco smoke. 'I'm living the consequences of forgetting that one.'

Snowy scratched in his notebook with a pencil.

'Do you remember that 109?' Bryan asked.

Snowy brightened: 'The one I shot down?'

'You didn't get a single bullet within five yards of it,' Bryan said.

Snowy's features sagged and he dropped his eyes to his notepad again.

'If it's possible, try to get closer before you open fire,' Bryan said. 'And use more deflection than you think you need until you're experienced enough to *feel* the angles. If you're bounced, turn towards the threat. If you are attacked, pull the tightest turn you can manage and stick with it.'

Snowy silently mouthed the words *stick with it* as he scribbled another note: 'Won't that leave you flying in circles?' he asked.

'Reversing the turn will take you across your enemy's gunsights,' Bryan said. 'Flying in a tight enough circle might bring him into yours.'

'Ah!' Snowy said, scribbling another note.

'If you're really in the shit and you're taking hits' – Bryan held out his flat hand between their faces to illustrate the movement – 'make a quick half-roll, pull the stick back when you're on your side, and then rudder into a steep dive.'

Snowy watched Bryan's hand descend vertically until the fingertips touched the table.

'But that only works properly' – Bryan arched an eyebrow at his friend – if you have sufficient altitude.'

Snowy picked up his book and scanned his notes: 'Very helpful,' he muttered. 'Solid information.'

'Good.' Bryan drained his tea. 'Because we're down for a patrol in half-an-hour.'

***

Snowy eased back on the stick, lifting the Spitfire off the ground. He pushed the lever to retract the undercarriage, checked he was a safe distance behind Bryan's port wing, then glanced into his mirror. This involuntary action brought a thrill to his scalp; he was getting better at his job. He checked his position again, adjusted his throttle, and flicked his eyes back to the mirror. The dust from their take-off drifted away revealing the expanding girth of Landing Ground 97 and the growing number of aircraft sequestered around its perimeter. This swelling of dispassionate armed force that was fighting on his side bolstered his spirit and helped quell the nerves that fluttered in his stomach. He shadowed Bryan's northward bank towards the coast, quartering the hostile western sky with growing confidence as the two fighters climbed through the clear air.

The glittering reflections of the sea rolled over the horizon as they levelled out at fifteen-thousand feet.

'*Turning onto patrol line now,*' Bryan's voiced buzzed into Snowy's earphones. '*We'll stay just this side of the lines. Keep your eyes peeled.*'

Snowy followed Bryan's wide left turn and settled into their southerly course. Snowy's head bobbled about, scanning the sky above his leader and behind his own starboard wing, checking his mirror, sweeping behind his port wing, and snatching a look at desert floor below. There were a few obvious signs of a defensive line in the sand and some tell-tale traces of moving vehicles, but nothing that chimed with Snowy's erstwhile sense of assurance.

'Now, now,' he muttered under his breath. 'We're very good at camouflage. Yes, that's it.' He went back to scanning the blue vault. 'Very good at camouflage.'

At the end of the run, the pair wheeled and back-tracked, crossing paths only with two other British fighters tacking south on the same patrol line.

As the coastline crept into view, Bryan's voiced crackled over the wireless: *'Let's get out a little way beyond the beach and I'll watch your back while you practise some tight turns and evasive action.'*

'Alright,' Snowy answered. 'That's sounds like a good idea.'

*'Just one thing,'* Bryan said. *'How are you for fuel?'*

Snowy had looked down at the panel before he realised the joke.

# Chapter 9

## Wednesday, 30 September 1942 – Landing Ground 97

Bryan roused from his sleep with a gentle jolt of unease. He lay perfectly still in the chill pre-dawn darkness, the follicles on the back of his neck tingling with instinctive warning. It took a few moments to separate a new sound from under Snowy's sonorous breathing; a dull rumbling wobbled the air's foundations. A thunderstorm perhaps? No. It was too constant; it whispered tidings of sustained violence. Bryan swung his legs out of the cot, pulled on his boots and shirt, and slunk out of the tent.

Outside, away from the rasp of Snowy's flaring nostrils, the grumbling dissonance became distinct: artillery, quite a lot of it. Bryan weaved his way through the canvas village, seeking a clear view of the western horizon. Passing between the last two tents, a dull radiance in the night sky confirmed his diagnosis, but it glowed deep inland, isolated in a corner of the desert directly south-west from the airfield.

Bryan lit a cigarette and pondered the coruscating patch of light. It was impossible at this distance to tell whose guns were delivering the barrage, but obvious it was too limited in scope to be a major offensive in either direction. He glanced around behind him; the pilots slept on and there was no-one coming to wake them. The tobacco smoke rubbed harshly in his throat and penetrated its bitterness into his sleep-furred tongue. He tossed the cigarette into the sand and set off towards the mess.

A figure stood by the main trestle waiting for the tea-urn to heat. As Bryan drew closer, the dim light of the urn's burner showed it to be the squadron leader. Barnard turned at the sound of Bryan's approach.

'Morning, Hale,' he said. 'You're about early.'

'Yes, sir,' Bryan said. 'I'm mostly a fairly solid sleeper, but I find an artillery barrage wakes me up every time.'

A smile crept onto Barnard's face and he lifted his gaze to the patch of distant iridescence that had begun to pale in the slowly lightening sky: 'A commendable talent,' he said.

'Do we know what it is?' Bryan asked.

'Yes.' Barnard poured two mugs from the urn and handed one to Bryan. 'It's nine regiments of British artillery dropping a creeping barrage into the Munassib Depression.'

'A creeping barrage?' Bryan said. 'Isn't that the way we fought the last war?'

'It's a probing attack,' Barnard answered. 'They're testing the German defences. I'm not an infantry officer, but I suspect there's no better way to advance on a defended objective over open ground.'

Bryan's head swivelled back to the south-west, to the twinkling lights and the savage significance they now reflected. As he watched, the flashing faltered and dimmed, and the rumbling rolled towards a chill silence.

'Will they be getting air cover?' Bryan asked quietly.

'The army's in amongst the enemy now; so it's become an overlapping target,' Barnard said. 'We're on standby. If they're successful, we'll support them against any counter attack. If it doesn't go so well, then they're lost, I'm afraid.'

Bryan held his gaze on the now anonymous spot on the rapidly brightening horizon: 'Testing their defences,' he murmured.

He turned to see the squadron leader walking away.

## Monday, 5 October 1942

The rain surged in intensity for a few seconds then abated, as if inhaling a breath, before redoubling its cudgelling beat on the tent. Cigarette smoke gathered along the apex, settling against the damp-darkened canvas in misty ribbons. Snowy and Bryan sat on their cots, raincapes draped across their shoulders in the expectation of inevitable leaks. Snowy stood into a half-crouch and shuffled to the entrance, pulling open a spyhole in the tent-flaps with his fingers.

'It's bloody vertical,' he said. 'Where does all this water come from in a bloody desert?'

'From somewhere else,' Bryan said. 'Obviously.'

Snowy carefully pulled the tent-flaps closed and returned to his cot.

'The heaviest rain I've seen before was one bank holiday in Hastings,' Snowy said. 'Not quite as hard as this, but hard enough to stop everything from moving and clear the streets. Judith and me got off the train and waited in the station for the rain to ease.' Snowy's features softened and his eyes sparkled with the memory. 'After an hour, it was still coming down like curtain rods, so we got on the next train home. Lots of other families and couples gave up and did the same. Judith suggested that we all open our picnics in the carriage and it turned into quite the party; sing-songs and everything.' A lone tear bulged into the corner of his eye and he wiped it away with a knuckle. 'Good memories,' he muttered. 'Good memories of a good woman.'

Bryan examined his friend's face for a moment: 'How are things?' Bryan tapped his chest to expand his meaning.

Snowy studied the glowing cigarette clamped between his fingers as he pondered the question.

'I know a lot better how I should react when it comes to the crunch,' Snowy began. 'I can only hope that I'll carry it through when it matters.'

'Let me make a confession,' Bryan said. 'When I was on Beaufighters flying night ops in England I had what you might call a bit of a turn.' Bryan squashed his cigarette out under his heel and lit another. 'A few bad things piled up, one after another and I didn't handle it as well as I should've. In fact, I went AWOL and they found me drunk and ranting in a hotel bar on the Norfolk coast. Anyway' – he took a deep draw on his cigarette – 'the upshot was, they diagnosed me with operational tiredness and I spent three months in a hospital with fops wearing white coats asking me stupid bloody questions.'

Bryan looked up to see Snowy gazing at him, open-mouthed.

'The point I'm making is, I got through it.' Bryan smiled at his blinking friend. 'You took a lot more damage than I did, a great deal more. They sent *me* to a sanatorium. *You* took yourself to Mary's House. I wish you'd been my doctor.'

Snowy barked a short laugh: 'Crikey, Bryan,' he said. 'Talk about skeletons in the closet!'

'Well, let's leave them there, please,' Bryan muttered.

The rain abruptly eased its clamouring and sighed away to silence as the canvas brightened with emerging sunlight.

'Come on,' Bryan said. 'Let's see if we can get to the mess before all the tables get taken.'

Snowy unlaced the tent flaps and the two men emerged onto the puddled earth. Activity was resuming around the field as the increasing warmth in the air drew the first tendrils of evaporating water from the ground.

'The leave rota has run its course,' Bryan said as they walked. 'The last of the lads will be coming back tomorrow. I suspect things will be getting busier around here quite soon.'

Snowy nodded in mute acceptance and looked away to the west in contemplation. A bar of black malevolence clenched that horizon, dragging beneath it a sodden petticoat of pummelling rain across the contested desert battlefield.

'It looks like we're on the edge of the storm,' Snowy said.

'Yes.' Bryan followed his gaze. 'That's exactly where we are.'

## Tuesday, 6 October 1942

Bryan sipped at his tea and stole a glance at Snowy's face. The other man's expression was unreadable, but his uncharacteristic lapses into silence reflected an inner disquiet. Bryan left his friend's introspection undisturbed and allowed his own gaze to blur into defocus. The battle that was now imminent would be fought for the prize of irreversible momentum. A plucky, hard-won score draw, like the English summer of 1940 was not an option; the desert in winter, unlike the English Channel, would not transform itself into a barrier to the conquering rush of the Wehrmacht. There would be no blitzing of cities because in Egypt there was nothing to be gained by terrorising the civilian population. This would be a battle between vectors of force applied against points of weakness; a game of chess played with blood and iron from a position of fluid fragility not seen since the tide of Panzers washed the BEF onto the beaches of Dunkirk.

The grumble of a heavy engine interrupted Bryan's reverie as a heavy truck pulled up outside the mess. He watched the tailgate drop and the returning airmen tumble from the back, pulling kitbags behind them. An orderly clutching a clipboard against his forearm checked off their names.

With all the men accounted for, the orderly raised his voice, swivelling his head like a town crier to take in the mess tent with his announcement: 'Firebird Squadron, ready to fly in one hour, gentlemen. One hour!'

Snowy lifted his head at the words and pulled a terse smile: 'I suppose that means that the game's afoot.'

*** 

The pilots stood around their squadron leader. The heavy humidity of evaporated rain thickened the air and the loose circle of men beaded sweat under their flying helmets.

'The rainstorms were far heavier in occupied Western Egypt, and we have intelligence to suggest that some of the enemy's airfields are waterlogged,' Barnard announced. 'It's suggested that the enemy won't be able to get any fighters off the ground for the next few days. Quite naturally, the bomber boys are keen to take advantage of this temporary opportunity to entertain a captive audience.'

A murmur of subdued laughter went around the pilots.

'A squadron of Bostons will rendezvous with us over the airfield and we're detailed to give them top cover. But, if the intelligence is right, it should be a milk-run.'

The pilots dispersed to their Spitfires, pulling on parachutes, clambering onto wings and slotting into cockpits. Bryan went through the familiar motions with a sense of relief; an easy trip would bolster Snowy's growing self-confidence.

The fighters taxied out, accelerating along the runway and lifting off in pairs. The damp-darkened earth held onto its dust and the squadron got away quickly, forming into a loose gaggle and settling into a wide, spiralling climb.

'*Bombers in sight now,*' Barnard's voice was clear and calm. '*Loosen up and follow them in.*'

Bryan glanced down to see the formation of straight-winged aircraft slide west across the landscape, their curved Perspex noses like blunt wedges pushing through the clear sky. Firebird Squadron spread out a few thousand feet above them, umbrellaing their tails against danger. Bryan edged out to the starboard fringe of the fighter canopy. He checked Snowy's presence in his mirror and swept the cloud-smudged sky for danger. The bombers angled inland onto their approach to the target and Firebird Squadron drifted across the sky to shadow them.

The clustered features of the enemy airfield resolved from the damp golden flatness of the sodden desert; trackways, canvas shelters, trucks, bowsers and dispersed aircraft inadequately concealed under drapes of netting dotted a wide area smeared with large patches of dark standing water. Bryan scanned the empty sky. The intelligence was right; there would be no fighter opposition today. He dropped his gaze to the bombers below, keen to watch their attack.

The formation lumbered closer, bomb-bay doors opening as they flew straight and level, locked into the tramlines of their bomb run. Around the airfield's perimeter, flashes of light sparkled, each one birthing a tiny puff of white smoke that drifted harmlessly aside on the sluggish breeze. Half a breath later, the shells they'd spawned burst like ugly flares amongst the bombers, spitting jagged metal through thin aluminium skins. One of the bombers spouted flames from its mid-section that quickly engulfed the entire tail. Irretrievable, it dropped from the formation like a torch, curving to its explosive termination in the rock-strewn sand.

Bryan flinched as another barrage of shells flashed into being amongst the advancing formation. One crashed into the nose of a bomber, flinging debris into the slipstream, leaving the eviscerated aircraft to side-slip and curve away, no-one left to heed its direction. Another bomber spouted flame and smoke from its starboard engine, losing speed but persevering on its course.

At last, small flecks of black dropped from the formation and the bombers banked away from the airfield, except the one trailing smoke, which continued west, its undercarriage sagging from its burning wing.

The falling objects curved down, lost from sight against the dark terrain, to hit a moment later, stitching trails of explosive destruction in ten narrow stripes across the airfield.

Firebird Squadron wheeled around to follow the bombers back towards the frontline. As they flew east, Bryan watched disconsolately as another of the big aircraft detached from the formation and steadily lost altitude. One parachute blossomed in the last minutes before the bomber ploughed a dark scar into the rock-strewn sandscape and burst into flames.

*** 

Firebird Squadron swept into land and taxied out in single file to dispersal. Bryan shut down his engine, pulled back the canopy and clambered out of the aircraft. The press of humidity gripped him, prickling sweat into his arm pits and beneath the leather of his helmet. He shrugged his parachute onto the fighter's wing and plucked the helmet from his head. Scrubbing his knuckles across his itchy scalp he walked to where Snowy stood waiting.

'That was a bit of a mess,' Snowy said.

'It wasn't great,' Bryan said. 'At least it put some holes in their runway.'

'Holes?' Snowy's brow creased with a frown. 'Four out of twelve shot down, and one parachute.'

Bryan rested a hand on his friend's shoulder: 'There'll be bigger cock-ups,' he said. 'Don't dwell on it.'

The squadron leader walked by: 'Time for a quick brew and a piss, lads,' he called over. 'Then back on stand-by.'

### Thursday, 8 October 1942

Bryan lay on the wing of his Spitfire, shoulder and hip against the warm aluminium skin of the fuselage, gazing up at nothing in the sky's azure-grey depths. Waiting was the part he'd always hated. Waiting on stand-by was the worst part of a bad thing, and knowing he was waiting for the army to pull itself together made it particularly hateful. A formation of aircraft intruded into the corner of his vision; tiny motes of darkness forming from the sun's glare. Bryan raised his head from its metal pillow and shaded his eyes with his hand. He watched the indistinct shapes getting closer and a thrill of adrenalin buzzed through his temples; something didn't look right.

Bryan slid down the wing and dropped softly onto the ground, moving like a wary cat, his muscles tensed in readiness to run. The formation was approaching from the east, which was reassuring; and nobody was shooting at the newcomers, another positive indication. Bryan relaxed as the fighter planes dropped into orbit and pulled away one by one to approach for landing, the white stars on their wings identifying them as American aircraft.

Bryan sidled around to the front of his Spitfire and leaned against a propeller blade to wait. Within a few minutes, the leader of the landed squadron taxied past him on his way to a more distant dispersal. The fighter in which he sat looked much like a Hurricane with a longer, deeper nose. The added depth came from a bulbous air intake below the engine compartment. Painted on this extra fuselage space was a snarling, tooth-lined mouth. Above it, just behind the propeller, was a savage, ire-filled eye. Bryan grinned in appreciation at this flamboyant belligerence, and the pilot grinned back and waved as he passed.

The procession of fighters trundled by; Bryan lit a cigarette behind cupped hands and watched them go. When the last of the Americans had fish-tailed away down the track, Bryan went back to his perch to resume his waiting with a slightly lifted heart.

\*\*\*

The orderly waltzed his zig-zag path through the tents, tapping a stick against each canvas wall.

'Firebird Squadron,' he intoned as he walked. 'Special briefing in the mess. Ten minutes. Firebird Squadron…'

Bryan and Snowy joined the drift of pilots moving across the field towards the large mess tent.

'Let's hope it's not the start of another cock-up,' Snowy said.

'I wouldn't place any large bets,' Bryan replied.

They walked into the mess. The American pilots were in one group, filling a couple of tables. The British pilots were shuffling onto tables on the other side of the room. Bryan winked at Snowy and went to sit next to an American.

Bryan slid onto the bench and the man turned to smile a greeting.

'Hi,' he said.

'Hello,' Bryan answered.

The man's smile broadened: 'Hell-low,' he corrected himself with mock formality.

'Do you know what's on the cards?' Bryan asked.

'Do I know what's cooking?' the man clarified. 'Listen, bud, we just go where they tell us, and they told us you could use a little help.'

A playful cuffing fight broke out between two pilots at the table.

'The guys might seem a little strange at the beginning' – the man nodded towards the rest of the group – 'but you'll soon get used to us.'

'I flew with an American back in England,' Bryan said.

'One of the pioneers?' The man pursed his lips and nodded in appreciation. 'Those guys had balls.'

'This one even wrote a book about his balls,' Bryan said.

The American's jaw dropped: 'Donaldson!' he gasped. 'You knew Gerry Donaldson? He was quite famous.'

'Was?' Bryan said.

'Rumour has it he went missing last month,' the American said. 'One of the boys said he read it in a paper. He ditched in the sea and they never found him.'

'The sea?' Bryan pressed.

'Yeah. The English Sea, or something,' the man replied. 'I don't know geography so much.'

'Good evening, gentlemen.' Barnard's voice stilled all conversations.

Firebird's squadron leader stood in a spot from where he could address all the tables and everyone swivelled to face his way.

'You probably noticed the arrival today of a squadron of Warhawks,' Barnard continued, nodding a welcome to the American pilots. 'They've been moved up specifically to help in another attack on the enemy airfield we visited the other day. I think we all saw that a straight forward bombing attack brought limited success on such a large, dispersed target. On top of that, slow-moving aircraft flying in a straight line are a bit of a gift for the AA defences. HQ are still very keen to neutralise this airfield and have detailed this new plan of attack to me this afternoon.'

'The Warhawk is well suited to dive-bombing, and a dive-bomber can choose an individual target with a high degree of accuracy. However, during its dive' – Barnard cast his eyes around his own pilots – 'an aircraft can obviously not manoeuvre and is therefore vulnerable to accurate ground fire, particularly as it pulls out of the dive. Which is where we come in.

'Firebird Squadron will go in first to attack the airfield's anti-aircraft emplacements at low level.' He paused, looking from face to face amongst his men. 'While this diversion is underway, the Warhawks will approach and commence their bombing attack.

'We're told by intelligence that the enemy's runways are still quite waterlogged, so hopefully there'll be nothing in the air to bother us.' He pulled a stiff smile: 'We go at first light tomorrow. Are there any questions?'

***

The pilots drifted away from the mess in small groups. The only sound of chatter in the encroaching darkness drifted along with an American accent.

Snowy and Bryan meandered shoulder-to-shoulder back towards their tent.

'Are you alright?' Snowy asked. 'You're normally a bit sparkier when you know there's a proper op on the horizon.'

'Yes. I'm sorry,' Bryan said. 'One of those yanks gave me some bad news about someone I knew.'

'A friend?' Snowy asked.

'We flew together,' Bryan replied.

They walked on in silence for a few moments.

'Seems like it might be a bit hairy tomorrow,' Snowy said.

'It'll be alright,' Bryan said. 'As long as they don't know we're coming.'

## Friday, 9 October 1942

Squadron Leader Barnard stood in front of a blackboard, a stick of chalk grasped in his fingers. A shallow U-shaped chalk line, representing the

119

coast, bisected the board. Landing Ground 97 was marked with a cross on the righthand side, the enemy airfield was a cross on the left.

'We're taking a roundabout approach to this mission,' he began. 'Success depends on surprise, so the fewer people see us, the better.' Barnard drew a line from the landing ground almost due north across the coastline, then extended the line following the coast towards the west. 'When we're due north of the target, we turn' – his chalk squeaked downwards to the second cross – 'and make our attack.

'The Warhawks will shadow us at an appropriate distance to arrive after our attack begins. We will fly the whole approach at low-level. The dive-bombers will, for obvious reasons, be at around nine-thousand feet. So, the Americans will take off first to gain altitude. Good luck, everyone.'

Firebird's pilots stood and left the mess tent, making their way through the pre-dawn gloom towards dispersal. The certainty of immediate danger subdued most of the men into contemplative silence. Snowy and Bryan walked side-by-side at the edge of the shuffling group.

Snowy cleared his throat and looked across at Bryan: 'This isn't a "just-stick-with-me" sort of situation, is it?' he asked quietly.

'No,' Bryan said. 'But you've done this before. Remember that truck convoy?'

Snowy winced inwardly at the memory of the running man.

Bryan continued: 'Anti-aircraft guns aren't much different from trucks, after all.'

'Except for the *guns* bit,' Snowy said.

They walked in silence for a few moments before Snowy cleared his throat again.

'Any last hints and tips?' he asked.

'If you're hit, gain altitude,' Bryan said. 'Give yourself time to make the right decision about what you do next.'

Engines kicked into life, ruffling the still air with their sonorous vibrations. The pilots reached the line of waiting Spitfires and turned as the engine noise roared louder. The Warhawks lumbered past, shark-teeth glinting with pearly iridescence in the breaking dawn light. Each aircraft carried six hefty bombs; two under each wing and two under the fuselage. The final aircraft waggled past and Barnard strode across in its wake, flying helmet clutched in his hand.

'Come on, Firebird,' he shouted. 'Let's get to it!'

Snowy taxied out and took his position next to Bryan at the end of the extended line of fighters that straddled the hard earth of the landing strip in the strengthening light. Snowy glanced up as the Warhawks crossed his field of vision, clawing their way up in a climbing circuit. The chunky American fighters wheeled out of view behind him, and he let his gaze fall back to Bryan's aircraft, ten yards to his right. For a few seconds his mind drifted back to the busy workshops and leisurely test-flights at Aboukir, then a chill gripped his vitals as he returned to the moment and the dangerous realities ahead.

Bryan's fighter eased forward, reacting to movement further down the line. Snowy nudged his throttle open and lurched forward. Rescued by the need for action, the knot of anxiety in his guts dissipated.

Firebird Squadron raced together down the runway. Snowy eased his stick back, pulling his Spitfire off the ground in ragged unison with the others. Wheels clunked into housings and the squadron levelled out at two hundred feet, banking gently onto a northerly course.

Snowy stole a quick glance behind him, relieved to see the dive-bombers, high above, wheeling to shadow the squadron. Then the speeding landscape pulled his attention back to his controls. The sand-yellow blur transposed in an instant to sparkling azure as Firebird barrelled over the beach and out to sea. Snowy flitted a look in his mirror every few seconds until the thin line of the coast was difficult to discern. Barnard called the course change and the squadron banked onto a westerly heading.

Snowy sat in his cockpit wrapped in the clamour of his engine, trusting his squadron leader to guide a dozen speeding aircraft to a small patch of desert where his enemies waited, unaware of their coming. He looked around at the others, bobbing slightly in the airflow, drifting a few feet this way and back, and a small swell of pride lodged into the base of his throat. A stray resonance from the clamouring pistons vibrated along a lever or a cable and for a few sweet seconds it seemed that Judith's voice hummed an aimless tune of contentment into his ear.

'*Turning back to the coast now, Firebird,*' Barnard's wireless-distorted voice crushed the ethereal music. '*Loosen up, line astern; give yourself the space you need.*'

The squadron banked to the south and its formation elongated. By the time they crossed the wave-lined beach, they flew in a straggling zig-zag as each pilot jockeyed to have empty air ahead of his guns. Snowy slid the safety catch off his firing button and squinted through the blur of his propeller at the landscape beyond.

'*Dead ahead,*' Barnard's voice bristled with tension. '*Tally-ho!*'

There! Blocky shapes, blurred with netting, dotted around on the desert floor, casting wide shadows in the beams of the rising sun. The dashing zig-zag splayed into a fan as each man chose his target, exposed and stark on the flat sandy expanse of the enemy airfield.

In front of Snowy's Spitfire an anti-aircraft gun resolved in a rush of urgent detail: a shirtless man worked frantically at a handwheel to depress the barrel enough to engage, his companion stood aghast and motionless, seemingly staring straight through Snowy's windshield. Snowy jabbed at the firing button and both men vanished in a storm of flailing ordnance and billowing dust.

Snowy flashed over the damaged gun to see another pointing skywards dead ahead. Men ran from the gun, diving into nearby slit-trenches. Snowy ignored them, pouring fire into the emplacement until ammunition near the gun exploded, buffeting the Spitfire with blast concussions. Snowy banked and climbed away from the detonations, flying out beyond the airfield's perimeter towards empty desert. The control column felt sound and the engine ran smoothly; confident that he had taken no damage he dropped into a wide turn back towards the target.

Spitfires slashed across the airfield from all directions, stitching lines of bullet-strikes around and across the gun-positions, before turning in wide loops to choose another track across the mayhem. In the centre of the airfield the first clusters of explosions from the dive-bombers flipped fighter planes onto their backs and detonated petrol bowsers in billowing roils of orange flame. The Warhawks flattened out of their dives and wheeled back to add their own raking gunfire to the carnage.

Snowy skimmed along the field's perimeter with waves of blast from the bombs banging like hand slaps on the Perspex of his canopy. He unloaded the remainder of his ammunition into an already burning gun emplacement and veered out and away from danger. He found himself flying alongside another of Firebird's Spitfires and the pair set their noses to the east and climbed away from the burning airfield.

\*\*\*

Snowy taxied into dispersal and shut down the engine. He sat for a moment, savouring the silence that pressed against his ringing eardrums. He pulled back the canopy and let the meagre breeze flit against his cheeks. High above, the Warhawks straggled past in twos and threes, overflying LG97 on their way back to their own airbase further east. Snowy undid his straps and climbed out onto the wing. Spitfires from Firebird meandered in, flattening out to land, their engines coughing and chuckling as if in pleasure at their homecoming. Snowy looked around at the busy disarray of engineers and armourers working on dust-mottled aircraft and a swell of emotion flushed his face. Relief? Vindication? Happiness? He dropped his parachute onto the wing root and jumped down to the ground, watching while the other Spitfires of his squadron snaked into dispersal, parked and dropped into silence like roosting birds with full bellies.

*\*\**

Snowy scooped a spoonful of watery soup into his mouth and glanced around the mess. Conversation buzzed amongst the men; those that had heard about the raid quizzed those that had flown it.

'I'll not forget this day in a hurry,' Snowy said, wiping a dribble of soup from his chin with the back of his hand.

'Well, while you're busy not forgetting this day, be sure to remember the fighters that should have been defending their airfield were bogged down in wet sand,' Bryan said. 'That probably won't be the case next time.'

'Even so.' Snowy scraped the last of the soup from his dish. 'That's the most exciting thing I've ever done. I'm beginning to think that getting this posting was absolutely the right thing to do.'

'Let's hope,' Bryan said.

The chill of the desert evening tightened its grip as Bryan and Snowy left the mess to walk back to their tent.

'I meant to ask you about that American friend you mentioned,' Snowy said.

'He wasn't a friend,' Bryan said. 'He was a pilot in my squadron at Kenley.'

'Must've been a brave man,' Snowy said. 'Volunteering when there was no need to do so.'

'Yes,' Bryan said. 'He was very principled. I suspect that's why he disliked me so much.'

'Come on,' Snowy chided. 'Disliked *you*? Whatever next?'

A frown creased Bryan's forehead: 'What's got into you today?'

'Ah! I don't know,' Snowy said. He cast a look across the gloaming sky. 'Just between you and me; I think I've finally let Judith go.'

Bryan's frown deepened.

'I know it sounds strange,' Snowy said. 'It *feels* strange. Especially because I hadn't realised that I was holding her back. But somehow, today, out there over the sea, I came to believe that she has stopped being sad. So, there's really no reason for me to burden her spirit with *my* sadness.'

Bryan remained silent.

'Ah, see?' Snowy said. 'You think I'm being soppy.'

'Not at all,' Bryan said. 'Something happened in your head, and it's made your heart feel better. If you could bottle that, you'd make a fortune.'

'If I could bottle it' – Snowy grinned at his friend – 'I think I'd give it away for free.'

# Chapter 10

## Sunday, 18 October 1942 – Landing Ground 97

Dust rolled in slow oscillations from the road, drifting south away from the airfield. It sprung from the constant passage of heavily laden trucks travelling sedately west, towards the rear of the British front-lines. Bryan squinted at their progress, watching with the intensity of a shaman witnessing the arrival of an omen.

'Is this good?' Snowy asked, shading his eyes and peering at the rumbling column.

'It's progress,' Bryan answered. 'Hopefully it means the army have decided it's time to get on with the job at last.'

Behind them, the swell of aero engines thundered across the field as another standing patrol climbed away into the western sky.

'Which means we can get on with *our* job,' Bryan continued. 'And when the job's been done and dusted, I can get back to my squadron.'

'Why would they let you go?' Snowy asked.

Bryan glanced sharply at his friend.

Snowy shrugged: 'But, why would they?'

'I have the squadron leader's word.' Bryan returned his gaze to the flow of heavy transport along the distant road.

'You may have his word that he'll put in a request,' Snowy persisted. 'But why would the person who got that request care about moving one person from Egypt to Malta?' He gestured towards the road: 'Moving one person about isn't what armies do.'

'Barnard's an honourable man,' Bryan countered.

'I'm sure he is,' Snowy said. 'So, let's say he insists on your behalf, and somebody somewhere agrees. How are you going to get to Malta? When is the last time a ship got through from Alexandria? I'm not even sure they try anymore.'

Bryan turned a baleful look onto Snowy: 'Have you quite finished?'

'I'm sorry, Bryan,' Snowy said. 'I suppose what I'm getting at is, the squadron leader is promising you jam tomorrow, and for that you're giving away the jam you have today.'

'Jam?' Bryan said quietly.

'Oh, you know.' Snowy pulled a beneficent smile. 'Alexandria; Cairo; your nurse.'

Bryan maintained his glare; Snowy's smile faded into chagrin and he looked back out towards the road.

'Oh, look.' Snowy pointed and Bryan followed his gesture.

A truck had turned off the road and was bumping across the rough ground towards the airfield. Bryan turned and started to walk back towards the mess. Snowy trailed after him.

The truck wallowed past them, the driver waving cheerily at them through his open window.

'I'm not sure *this* is a good sign,' Bryan muttered.

By the time the pair reached the mess tent, the truck had found a patch of open ground on which to park. The driver clambered out, dropped the tailgate and climbed onto the flatbed. He opened the large wooden trunk that stood there and rummaged about inside.

Bryan poured a mug of tea from the urn outside the mess.

'Is it Sunday?' he asked.

'Er, yes. I think it is,' Snowy replied.

'Then I'll bet you that's a bloody mobile priest.' Bryan turned to watch the rummaging man. 'They generally turn up just before a considerable amount of people start getting killed.'

The man pulled a square of heavy cloth from the trunk and draped it to hang over the tailgate. The cloth gleamed in the sunlight like shot silk and a large embroidered cross occupied its centre.

'See?' Bryan said.

'Well, maybe we should attend,' Snowy said. 'It can't hurt.'

'You go,' Bryan said. 'I'm not in the mood.'

Snowy drifted off to join the crowd that was gathering around the back of the truck. Bryan retreated into the shade of the mess tent and sat at an empty table. He watched through the mess entrance as the priest pulled on a surplice over his uniform, closed the trunk and placed a dull brass crucifix upon its lid. The man jumped to the ground and began handing out hymn books to his growing congregation.

Bryan sipped at the bitter tea and mulled his situation. Snowy's glib assessment was brutally realistic on the face of it, but the submariner's idle speculation about invasion over poolside drinks at Gezira added an unpredictable spin to the mix.

The impromptu service outside reached its first hymn, and the tuneless drone of half-hearted singing drifted into the mess tent. Bryan gritted his teeth in irritation: 'Why is it always Onward bloody Christian Soldiers?' he muttered to himself.

A low rumbling noise impinged on the atonal hymning, rising quickly to a full-throated, rasping roar. A twin-engine aircraft flashed over the service, scattering the men at the edge of the crowd, and dropping the rest to the ground. Another dark shape barrelled over, lashing the huddled congregation with a sweep of prop-wash as it peeled away. Bryan sprang to his feet and loped to the tent's entrance. A third and fourth aircraft swept low across the field and Bryan smiled in recognition: 'Fuck me,' he muttered. 'Beaufighters.'

The realisation they weren't under attack spread amongst the floundering congregation and the air filled with their ungodly curses as they stood, brushing the dust from their shorts and scrabbling to retrieve their hymnbooks.

The rest of the Beaufighter squadron traversed the airfield and banked away to join the landing circuit. Bryan left the mess tent, skirted the recovering throng at the church service and wandered out towards dispersal to watch the Beaufighters come in.

As Bryan arrived, the first of the heavy fighters crawled its way along the track, an airman walked backwards in front of the big machine, beckoning the pilot onwards. The aircraft's pugnacious snub nose was set back behind the spinning propellers and the pilot's face pressed close to the large windshield, concentrating on his guide.

Bryan stood back as the Beaufighter approached, and then walked with it, a distance off its starboard wingtip to avoid the dust it kicked up. The observer watched Bryan dispassionately from the dorsal blister just aft of the wings, until the craft swung off the track and came to a halt.

The airman trotted off to other duties and Bryan stood to one side as the pilot closed down the engines. After a few moments the hatch under the nose fell open and the pilot dropped to the ground. He closed the hatch and regarded Bryan from under a mild frown.

'Hello?' he ventured.

'Oh, don't mind me,' Bryan said. 'I used to fly a Beaufighter. It's a nice surprise to see one again close up.'

'When were you on Beau's?' The pilot pulled off his flying helmet.

'The winter of 1940,' Bryan said. 'Night fighters out of Middle Wallop.'

'Really?' The pilot walked across and offered his hand. 'You must have some stories to tell. My name's Jim. Jim McCaffrey.'

'Yes, quite a few. Bryan Hale.' Bryan accepted the shake. 'What brings a squadron of Beaufighters to this shitty little corner of the desert?'

'Coastal patrols,' McCaffrey said. 'Mostly long-range stuff.'

'Invasion prep?' Bryan asked.

McCaffrey looked him in the eye and said nothing.

'Of course,' Bryan said, nodding. 'Rumours and gossip…'

The hatch at the back of the Beaufighter dropped onto the ground and the observor emerged, bowed under the weight of two kitbags.

'Well, enough of that.' Bryan raised his voice against the oncoming clamour of a second Beaufighter. 'Let me show you where the mess tent is.'

***

Snowy was content to sit and listen to Bryan and McCaffrey talking shop about the virtues and vices of the big twin-engine fighter while he ate his dinner, leaning in occasionally to question and clarify a technical detail. He watched Bryan's face as he described night-time combats with near-invisible adversaries intruding through the winter sky to strike random blows at the sprawling mass of London. He listened in quiet awe as McCaffrey described mast-hopping attacks on coasters, the puncturing assault of cannon-fire in pass after pass, churning the sea to foam around them until the ships settled, wallowed and overturned in defeat like dying whales.

'Tell Jim about the high-altitude Spitfires, Snowy,' Bryan urged.

'Really? Alright,' Snowy said. 'Have you ever heard of a Junkers 86…'

The banter flowed back and forth as the day deflated to evening and the sky outside darkened like portent.

### Tuesday, 20 October 1942

'Things are getting livelier.' Barnard stood in front of the assembled pilots in the mess. 'I'm sure you've noticed, and if *you've* noticed, it's a safe bet that the Germans have noticed as well. We've been tasked' – he brandished a sheet of paper in his hand – 'with excluding all enemy planes from the sky. By so doing, reconnaissance will be disrupted and the army's preparations can be kept as discreet as possible.

'So, we'll be ramping up the patrols from LG97. We will be flying at full squadron strength, and we'll be flying more often. Be ready for take-off in thirty minutes.'

The pilots shambled out of the mess and headed towards dispersal.

'This is the bit I can't get used to.' Snowy waved a hand to encompass the loose body of men trudging across the hard-packed, sienna earth. 'It feels like I've been picked for first-eleven.'

'And there's everything to play for,' Bryan said. 'Like you said, there's nothing beyond the shit-house this time.'

***

Firebird Squadron circled the airstrip, spiralling upwards to ten thousand feet before vectoring towards the coast in a shallower climb. As they reached the shore, Barnard levelled them at fourteen thousand and began a slow bank to port to bring them back to a landward heading.

Snowy gazed down at the water, entranced by the sparkling reflections of the sun that danced across its surface. He looked up to check his position behind Bryan's starboard wing, then scanned the sky above and behind. The ghosts of the glinting reflections swam across his vision, blurred motes that floated lazily across his eyes. Snowy blinked against them, but they multiplied. Then one sparkled...

'Shit!' Snowy pressed transmit: 'Bandits coming down now!'

Bryan's tail twisted through ninety degrees and vanished to Snowy's left. Snowy wrenched the control column over and pulled back hard to follow him, gasping as the force of his lurching manoeuvre compressed his spine and contorted his eyeballs. Two aircraft flashed past his canopy in quick succession, their yellow noses the only feature that registered. Snowy fought against the grinding in his vertebrae to force his head back, then scrunched his eyebrows upwards so he could swivel his eyes in a bid to find Bryan. The edges of his vision shaded black... Bryan was gone... The darkness advanced...

'Shit!'

Snowy levelled out, panting from exertion, his head throbbing in protest as the blood seeped back and the darkness slowly receded.

A dun-painted aircraft with a yellow nose traversed his windscreen from the left. Snowy snatched a glance into his mirror and kicked his Spitfire into a hard right turn to follow it.

'109,' he hissed to himself through gritted teeth. '109.' The enemy crept back across his nose. '109.' The German's fuselage centred in his sights. Snowy jammed his thumb into the firing button. His tracers flashed wide and the Messerschmitt flicked onto its back and darted away like a swallow.

'Shit!'

Something fell towards him, blazing a vivid orange trail behind it. Snowy banked to keep it in vision, momentarily distracted by the sweep and spin of elliptical wings and the flash of the Spitfire's roundels as it pitched and wallowed its fiery way towards the sand.

Tracer flashed over his cockpit, terrifyingly close.

'Shit!'

Snowy flicked into a half-roll, yanked the stick back and jammed his boot against the rudder, flailing his fighter into a sickening dive that scythed through the oily black smoke trailing behind the stricken Spitfire. Snowy eased back on the throttle, jinked past the windmilling conflagration, pulled the control column back steadily and pushed the throttles open to zoom out of the dive and climb back into the battle.

After throwing a quick glance into the mirror, Snowy surveyed the planes whirling above him. One small shape spewed a lashing coil of tracer across the sky, then dipped into a dive, dropping away from the fight. A flash of yellow gave it away as it flattened out, fleeing westwards on a perpendicular course. Snowy adjusted to put his sights far ahead of the yellow nose and gently squeezed the firing button. Tracers flashed out into shallow, downward curves and Snowy nudged the stick to hold them steady as the Messerschmitt blundered straight through them, taking sparkling hits along its entire fuselage.

Snowy's guns clanked to empty and he dipped his wing to watch the 109 slide into an irretrievable plunge earthwards.

'*Reform, Firebird.*' Barnard's voice crackled into his ears. Snowy held his gaze on his adversary until it hit the ground, throwing a brief flash of fire into the surrounding sand, then he banked back into his climb. The sky above him now held only Spitfires, gathering into a ragged formation and heading east. He counted nine, two of which trailed thin lines of white vapour. Snowy accelerated to catch up, flying between the columns of black smoke that bore mute testimony to the squadron's loss. He recognised Bryan's markings and crabbed across the rear of the formation to ease in behind his friend's starboard wing. He fell to the routine scanning of the sky above and behind, while his fingertips numbed with the dissipating excitement of battle.

***

Bryan climbed out of his cockpit, stood on the wing root and gazed back to the runway. One of the battle-damaged Spitfires stood there blazing fiercely with airmen and groundcrew gathering around to fight the fire. He grunted with relief as the pilot emerged from throng of bodies and walked away unaided.

Bryan slid off the wing to where Snowy stood waiting.

'Ah, Snowy White,' Bryan said in mock announcement. 'The newest batsman in the Firebird first-eleven, a surprise appointment for some, but nonetheless, still Not Out.'

Snowy grinned at the absurdity and the pair started towards the mess while airmen swarmed over their aircraft to make them ready for the next patrol.

'I did that thing you showed me.' Snowy mimicked the roll and dive manoeuvre with his hand. 'It worked a treat.'

'It's good, isn't it?' Bryan said. 'It's basically what pigeons do.'

'And then I shot down a 109,' Snowy said. 'Properly this time.'

'Well done.' Bryan slapped him on the back. 'If we ever get back to Mary's House, I'll buy you a sausage, a drink and a whore to celebrate.'

### Thursday, 22 October 1942

Firebird Squadron meandered across the sky on a patrol route that took them close to several German airstrips, hoping to prod the opposition into response. They attracted an occasional speculative AA shell, but no-one came up to fight.

Bryan looked down at the runways they skirted, picking out tiny shapes that could be fighters; targets that might be strafed. Bryan chafed against his seat-straps, but Barnard preferred to fulfil his orders in the simplest way possible; no enemy planes were in the air, so his brief was being filled.

Maintaining altitude, as much in defence from twitchy British fingers, the squadron drifted east and descended the length of the front line to its termination at the edge of the Qattara Depression. Wheeling around over the darker, marshy ground of the depression they retraced their flight northwards.

Bryan scanned the British hinterland, zeroing in on tiny smudges of dust that hazed the ground here and there. These were the clear signs that troops and artillery shells were riding trucks to the front line; evidence that an offensive loomed.

The coast rolled over the horizon's edge and the squadron banked to starboard and dropped altitude rapidly on a descent for home. The road that ran tangentially to the southern edge of Landing Ground 97 bore a snaking stream of trucks that draped the sky with a roiling curtain of dust.

'*Let's give our boys a show, Firebird,*' Barnard's voice crackled over the wireless.

The squadron loosened into a long line of pairs as Barnard led them down to treetop height, barrelling east, parallel to the loaded trucks grinding west, before curling up and over the road to climb into the landing circuit of their airfield.

Bryan glanced down at the men waving from the packed trucks that hauled them into the battlefield and found himself grinning with mad joy at the calamitous, monumental folly of it all.

### Friday, 23 October 1942

The squadron gathered in the mess, brought there by a word-of-mouth summons to attend an important briefing. The weariness of constant flying sagged the core of every muscle and weighed on the cheeks of every man's face. Bryan shifted his weight on the bench to relieve the ache in his buttocks and let his gaze settle through the mess entrance where darkness battled with the serene luminosity of a full moon to seal its cold grip on the day.

Snowy brought two mugs of tea to the table and sat down opposite Bryan.

'Where'd you grow up?' Snowy asked.

The question caught Bryan off guard and he snorted an explosive laugh.

'In a fucking church.' He lit a cigarette and tossed the pack across to Snowy. 'I wouldn't recommend it.'

'I like churches,' Snowy said. 'I think most churches are very pretty.'

'Perversely, so do I,' Bryan said. 'But their charm depends on you being able to go home afterwards. When your father is the vicar, there's no respite, no escape.'

'Which church was it?' Snowy asked.

'It was – it still is – St John's in Hampstead,' Bryan answered.

'Is it pretty?' Snowy took a cigarette and pushed the pack back across the table.

'From the outside, it looks a bit like a soul-grinding factory,' Bryan said. 'But once you get inside, I suppose it has a certain spartan charm.'

'Do you visit?' Snowy asked.

Bryan's brow furrowed slightly at the memory of a warm kiss in the frosty night air and a love lost forever: 'I was last there at Christmas,' he said. 'Christmas 1940.'

Snowy sensed he'd inadvertently rattled the skeleton in its cupboard and fell to sipping his tea in silence.

The low murmur of conversations tapered and heads turned as the squadron leader and the intelligence officer walked into the mess.

Barnard looked around the faces of his men, an almost sad half-smile playing on his lips: 'It's on,' he said.

A ripple of reaction circulated amongst the pilots; a combination of exhaled breath and slumping shoulders, sprinkled with muttered, indiscernible oaths.

'A thousand-gun barrage will begin later tonight,' Barnard continued. 'This will last around five hours and then the infantry will start crossing the minefields.'

Someone muttered: 'Poor bastards.'

'We're in for a busy time, and that starts with a pre-dawn muster here in the mess, when I'll have our specific orders for the day.' Barnard looked around his pilots once more: 'Get the best sleep you can, gentlemen.'

***

Bryan lay back on his cot and listened to Snowy's ragged breathing. The watery light of the full moon backlit the tent's roof, lending it a ghostly luminosity. From the warm blood that pulsed in his ears, to the chill desert air that made up the presently quiet night sky, to the silent, frozen face of the grey, lifeless moon that reflected the cold light from the hidden sun, all these conspired to create this single moment. Bryan lit a cigarette, inhaled deeply of its smoke, then held it in front of his face, examining the glowing coruscations of its burning tip as if it were finely cut andesine.

The air split with a sudden thunderous boom, like the unleashed fury of jealous gods from atop a distant mountain. The cacophony swelled to its apex then rolled across the desert in continuous, unabated waves of monstrous rage.

A smile crept across Bryan's face: the moment had changed.

## Saturday, 24 October 1942

Firebird Squadron cruised at fourteen thousand feet above the sea, travelling west for the second time this day through the safer maritime corridor that led to occupied territory. Bryan glanced away to the nearby coastline on his left, and beyond that to the desert, where battle was now joined. A continuous pall of smoke and dust kicked up by the night's bombardment swayed sluggishly in the thin breeze over the front line, ascending on the developing thermals to be decapitated by faster streams of air that raced across at higher altitude. West of the frontline, new plumes ascended from concerted bombing attacks on entrenched anti-tank positions that had started at dawn.

Bryan's gaze dropped to the aircraft below, silhouetted sharply against the deep blue of the dashing water. Eighteen American-built bombers bearing British roundels flew in close formation; compact, twin-engine craft, their tapered fuselage gave them a hunched, nose-heavy demeanour. A distance behind these, a squadron of bomb-bearing Hurricanes progressed in a wider, looser formation. Their targets had to be neutralised to open the way for the planned breakthrough of British tanks.

The combined force wheeled south, over the coast and into the occupied hinterland. Bryan squinted at the empty western sky and licked his lips underneath his mask. Where were they?

The Hurricanes dropped away like wraiths, heading for targets further west, while the main bomber force held its southerly run.

'*Bandits, three o'clock high*,' Barnard's voice was measured. '*Keep an eye on them.*'

Bryan looked up to his right. Six fighters flew a parallel course to Firebird at the same speed. They had yellow-painted noses, but weren't quite the right shape to be 109s.

Below, the bombers unloaded into the burgeoning dust clouds and wheeled away east. Barnard started a banking climb to engage the shadowing fighters but they turned away and accelerated westwards. Barnard turned the bank into a circle and led Firebird back to cover the tails of the retreating bombers.

***

The pilots sat in pairs and groups, cross-legged on the hard ground in dispersal, passing around water canteens and watching the groundcrews refuelling their fighters.

'What were they up to?' Snowy asked. 'Why didn't they attack the bombers, or us?'

'Italians,' Bryan said.

Snowy paused a moment to reflect.

'That Italian that shot holes in me wasn't so backward about coming forward,' he said.

'They're spirited fighters, there's no doubt about that,' Bryan said. 'I just think they have a better developed sense of odds than we do.'

'Perhaps they see it as a German war,' Snowy mused.

'Perhaps,' Bryan said. 'But that point of view may well be a short-lived luxury.'

'Alright Firebird!' Barnard walked in amongst the group. 'Another escort mission. Let's get moving!

### Monday, 26 October 1942

'Some good news for a change, gentlemen.'

The scraping of forks on tin plates ceased and mugs descended quietly to tabletops as faces crumpled with weariness turned to regard their squadron leader in the pre-dawn gloom.

'Yesterday, the army chucked its main force against the spot in the enemy line where German and Italian forces meet,' Barnard continued. 'Their hope that this might represent a fracture point was vindicated; they've broken through the minefields and are in the process of consolidating a bridgehead. They are, of course expecting a counter-attack, and we'll be working hard to disrupt that as it develops.

'We'll be going in low and hunting in pairs. There will be Hurricane and Warhawk squadrons looking for any armour that's on the move. So, don't attack tanks unless you can see the crew is dismounted. Our main targets today will be troop trucks and supply vehicles heading towards the front-line. We've got our toe in the door, let's make sure it stays there. Take-off in thirty minutes.'

Barnard left the mess and the humdrum of muted conversation and the clink of cutlery rekindled.

'It feels a bit one-sided,' Snowy said. 'A bit like shooting at cows from a sports car.'

Bryan nodded: 'It's not the kind of thing that will likely win you a medal. It just needs to be done.'

135

'Back and bloody forth, though Bryan.' Snowy's voice dropped to a whisper. 'Then weeks of delays before it starts all over again. It makes you wonder if there's actually a bloody plan at all.'

'I'm convinced there's an invasion planned,' Bryan said.

Snowy's eyebrows jumped in surprise: 'In Africa?'

Bryan nodded: 'The Americans. They may well already have sailed. I met a chap from *The Unheard* in Cairo, he convinced me it's on; it's the only thing that makes sense.'

'Americans.' Snowy's eyebrows relaxed into a gentle frown. 'Sailed. From America.'

'That's the dead-cert rumour.' Bryan stood up. 'Come on, Snowy. Let's stay alive to see it happen.'

***

Bryan pulled his Spitfire off the hard-packed earth, retracted his wheels as soon as they left the ground, and levelled out at fifty feet, veering south-west across the coast road and into the desert beyond. He glanced in his mirror to see Snowy's fighter climb above him, wallow from side to side searching for him, then descend to slot behind his starboard wing.

'That's it, Snowy,' Bryan muttered to himself. 'As low as we can go.'

The two Spitfires darted towards the breakthrough, skimming through the dawn air, backlit by the rapidly rising sun. For the first few miles, the desert remained desolate, empty of artefact. Then they crossed tracks that ran towards the front, makeshift thoroughfares dotted with vehicles; laden trucks heading west, empty trucks heading east.

Smoke and dust shrouded the horizon ahead, and the two sand-coloured Spitfires rushed towards the battlefield that spawned it, like dragonflies drawn towards a mesmerising point of dazzling light. The desert flashing by beneath their wings now revealed its scars of war; the pock-marked aftermath of artillery and bombing raids that had disfigured its flat face, disrupted and discoloured its soft complexion. Amongst the sand-blurred craters stood blackened tanks and personnel carriers, like the crisped corpses of burnt beetles; carapaces split asunder and innards incinerated.

These charred stains on the sand multiplied and funnelled westwards towards the narrow passage cleared through the minefields. Amongst, and around them, armoured vehicles laboured forward, shadowed by infantry moving in shifting and straggling columns. An occasional shell burst in their midst, dropping from the brightening daybreak to maim and disable, sent in the certain knowledge that a target would be waiting amongst the converging herd of soldiers.

The Spitfires sped over the soldiers' heads, intersecting their constrictive corridor and banking west across the empty terrain with its unharvested seeding of mines. Ahead, on the other side of the minefield the army oozed into enemy territory, forming a delta of fury. Stationary tanks in echelon hurled high explosives towards enemy positions, adding their gun smoke to the choking dust thrown up by the intensifying artillery barrage.

Bryan and Snowy swept over the southern edge of the British incursion and barrelled over the enemy's defensive line of hull-down tanks and entrenched infantry. Bryan felt the familiar expectation of bullet strikes tighten the muscles across his shoulders, then they were over the empty sand behind the lines, criss-crossed with tyre and track marks, littered with an army's detritus. The pair flew on, leapfrogged the artillery emplacements belching fire eastwards, and snaked into their hunting ground; the enemy hinterland and his soft-skinned supply lines.

Snowy glanced in his mirror at the bank of artillery gun-smoke receding at speed and a tingling chill percolated his limbs. This time it was not anxiety; this time it was poise. He dropped his eyes back to Bryan's Spitfire, bobbing gently on the cushion of warm air that sat on the radiant sand, close by on his port quarter. Instinctively he eased back on the throttle, allowing the gap between his nose and his leader's tail to lengthen, opening up the time he had in hand to react when Bryan attacked something. He fell back a hundred yards or more, then squeezed the throttle open to hold the gap.

Dust columns rolled onto the horizon, rising like leaning pillars of gaseous sandstone, betraying the motion of tracks and wheels hurrying toward the battle. Bryan's wings tilted towards the nearest; Snowy angled after him, drifting slightly wide and pushing the safety off his firing button.

The desert ripped by and blocky, dun-coloured shapes resolved from the obscuring dust, a column of eight, maybe more. No gun-smoke trailed from Bryan's wings as he sliced through the dust cloud. As Snowy bore down in his wake, the hazy hulks crystallized into tanks, shuttered and sealed against his puny guns. The white-edged black cross on the side of a squat turret flashed with awful clarity and was gone as Snowy careened across the unheeding armoured column, banking to follow as Bryan's flight path curved towards the next haze of rising dust that followed closely behind the tanks.

This time streamers of gun-smoke ribboned away from Bryan's wings and detonations flashed ahead of him in the dust. He lurched to the left and fired again. Snowy copied Bryan's violent correction and a second later the sand-coloured blocks emerged from the haze ahead of his nose; trucks in a straight line, the first two with shattered windscreens, torn canvas and nascent fires licking from their engines, the rest alive with desperate men tumbling from their tailgates, skidding in the sand to find their feet and run. Snowy jabbed his thumb into the firing button and swathes of ordnance slashed along the column, tearing through metal, cloth and flesh, flailing the sand on either side of the vehicles into tumult. The last truck dashed away beneath his tail and Snowy glanced into the mirror at the charnel hell he'd drawn in the sand, then sought out Bryan's silhouette in the distance and surged after him.

Bryan pulled a wide turn to starboard. Snowy stole the odd glance at his compass, expecting Bryan to head east. But the dial ticked past east, and the turn continued.

'*There's a tank that's all on its tod.*'

Bryan's voice buzzed in Snowy's ears and he looked to his right into the centre of their orbit. He spotted the tank, seemingly bogged down in a darker stretch of sand.

'I see it,' Snowy said.

'*I reckon the crew are either in it or under it,*' Bryan said. '*Let's make things noisy for them.*'

Bryan tightened his turn to come into a low broadside approach at the tank. Snowy continued his turn and watched.

Bryan's fire plastered the side of the tank, displacing dust and ricocheting hot bullets to flare in sputtering arcs over the motionless bulk.

Snowy banked around, climbing slightly for leeway, and lined up on the other side of the tank. The impassive bulk of armour expanded quickly in his sights and he stabbed at the firing button. The dancing sparkles of bullet impacts sprinkled mesmerising patterns over the metal hulk, and Snowy pulled hard at the last second to break the spell and skim over Panzer's silent turret.

'*That'll teach them to break down in the middle of bloody nowhere.*' Brian said. '*Form up on me, let's be on our way.*'

Snowy clawed his way back to his place on one side of his leader's tail as Bryan lofted into a healthy climb to put some air between them and the rock-strewn sand. To the east, the battle of the breakthrough belched thick curls of heavy smoke skywards. Above that smoke, aircraft left tiny scuds of vapour against the blue. As Snowy watched, something flared in the heights, its flame drawing a curling spiral towards the ground.

The pair flew north-east into calmer skies, ascending as they travelled towards the coast. More columns of smoke caught Snowy's eye. These rose over behind his port wing, far away on the coast. He'd heard gossip the previous day about diversionary attacks to draw away the best of the German forces. He wondered idly if the soldiers were told they were dying for a trick.

Snowy shifted his gaze back to Bryan's tail and followed his bank onto an easterly course and the long descent to base.

### Wednesday, 28 October 1942

Bryan lay awake, smoking a cigarette and staring at the canvas roof of the tent. He'd focussed too long on a single spot and the material seemed to squirm and shimmer as the fabric's coarse familiarity dulled his retinas. Across the field, engines coughed into life and vibrated the night air with purring resonance. Their deep timbre, isolated in the otherwise silent darkness, reached a probing finger into Bryan's chest and touched his heart. He rolled out of his cot and dressed; the glowing cigarette clenched between his teeth. He tied his boots, left the tent and set off across the field, gravitating towards the grumbling roar of many mighty pistons.

White-painted marker stones reflected the moonlight like the scattered teeth of long extinct creatures. The same glow danced and shimmered in the spinning propellers of warming engines, and drew luminous lines along leading edges and across the tops of the Perspex domes on the backs of the readying Beaufighters.

Bryan kept a distance in the darkness. He itched to know the details of the mission, but the aircrews were already on board and only groundcrew moved around the bellies of the aircraft, muffled with scarves and goggles, checking hatches and dragging away the heavy chocks. Instead, Bryan watched a pilot in his dimly lit cockpit; the man's torso twisted back and forth as he checked his instruments in preparation for take-off. The ingrained take-off routine intruded unbidden into Bryan's mind, and with it came the remembered voice of his erstwhile operator: '*All set back here, Flight.*'

Bryan pushed the memory away and swept a look across the star-spattered vault. It would be a perfect night to hunt an intruding bomber, jockeying around the sky to silhouette its dark outline in the moonlight, to creep into its wake until its shadowy form filled the gunsights. But the Beaufighters arrayed before him carried racks of rockets beneath their wings, which revealed an intent to assault earthly targets, and such an early take-off suggested those targets were a long way from LG97.

One of the pilots flicked on the spotlight mounted in his port wing and edged forward onto the track that led to the landing strips. The light's beam swept over Bryan, dazzling him for a moment and forcing him to step backwards. Squinting against the receding dazzle he watched the big aircraft creep past him. The pilot leaned in Bryan's direction and waved. Bryan waved back, assuming the ghostly face in the dim cockpit cabin to be Jim McCaffrey. Other lights clicked on and the aircraft that bore them creaked into motion one by one, parading past Bryan like a train of elephants, moving with careful, solid purpose. Bryan cursed himself for not bringing a neckerchief, cupping his hands over his nose and mouth, and narrowing his squint against the whipping dust.

Ahead of the creeping column of aircraft a flame danced in the darkness, moving across the field, its orange glow dimly illuminating its bearer's pale face and arm. The flickering light dipped to the ground, vanished for a moment, then raced away in a straight line, leaping tongues of flame into the air and blurring the stars on the horizon with black smoke and heat haze. The airman carrying the torch progressed for about forty yards, his trotting form now clearly backlit by the firelight. He stopped and crouched again, sending the other side of the flare-path dashing along its parallel runnel.

The gelatinous rumble of engines took on a fiercer overtone as the lead plane roared down the flare-path and lifted off the ground. The spotlight in its wing extinguished, leaving only its navigation lights to bracket its dark shape as it climbed away. Fighter after fighter hauled its payload off the ground, dimmed its light and ascended into the dark vault. Bryan watched them until distance silenced their roar and their navigation lights melted into the stars. The flare-path guttered, sputtering its weakening flames and dying in sporadic sections, until it finally surrendered the field back to the night.

***

'Yesterday, counter-attacks attempted by a division of Panzers were held at bay by the army's anti-tank batteries.' Barnard held his voice steady, but a weary vibrato underpinned his tone. 'Montgomery has taken this as an opportunity to pause Operation Lightfoot and regroup.'

Howls of protest erupted from the pilots gathered around the mess tables.

Barnard held up a hand to quell the commotion: 'We still have work to do while the army regroups,' he said.

Barnard waited while a few sullen mutterings faded to silence.

'We'll be flying cover for our American dive-bomber friends again this morning. They'll be seeking out and discouraging any enemy forces from mustering another counter-offensive against our bridgehead. We'll stay high and keep any fighters off their backs. Any questions?'

'When's the bloody army gonna' pull its weight?'

Barnard glanced around but failed to find the source of the muttered question.

'I understand your frustrations,' Barnard said. 'If we win this war, we will win it in stages, every stage well planned and well executed. I'm sure you appreciate that everyday supply issues are just as important as courageous actions at the front. If that weren't the case, we'd probably be sitting in a prisoner-of-war camp right now, arguing about who has the last cigarette.' He smiled at the band of grubby men before him and looked at his watch. 'Take-off in twenty minutes.'

***

Bryan drifted out to starboard and looked down, under the bellies of Firebird Squadron, to the gaggle of Warhawks that flew a lower, parallel course. Their dun green paintwork contrasted sharply with the luminous blue of the Mediterranean over which they flew and the white stars on their wings glinted in the strengthening sunlight. His eyes wandered beyond the American formation to the coastline behind them and the smoke that rose from continued skirmishing there.

Bryan returned to scanning the sky ahead and a movement caught his eye. Heading towards the Spitfires from seaward, a scattering of motes dotted

141

the sky. Tension crept into Bryan's neck muscles as his eyes flitted from one tiny shape to the next, then dissipated with the relief of recognition.

He thumbed transmit: 'Friendlies at one o'clock,' he called. 'Beaufighters heading home.'

The Beaufighters' course took them between the two fighter formations, on a diagonal towards the south-east. Bryan craned his neck around to count them as they receded towards the coast: there were two missing, and one of the remaining number trailed a white ribbon of vaporising coolant from its port engine.

Bryan turned back to his front. Two crews who'd taxied past him a few hours ago, four men intent on their task, were missing, almost certainly dead. Reflexively, Bryan glanced into his mirror to check Snowy was there, close behind his starboard wing.

The Warhawks banked south towards the coast and Firebird wheeled to match their course, flying on the dive-bombers' western flank to buffer them against those hostile skies. The formation drifted south towards the smoke and dust clouds of previous bombings, and Bryan fell to scanning the sky beyond his starboard wing. Speckles against the blue drifted into his vision. He focussed on them, then looked beyond them, trying to coax some clarity into the tiny shapes.

'*Bandits, three o'clock high,*' Barnard called. '*Keep an eye on them.*'

The flecks in the sky grew enough to count; there were six. As they converged, they dropped their altitude to match the Spitfires. An American voice called something across the wireless, too modulated by accent for Bryan to catch. He glanced left to see the Warhawks accelerating away towards their targets. He swivelled his head back, expecting the hostile force to pursue, but the gaggle of aircraft continued its course undisturbed. They drifted close enough to be recognised as 109s; their black crosses on sandy camouflage being stark enough to register over the distance.

'*Alright, Firebird,*' Barnard called. '*They've paid their admission, let's give them their show.*'

Barnard banked right to cut off the enemy formation, dragging the squadron around behind him. The Messerschmitts immediately curved away in the same direction and dived away westwards.

\*\*\*

The pilots dropped from their aircraft and pulled parachute packs off their sweat-soaked backs. They drifted towards an orderly festooned with water canteens that he gave out as they passed him. They settled on the warm ground and watched as ground crew began refuelling their fighters. Armourers walked from plane to plane, checking the still-sealed gun-ports before wandering off in search of something else to do.

Bryan took a swig of water and passed the canteen to Snowy.

'Germans flying like Italians,' Bryan said. 'Perhaps they think the game's up.'

'Why would they?' Snowy asked. 'We've just called a halt to the offensive to regroup, after spending well over a month bloody regrouping.'

'They can see what's happening on the ground as well as we can,' Bryan said. 'It's turned into a slogging match, pure and simple, and they've never been afraid of those. They've invaded Russia, for heaven's sake. That's hardly a subtle move.'

Snowy glugged at the canteen, his Adam's apple bobbing in beat with the noise.

'Perhaps they know something we don't,' he said, wiping dribbles of water from his chin.

'It can't be possible to hide an invasion fleet for long,' Bryan said. 'Perhaps that's what they know; they've discovered the Americans are really on the way.'

'So, perhaps that's why old Monty has called halftime,' Snowy said. 'Could be a top bit of generalship right there.'

Bryan cast a sidelong glance at Snowy, but remained silent.

# Chapter 11

## Sunday, 1 November 1942 – Landing Ground 97

'Just like a vulture drawn to a carcass,' Bryan said.

Snowy craned his neck to look out of the mess entrance to where the church-truck was parked. The priest standing in front of its flat-bed intoned and gestured his way through a sermon; '*patriotic*' and '*courage*' rose above the nasally drone of unintelligible verbiage, closely followed by '*righteous*'.

Snowy turned back and looked Bryan in the eye: 'If your father was a cricketer, would you hate cricket?'

Bryan held his baleful gaze on the gesticulating preacher.

'I do hate cricket, on its own merits,' Bryan said. 'Which rather pops your bubble, doesn't it.'

The turgid strains of a hymn drifted into the mess and Bryan dropped his head into his hands.

'Onward Christian Soldiers. Who would've guessed it?' he moaned.

'Oh, come on, now. As hymns go, it *is* quite' – Snowy screwed his mouth up, searching for a word – 'marchy.' He rocked his shoulders to the tempo, humming under his breath.

Bryan looked up at Snowy in silence for a moment.

'You know, I think they can smell fear,' Bryan continued. 'They use other people's weakness to bolster their own delusions of power. Then, when they get to like the taste of power, they pretend their craving for more power is an irresistible vocation. Then there can be no arguing with them, no limit to the size of the churches they'll build, no limit to the sacrifices they'll demand.'

'Tell me,' Snowy said. 'Was your father *really* that unkind to you when you were a child?'

'Shush,' Bryan said. 'Look.' He nodded over Snowy's shoulder towards the truck.

The hymn had ended and the intelligence officer had clambered onto the flat-bed. Bryan and Snowy stood and drifted outside to listen to the man.

'We've received orders for the renewal of the offensive,' he held up a sheaf of papers. 'Operation Supercharge begins tomorrow. We are tasked to impose and maintain air superiority over the armoured breakthrough. Individual squadron briefings will take place this evening. Thank you, gentlemen.'

The intelligence officer jumped to the ground and elbowed his way out of the dispersing congregation.

**Monday, 2 November 1942**

'Are you alright?' Bryan asked. 'You look a bit green about the gills.'

Snowy glanced up at his friend and swallowed hard: 'I do feel a bit queasy,' he said. 'Breakfast isn't sitting well.'

'We'll take it up with the chef,' Bryan said. 'Just as soon as we get back.'

Snowy nodded, pulled a wan smile and trudged on.

The pair straggled at the back of the group as Firebird Squadron walked across the airfield towards their dispersed Spitfires. The air rumbled and quaked with concussions as the British artillery hurled high explosives ahead of the assault force on the ground. They'd shattered the desert night hours ago and the tempo had been frenetic ever since.

The pilots reached the track and spread out, each one heading for their own aircraft. Snowy and Bryan diverged wordlessly and Snowy rubbed his knuckles below his sternum, trying to dislodge the bubble of unease that nestled there while he covered the last few yards to his fighter. Groundcrew bustled him into a parachute and strapped him into his cockpit, where he sat waiting for his turn for the starter battery to come round. The acid burned at the top of his stomach and his hand strayed towards his straps; if he could just get out for a moment and stick his fingers down his throat...

A hand banging on the side of the fuselage stopped the motion. He looked down to see the starter attached and an airman staring at him expectantly. Snowy gave the man the thumbs-up and pressed the starter buttons. The engine barked into motion, belching a swathe of blue smoke past the cockpit. Two airmen clambered onto the wings, one on each side, faces swathed in grubby bandanas and eyes hidden behind darkened goggles. One of the men gesticulated, jabbing his fingers forwards, and Snowy released the brakes and rolled gently onto the track.

Firebird Squadron assembled in a ragged line across the landing strip. Snowy looked out at the airman on his right; the man gave him a good-luck wave and slid from view. Snowy glanced to his left where the wing was already empty. He looked into his mirror to watch the two men loping away like desert wraiths until they blurred and vanished into the swirling dust behind the squadron's whirling propellers. Moments later the aircraft beside

145

him lurched into motion and Snowy pushed the throttle forward to match its pace.

Lifting free from the ground, Firebird lofted into the clean morning air to see the horizon ahead blackened with smoke from the distant battle lines. With no use for subterfuge, the squadron headed directly west, climbing hard for altitude. Snowy identified Bryan's aircraft and crabbed across to settle in behind him.

The clatter of his labouring engine rattled through Snowy's skull, cycling from ear to ear across his forehead. The upward pitch of his Spitfire blocked the view of the horizon towards which he sped. A creeping, irrational notion that his pale blue underbelly was exposed to enemies he could not see tugged tension into his neck muscles and bubbled more acid fumes into his oesophagus. He took a deep breath of oxygen and glanced at the altimeter; they were approaching eighteen thousand feet. He returned his gaze to Bryan's tail and the vast blue curve of the sky beyond it.

'*Levelling out.*' Barnard's voice sounded distant on Snowy's pressure-stretched eardrums. '*Keep your eyes peeled.*'

Snowy sighed relief into his mask and eased the stick forward. He swallowed hard to equalise the pressure in his ears and his stomach flared another spike of acid into his throat. The horizon swung back up across his windshield, the streamers of black smoke underscored with billowing dust now frighteningly close. Barnard eased into a shallow bank to starboard, aiming to cross the lines through a clear patch of air. Snowy checked left and right, then eased his control column to match the tilt of Bryan's wings.

'*Look out!*'

Instinctively, Snowy snapped his head upwards. Black shapes dropped, expanding quickly. Flashes streaked towards him. Two metallic clangs juddered his nose, like the blows of a lump-hammer. The shapes flashed by on either side; stiff-winged stooping eagles curving out of their dive. The engine note changed, strangled by blunt trauma; rhythmic knocking vibrated through the airframe. Snowy sat for a moment in chilled inertia, still staring upwards. A gasping intake of breath into empty lungs broke through his shock. He pulled on the control column, banking away, heedless of anything around him, his eyes fixed on his compass, watching it creep around the dial until it indicated east. The engine's rattle ascended and the controls vibrated in sickening resonance. Snowy gripped the stick in both hands, fighting to control his heaving chest, concentrating desperately on the sky ahead, where safety waited.

Streaks of light whipped over his head, fanning out like malevolent tongues over his canopy. Snowy screwed his head around, searching for his tormentor. A shape flashed over, buffeting the Perspex with a slap of backdraft, and vanished into the heedless blue.

'Fuck!' Snowy wailed into his mask, using the raw rasp of fear in his larynx to push back the rising pulse of panic in his guts. He pushed the stick forward, tilting the horizon up, diving towards the sand, diving away from danger.

A tendril of cold rationality slithered into his blood-clamoured brain and he reached a shaking hand up and pulled back the canopy. The lopsided roar of the engine redoubled its hammering on his temples, but the rush of the slipstream smacked him back to clarity. He pulled out of his dive smoothly, checked his heading was still true and eased back on the throttle to preserve his labouring engine. The desert dashed by no more than one hundred feet below his wings. Snowy scanned the sandy landscape ahead. Over to his right, a burst of white smoke drew his attention. As he flew past, Snowy saw the angled barrel of an artillery piece pointed back the way he had come. Relief flooded through his limbs like crystals glittering along his nerves, and he flew on, straight and level, his mouth gaping as the heaving of his chest slowed.

The blast flashed a blinding light into the bottom of the cockpit, the concussion blew Snowy's legs against the fuselage, and something warm splashed into his face. The fighter roared over the open canopy in a slashing diagonal, banking lazily away, flashing the black crosses atop its wings.

'Enough!' Anger bubbled into Snowy's throat. 'Enough!'

He shut off the throttle and let his aircraft sink towards the sand. His right leg was numb and he snatched a quick look down. A ragged hole to the right of the rudder bar cast a patch of dim illumination onto a shredded boot where creamy-white shards reflected the light. Snowy gritted his teeth and braced his arms against the control panel.

The Spitfire's belly hit the ground, crunching the windmilling propeller to a grinding halt, and skidded to a stop in a shallow arc through the pliable sand. Snowy undid his straps, pulled off his mask and helmet, and pushed himself upright with his good left leg. The background rumble of artillery acquired a sharper edge of engine noise and Snowy looked up to his left;

the 109 had completed its turn and lanced towards him in a shallow dive. Snowy flopped out of the cockpit onto the starboard wing. He landed heavily, knocking some wind from his lungs. Encumbered by his parachute, he floundered for a moment before finding the leading edge with his fingers and dragging his weight onto the hot sand, pushing against the wing-root with his left foot to get his torso behind the protective bulk of the engine.

Ordnance clattered into the aircraft, ripping holes through the fuselage and cascading shattered Perspex onto the wing. Snowy's head resonated to the metallic clang of strikes on the engine and he clenched his teeth against his hollow fear of the flying metal that flailed around him. The clattering ceased as the 109 tore its path through the sky a few yards above its supine target, blasting its backwash into the sand as it climbed away.

Snowy hauled himself into a sitting position and glanced briefly at his mangled foot as the numbness receded and gave passage to the first bright stabs of pain. He diverted his gaze to the German fighter, unclipped his holster and pulled out the revolver as his enemy banked around for another pass. Snowy held the gun in both hands in front of his face, following the 109's arc over the notched sight of the weapon. The fighter flattened out and dived towards him. Snowy pushed the safety catch off with his thumb and pulled the trigger.

The revolver bucked in his hands and Snowy screamed his defiance in one long banshee wail through clenched teeth. He brought the gun down to bear on the growing shape and fired again; down, screaming, fire again, down...

Vivid yellow light sparkled along the shape, and one hundred yards away the sand erupted into spattering tracks that rushed forwards...

Fire again, screaming, down...

The sparkling stopped, the sand fountains quelled, Snowy's head cracked onto the fuselage as the German fighter slammed overhead, one last bullet fired into the space behind its tail, and his scream wound down to a whimper that expelled bubbles into the spit that dribbled from his lips.

Snowy stared upwards into the serene blue sky, listening as the rasping engine receded in volume until it was lost in the gentle growling of the British artillery.

'Out of ammunition.' Snowy dropped the revolver into the sand. 'He ran out of fucking ammunition.'

A concussive jab of electric pain stiffened his right leg and Snowy looked again at his foot. A slow pulse of blood leaked from the shredded leather of his boot, colouring the sand black like an oil stain. Pushing with both hands he shifted himself into a better sitting position with his back squarely against his aircraft. He pulled the bandana from around his neck and looped it around his calf below the knee, tightening it to slow down his bleeding. The pressure of the tourniquet calmed the shooting pains and Snowy leaned back on the aluminium skin behind his head. The sun was climbing higher in the sky and he was laying exposed in its full glare. He looked again at the weeping mess at the end of his leg and the flies that now buzzed around its oozing bounty. He squinted up at the strengthening sun and clacked his dry tongue against the roof of his mouth. He picked the revolver out of the sand and blew away the grains that stuck to its dull metal. He opened the gun's cylinder to see the rounded head of the single remaining bullet gleaming dully in its chamber. He pushed the cylinder back into the weapon's body, feeling the solid click as it locked home. He laid the gun in his lap, resting his hand on its reassuring bulk. There was at least a quicker way out if the waiting became too arduous. He closed his eyes against the beat of the sun.

***

Images swirled. Snowy stood on the street, mildly surprised that his right foot was intact. Stranger still was the pinstripe suit he wore and the polished black shoes. His wedding suit; expensive, but money spent on good cloth was always money well spent. He knew this street; he lived in this street. He walked, enjoying the click his heels rang from the pavement. People nodded and smiled as he passed. Suddenly he noticed he was wearing a hat; he tipped it and smiled back. He stopped at a door. He remembered its colour; he'd wanted black but Judith had insisted on post-box red. She'd said things would likely get black enough for everyone without having a dreary front door to look at every day. He pushed the door and it opened, swinging easily on its hinges. He stepped into the hallway with its crowded coat rack and large round mirror. A familiar scent of lavender talc hung in the air. He wondered if Judith was home, but his call for her died in his throat. Judith had gone; she didn't live here anymore. He knew that, of course he did. Maybe it was time to go and find her, to tell her again how much he loved her. He stepped back onto the street and closed the door.

'He's dead.' A man's voice.

The street vanished, as if it was a film projected upon the oily surface of a bursting bubble.

'It's not safe in the open.' The voice continued. 'Not even this far back. Let's be getting along.'

Snowy groped into the darkness, confused. His right foot throbbed burning pain up his leg.

'I reckon he's breathing.' A second man.

Snowy opened his eyes and blinked against the sun's glare, struggling to focus his eyes.

'See?' The second man said. 'He *is* alive.'

The man swam into view, crouching next to Snowy, peering into his face. Snowy tried to form a word, but his tongue sat like a piece of wood in a leather bag.

'We've got to get these shells to the guns.' The first man again. 'There'll be hell to pay if we don't.'

The second man stood and turned to his companion. Snowy's vision squirmed to focus on the other. Behind him, two trucks stood, engines running.

'It's the bloody breakthrough,' the first man continued. 'The guns *need* these shells.'

The second man turned to look at Snowy again, hands on hips, weighing up the situation.

The rumbling that had knitted the land to the sky since the early hours of that morning gently echoed away to cool, clean silence.

The second man cocked his head at the change: 'The barrage is over,' he said. 'End of argument; we're going to help this poor fucker.' He strode over to one of the trucks. 'We'll drop your load here and you can take the fly-boy back with you. I'll take my load to the guns and come back for yours. Let's get on with it, and somebody give that poor bastard a drink of water.'

***

Bryan shut off his engine and pulled back the canopy. He unhooked his straps and stood up. Leaning on the top of the windshield, he watched the stragglers of Firebird Squadron taxiing in. Three aircraft were missing. He squinted against the sun to make out the identification letters on the Spitfires as they emerged from the swirling dust. The last one trundled past.

Bryan scanned the distant runway for a latecomer, then lifted his gaze to search the western sky. No Spitfire flew there.

Bryan punched his parachute release and let the pack fall into his cockpit. He climbed out, cursing at the webbing that tangled momentarily on his boot. He jumped to the ground as another pilot trailed past with shoulders slumped.

'Did you see what happened?' he asked. 'Did you see Snowy?'

The pilot stopped and looked at him; his sweat-soddened hair plastered across his forehead, forming a dark pelmet over his dazed visage. He blinked several times, absorbing the question.

'Messerschmitts,' he said quietly. 'That's all I saw. All over the fucking sky. Messerschmitts.'

Bryan strode past him, along the extended line of Spitfires, checking the letters on each fuselage he passed. He stopped by one and watched two airmen helping its pilot out of the cockpit. Blood saturated the pilot's shirt-sleeve and dripped like a litany from his fingertips. The man keened constantly through gritted teeth, moving with the infinite care demanded by the strictures of acute pain. An ambulance rumbled to a halt next to the fighter, shedding stretcher-bearers from its tailgate.

Bryan turned away and walked towards the orderly holding the water canteens. There was nothing else to do.

***

Snowy swam back into consciousness, the rattling of his damaged engine ringing in his ears. He gasped a shocked inhalation and lurched his torso forward. A shock of pain stalled the movement and a palm pushed his chest back.

'Steady on, son.'

Snowy looked into the face of the soldier who leaned over him. It was a different man from the two who had debated over his fate.

'Call me Snowy,' Snowy said, although it didn't come out sounding like that.

'Yes, mate. Here you go.' The soldier opened a canteen, lifted Snowy's head with his free hand and trickled warm water between his lips.

Snowy held the water in his mouth, undulating his tongue in its sumptuous fluidity before swallowing it. Abandoning attempts at speech, he nodded his gratitude and settled back.

The engine noise was behind his head, at the front of the truck; the rattling came from the lengths of chain that secured the tailgate. His head rested on his parachute pack and his body swayed in gentle resonance with the creaking suspension as the truck made good speed eastwards across the desert.

*** 

Bryan sat apart in the mess, chain-smoking cigarettes and stubbing them out in the remains of the lumpy mashed potato on his plate. He didn't seek company, and his demeanour did not invite it.

The squadron leader walked in, casting a weather eye over the eating men as he poured a mug of tea from the urn. His gaze dropped onto Bryan. He shut off the tap and threaded his way through the tables to the solitary man.

'How are you, Hale?' Barnard asked as he sat down across the table.

Bryan looked up into the other's face: 'We lost three.' He shrugged. 'That's always going to hurt.'

'Four,' Barnard said. 'The wounded lad didn't make it.'

He pulled a hip flask from inside his tunic and flipped it open. He poured a slug into his tea and handed the flask across. Bryan took a swig and rolled the rich, woody rum around his mouth, allowing its alcohol to sizzle on his gums.

'I've talked to most of the pilots,' Barnard continued. 'No-one saw exactly what happened to anyone else, but nobody saw any parachutes.' He took a sip from his tea, flushing the liquid through his teeth in contemplation. 'I think they hit us with two squadrons; the one that bounced us, and another one arriving a touch later to pick off the stragglers. No-one's claimed a kill, so it looks like the Germans kept a clean sheet.'

Bryan shook his head slowly: 'Snowy just vanished. Someone called the bandits, then bang; Snowy was gone.'

'You know yourself, Hale, dogfighting is little more than opportunistic thuggery. If you're in the wrong place, looking the wrong way, chances are you'll buy it.'

Bryan sighed and leaned forward onto the table: 'He was just getting good at it. I was beginning to believe he'd get through it all.' He sucked another draft out of the hipflask and handed it back. 'Snowy didn't have to be here,' he continued. 'He'd done his bit for this battle with his work at Aboukir; he's a boffin first and a fighter pilot second. He followed me because he thought I was his friend.'

'Well, aren't you?'

Bryan looked down into his despoiled mash: 'He believed I was. And I suppose I tried to be. But I've never really understood how to do it properly.'

'I think you're mistaken on that.' Barnard stood up. 'And I'm sure Snowy would agree with me.'

Barnard placed the hipflask down in front of Bryan, turned and left the mess.

### Tuesday, 3 November 1942 – Cairo Hospital

Snowy's world pressed in on him like a claustrophobic fog, as if he stood (or lay; he couldn't discern) in a fleece lined box, warm and muffled. Yet when he reached out, these dark and fuzzy constrictions were infinitely distant; blocks of immeasurable size that bulged and distended like monstrous intestines, and he floated, lost in the vast space between them. Something brushed his face; a movement of air. Snowy focussed on the sensation, rediscovering the boundary. His nerves tingled, redrawing the physical limitation of his skin. The bloated shapes pressed closer in a sickening rush, but Snowy opened his eyelids.

A dull white surface reflected harsh electric light and Snowy squinted to protect his throbbing eyes. The sound of breathing crept into his consciousness and he listened with fascination while his vision adjusted. Tiny points of fluorescence wavered against the wash of white, spinning a momentary dance before vanishing to be reborn elsewhere. A ceiling fan coagulated out of the blur, wood and wicker blades chasing each other around in sweeping circles, its pull switch swaying lazily in rhythm with the oscillation. Snowy's head lolled to the right as something loomed over him, large and blue. He blinked rapidly, willing his eyes to focus on this new shape. The blue resolved to the dark fabric of a dress and a face emerged to sit atop it, crowned with a luminous white cap.

'Nurse?' Snowy's voice scratched in his throat.

'Matron,' the face corrected and receded back into obscurity.

### Landing Ground 97

Bryan was the last to take off. Emerging through the dust bank raised by the others, he climbed after the depleted squadron. Firebird's losses had yet to be replaced, and today they could muster no more than seven. Bryan dropped into the role of solitary weaver – watching everyone's tail and guarding against another catastrophic 'bounce' – with quiet relief. He didn't want another wingman; someone who would sit with him in the mess, talking at him, being friendly. He didn't need to look into another eager face, bright with the metallic expectation of battle, and know that they were wanting, that blind luck was their best hope of coming back.

Bryan pulled into a shallow left bank, beginning his weave and easing his throttle forward to maintain his distance. The squadron drifted across his windshield. He reversed the bank and they drifted back. Bryan eyed the six Spitfires flying in pairs arrayed before his nose with flat dispassion. His gaze settled on the Spitfire flying at the apex. It contained the squadron leader. Barnard was valuable; made so by his promise.

Barnard led the formation into a wide left bank, heading onto their southerly patrol line. Bryan adjusted to follow and dropped his head back to scan the blue vault above, seeking the tiny portents of diving danger. The blue was the battleground; a friend and an enemy in equal measure. It was clean and brisk; it was the antithesis of the gritty, stinking sands of the filthy sweating desert that he was coming to hate more and more as the days crawled by.

His displacement and continued exile from Malta had carved a chasm in his chest. Katie hadn't softened his plight with her tenderness: *'Dear, dear Katie, I wish you contentment.'* Snowy had distracted and amused him like a faithful school chum: *'Poor Snowy, I hope it was swift for you in the end.'* But now the pangs of rancour had no salve; the resentment scratched at his soul and simmered a rising malcontent.

The squadron reached the end of its patrol line and wheeled around to return north. Bryan looked down under his port wing, studying the landscape for long moments; there was something different about the battlefield. He pulled himself back to scanning the sky, forcing himself not to hurry, methodically quartering the dome from left to right, front to back. Then he dropped his gaze once more to the desert floor. The smudges and flecks that betrayed the presence of guns, trucks, men and tanks were spread thinner on the ground. Bryan made another sweep of the sky and looked back at the ground rolling past beneath him. The battlefield was wider – much, much wider than yesterday.

'Oh, my word,' Bryan muttered to himself. 'The bastards are pulling back.'

## Cairo Hospital

Snowy woke from a shallow snooze to the sound of swishing fabric. He blinked the sleep from his eyes to see a nurse work her way down the ward, closing the curtains against the gathering dusk outside. He wriggled his shoulders against the pillows that propped him in his bed and swallowed against a vestige of acid nausea. His right foot tingled with irritation, as if thousands of ants crawled there, testing his skin with their mandibles and scurrying on to scratch and nip elsewhere. He looked down at the cage that held the covers off his legs. He made an attempt to lean forward but a dense fatigue pushed him back into the soft embrace of his pillows.

A woman he recognised strode into the ward.

'Matron?' Snowy called.

The matron stopped at the foot of his bed.

'My foot is itching like mad,' Snowy said.

'Which one, Mr White?' the matron asked.

'My right foot,' Snowy said.

'Not possible, Mr White.' The matron pulled a straight-lipped grimace. 'I'm afraid you no longer *have* a right foot.'

## Landing Ground 97

Bryan twiddled his cigarette around in his fingers watching the smoke curling up in dancing spirals in front of his face. He eavesdropped on the conversations drifting from other tables; voices were lifted with optimism, discussion was sometimes robust, but most in the mess had noticed what he had seen and come to the same conclusion. Bryan sipped his tea, feeling the stewed tannins settle their roughness onto his front teeth.

Barnard walked past the marquee's entrance, dragged to a halt by a pilot's shouted question: 'What do *you* think, sir? Have we got 'em on the run?'

Barnard hesitated in the darkness, then stepped inside. He directed his answer to the questioner, and Bryan had to lean forward to decipher his words.

'It's really too early to draw any conclusions,' Barnard said. 'What looks to be the case from the air is often very different on the ground.'

Bryan gazed directly at his squadron leader's face, but Barnard avoided his eyes.

Another airman: 'Oh, come on, sir. You must have *some* idea.'

Barnard turned to the man, again speaking directly to him: 'Let's see what the army has to say about it. We should be getting reports throughout the day tomorrow.'

Bryan braced his hands on the table ready to rise to his feet. Barnard turned and caught his eye, freezing the action. Barnard's face was resolute, but his gaze carried the softness of empathy underscored with the tension of some hidden and reluctant necessity.

Barnard turned abruptly and left the mess. Bryan settled back onto the bench. Unbidden, Snowy's words replayed in his mind: *How are you going to get there? When is the last time a ship got through from Alexandria?*

Bryan lit a fresh cigarette and softly ground his teeth together.

### Wednesday, 4 November 1942 – Cairo Hospital

'Katie! Will you come here for a moment, please?'

Katie skidded to a halt halfway across the hospital lobby and diverted to the reception desk. She leaned on the polished counter, questioning eyebrows raised.

The nurse behind the counter held out a brown envelope.

'This needs to go up to the wards,' she said. 'It's for the amputee, White, D, RAF. Matron's waiting for it.'

Katie took the envelope and trotted up the stairs. She ducked into each ward, scanning the names scrawled above the bedheads until she found White, D, RAF.

'Hello Mr White,' she said, glancing around the ward in search of the matron.

'Call me Snowy,' the man said.

The matron bustled into the ward and made for the bed.

'Ah, you have it,' she said, taking the envelope from Katie. 'Thank you, Nurse Katherine.'

The man's attention snapped from the matron to Katie's face. His gaze dropped furtively for a moment and then returned to her eyes. Something unreadable there intrigued Katie; she stepped back, but did not leave.

'They've been looking for you, Mr White,' the matron said.

Snowy dragged his gaze to the matron's face: 'They?' he asked.

'When our admissions list went in, we got a call from RAF HQ in Alexandria,' she continued. 'They're flying you home as soon as possible.

Apparently, someone at the Air Ministry wants to know all about some work you've been doing on Spitfires.'

She handed Snowy the envelope: 'You'll need these papers. Keep them safe.'

Snowy took the envelope and turned it over his hands like it was a fragile artefact.

'If you carry on progressing as you are' – she patted his forearm in reassurance – 'we can discharge you in a day or two.'

The matron moved on to check something at the next bed along and Katie took a half-step forward.

'Are you alright... Snowy, isn't it?' Katie asked. 'Is there anything I can get for you.'

Snowy's eyes flicked from the envelope to Katie's face, and the warmth returned to his features.

'Are you Katie? Bryan's Katie?'

A shock of electric surprise ran through Katie's body, suddenly weakening her elbows and knees. To dissemble long enough to recover, she moved the visitors' chair closer to the bed and sat down.'

'No,' she said eventually. 'That nurse doesn't work here anymore.' Katie allowed a sad smile to creep onto her lips. 'I knew her quite well while she was here. But now she's gone.'

'That's a shame.' Snowy's eyes dropped back to his envelope. 'Bryan talks about her a lot, but, if you ask me, I reckon he never told her how much she really means to him; I mean, deep down.'

'Don't worry, Snowy,' Katie said. 'I think she knows.'

Moisture pricked into the corners of Katie's eyes; she stood and replaced the chair, a chance to turn her face away from the man in the bed.

'Good luck, Snowy,' she said as she smoothed her apron, her face still averted. 'Have a safe journey.'

'Thank you,' Snowy said and watched Nurse Katherine as she walked quickly along the ward and out through the door.

## Thursday, 5 November 1942 – Landing Ground 97

Firebird Squadron crabbed further west into a sky empty of adversaries. Bryan paused his weaving flight to survey the terrain below. There was no longer a battlefield of lines; everything was in motion swathing vast tracts of the desert in drifting dust clouds. From this height it was impossible to define which dust bank hid the fleeing enemy and which streamed from the wheels and tracks of their pursuers.

Barnard's order crackled across the ether and the squadron wheeled eastwards for home. Bryan continued his search of the empty sky above and behind as the formation bled away its altitude. They crossed the line of entrenched British artillery, standing silent now that their targets had retreated out of range, and Bryan stopped searching for an enemy that was obviously too busy packing up their airfields and heading west ahead of their vanquished army.

The squadron flattened out to land, Bryan coming in behind the others. He taxied carefully through the roiling dust until two airmen appeared at his wingtips to guide him out to dispersal. As he shut his fighter down, he glanced around, looking for Barnard. He spotted him with a couple of other pilots, drinking and washing his face with water from a canteen. By the time Bryan had got out of his aircraft, Barnard had left the group of drinking men and was on his way towards the admin tents.

'Perfect,' Bryan muttered to himself, and walked after his leader, his eyes locked at a point between the man's shoulder blades. Barnard ducked into the tent. Bryan paused for a moment to allow the man to dump his flying gear and get behind the trellis table that served him as a desk, then followed him in.

'Excuse me, sir.' Bryan straightened his back into a semblance of attention. 'May I have a word?'

Barnard looked up. His features fluttered as he considered refusing, then settled into resignation.

'Yes.' – it was almost a sigh – 'Sit down, Hale.' He indicated the chair in front of his desk.

Bryan sat down and regarded Barnard in silence. Bryan's very presence was the unvoiced appeal; the other man's promise was the longed-for prize.

'We're expecting a full complement of replacements tomorrow,' Barnard began. 'And it's obvious that Rommel is in full retreat.' He clasped his hands together and looked down at his desk. 'And I'm aware that I made certain commitments to you.'

'But?' Bryan intoned.

'But,' Barnard echoed and looked up into Bryan's eyes. 'Things have got a bit complicated.'

Bryan remained silent, clamping his jaw shut to remain that way.

'I can take you off operations,' Barnard said. 'That's easy enough. I can get you a staff position in Alexandria or Cairo; something comfortable for a few months and then-'

'Malta' – Bryan interrupted – 'was your promise.'

The conflict flickered again across Barnard's features. After a moment, he leaned forward and lowered his voice: 'Look,' he said. 'A British invasion fleet has just entered the Med heading towards Algeria. An American fleet is approaching Morocco's Atlantic coast. It's a matter of days before the biggest operation of the war kicks off. Even if I put in the request for your transfer, no-one would have the time to even look at it for weeks, probably months.'

Bryan narrowed his eyes as he absorbed the information.

'I'm sorry, Hale,' Barnard continued. 'To be honest, it would be easier to get you down to the west coast and on to a Sunderland for a flight back to Britain.' Barnard's face brightened at the thought. 'We could organise that. I can authorise an extended leave and you'd be home in a couple of days.'

'I don't want to go home,' Bryan said. 'I want to go to Malta.' He stood up and again straightened his back, looking dead ahead at the tent's back wall: 'May I leave, sir?'

Barnard regarded Bryan for a moment, then nodded sadly.

Bryan left the tent and headed back towards dispersal. The horizon out over the sea had darkened with storm clouds, and the first few drops of rain hit the sand around his feet as he walked.

# Chapter 12

## Friday, 6 November 1942

The rain swept in on buffeting winds; it lashed the canvas, quelled, then lashed again with renewed malice. Bryan lay on his cot smoking. The close confines of the tent suited his mood and the rain prevented his further participation in what he regarded as a won battle; at least for today. The options of a desk job or a ticket home were tantamount to open insults, and the certainty that he would be kept here in Libya indefinitely sat like a puddle of gall in the pit of his stomach.

Something bumped against the tent-flaps, then fingers fumbled with the ties. The flaps opened and a man pushed his way in, water dripping from his rain-cape in tiny cascades. The man turned to refasten the ties.

'Who the fuck are you?' Bryan said, sitting up and swinging his feet onto the floor.

The man finished with the ties and turned, pulling his hood back from his face.

'Simon,' the man said, shrugging his kitbag from his shoulder onto the floor. 'Replacements. Just arrived. Twelve of us.' He glanced at the empty cot. 'I was told this was a spare bed.'

Bryan looked across at the empty cot and nodded slowly.

Simon pulled his rain-cape off, rolled it into a bundle and shoved it under the cot. He wiped the spatters of water from his face and sat down on the thin mattress.

Bryan dropped his cigarette onto the ground and crushed it under his boot. He pulled the pack from his shirt pocket and held it out to the newcomer.

'No thanks,' Simon said. 'I don't smoke.'

Bryan pulled a fresh cigarette for himself and lit it, all the while studying Simon's face.

'You look about twelve,' Bryan said.

'I'm twenty,' Simon said.

'Any combat experience?' Bryan asked.

'None as yet,' Simon replied. 'Perhaps you could show me the ropes.'

The rain drummed onto the canvas, filling the space between the men with its noise.

'The last man I taught' – Bryan blew smoke from his nostrils like a sigh made visible – 'no longer needs the bed you're sitting on.'

Outside someone raised their voice, shouting a single word over and over, unintelligible under the hammering rain.

'We all start somewhere,' Simon said. 'I expect there was a time when you were green.'

Bryan nodded: 'Indeed, there was,' he said quietly. It seemed a long time and a lot of people ago. He glanced around the tent, which suddenly looked even shittier, and pushed the clamouring memories from his mind.

The shouting outside persisted, growing louder. Simon started to say something and Bryan held up his palm to forestall him, cocking his head in an attempt to decipher the cries.

The shouting moved closer; close enough to carry above the storm: 'Hale! Hale! Bloody hell! Hale, where are you?'

Bryan recognised Barnard's voice, leapt from the cot and untied the tent flaps. He ducked out into the gloom of a premature dusk and the stinging lances of the saturating rain. A figure was zig-zagging through the tents, repeating his call over and over.

'Sir,' Bryan shouted through the storm. 'Over here!'

Barnard spun on his heel and dodged through the tents towards him.

'Hale!' he gasped. 'Thank Christ I found you. Listen, man. The Beaufighter squadron has been ordered to Malta to cover the Algerian landings. I've talked to McCaffrey; he's willing to take you with him.'

Bryan stared into the squadron leader's eyes. Rain plastered his hair across his forehead and ran down his cheeks. Bryan blinked against the water and his jaw dropped open.

'They're running up their engines now,' Barnard shouted into his face. 'They're leaving in a few minutes. You need to get out to dispersal. They can't wait in this weather.'

The numbing spell of Bryan's surprise shattered; he turned and lunged into the tent, grabbing at his case under the cot.

'It's all yours, Simon,' he said through a fierce grin. 'Freehold.'

He ducked back out into the rain and stood nose to nose with Barnard.

'Thank you,' he said.

Barnard nodded once: 'Go!'

Bryan set off at a trot, vaulting guy-lines until he was clear of the tents, then accelerating to a sprint. His sodden clothes stuck flat to his skin and he ran through the failing light like a naked wraith, feet pounding into the rain-soaked sand with wet slaps that cascaded mud up his legs.

The roar of engines undercut the thrumming rain, and lights blinked into being through the deluge. Bryan veered towards the first set of twinkles in the dark, pounding his legs like fury, his throat rasping with the acrid bitterness of old tobacco.

The sparkling navigation lights accreted dark shapes around them, a row of brooding behemoths looming in the deepening dusk, standing like monstrous raptors stretching their wings in preparation for an imperative migration. Bryan slid to a halt in front of the lead Beaufighter and squinted up at its large, sloping windshield. Haloed by the golden glow from his instruments, McCaffrey's face appeared like a benevolent messiah behind the glass. McCaffrey gazed down at the dials before him, eyes flitting from one to another as he made final checks on the twin engines that roared their ardour either side of his cockpit.

Bryan skirted around the aircraft's wingtip and loped towards the fuselage. The blast of the propeller lashed the rain horizontally into his body and he fought to stay upright, slipping in the thin layer of mud that greased the soles of his boots. He flattened his torso against the wet fuselage and hammered the heel of his hand against its painted roundel that streamed with runnels of water. He thumped an urgent rhythm on the metal while the roar of the engine ripped away his shouts, flinging them unheard beyond the tail of the aircraft. The underside hatch swung open, hitting the ground by his feet. Bryan gasped with elation, ducked under the fuselage and pulled himself inside. The observer grabbed Bryan's arm, helping him aboard, then closed and locked the hatch. The man turned to regard Bryan.

'We'll be staying low,' he shouted. 'So there'll be no need for oxygen. But I'm afraid we don't have a spare parachute.'

Bryan shrugged at the man, his face wreathed in a beaming smile. The observer pointed at four kit-bags laying against the fuselage wall.

'That's the best we can do,' the man shouted. 'We're not really equipped to deal with passengers.'

Bryan settled down onto the bags and wedged his case next to them. He watched the other man climb into his seat under the rain-streaked observation blister, re-attach his wireless cable and hold his mask to his face to talk to McCaffrey on the other side of the armoured bulkhead. The observer caught Bryan's eye and winked just as the engine noise surged and the aircraft rolled into its taxi.

Bryan exhaled a ragged breath and looked for handholds on the strutting around him. His wet clothes chilled his flesh in the cooling air, goading his muscles into intermittent shivers as the Beaufighter bumped its way towards the runway.

## Saturday, 7 November 1942 – Ta'Qali Airfield, Malta

Something prodded Bryan in the shoulder, nudging him out of his fitful doze. He blinked the slumber from his eyes to see the observer sitting in his elevated seat, his leg at full stretch to poke at him with the toe of his boot. Bryan slapped the man's foot away and sat up. The observer made a swooping motion with a flattened hand and mouthed the word 'landing'. Bryan nodded his understanding and reached for his handholds. The Beaufighter banked into its circuit. The hydraulics hummed and the landing gear clanked into place. As the illusory warmth of sleep deserted him, Bryan's body quaked with shivering beneath his still-damp clothes and his jaw started chattering. He clamped his teeth together to still the rattling and waited.

The big fighter levelled out and the engine noise reduced. It flew on for a few serene moments before it bumped into contact with the ground and the rumble of its wheels overpowered the purring of its engines. Bryan dropped his chin to his chest. After nearly three months, his exile was over; he was finally back.

The Beaufighter slowed and turned, taxied a short distance, then stopped. The engines dropped to silence, first starboard, then port, leaving the propellers to tick the sound of their slowing revolutions through the airframe until they too were mute. The observer clambered down and grimaced with pleasure as the blood returned to his buttocks. He undid the hatch, let it fall open and dropped to the ground.

Bryan dragged himself to his feet and arched his back against his stiffened muscles. He grabbed his case and followed the observer through the hatch. He stood next to the fuselage, by the roundel that he had thumped in desperation only five hours before, and looked around.

The night was perfectly clear and black; a thin crescent moon hung in the sky like a maniac's smile surrounded by the crystal glimmer of the stars. Beyond the tail of the aircraft, the flaming flarepath danced in bright parallel lines. Disembodied lights descended towards it until the orange glow of the fires illuminated another Beaufighter on its way to roost.

Bryan blinked the ghosts of the flames from his retinas and looked towards the front of the plane. The observer had sat down with his back against the Beaufighter's big tyre, seemingly already snoozing. At the nose, the pilot's hatch hung open and McCaffrey stood talking with an airman. Bryan watched for a while, but McCaffrey walked off with the airman still deep in conversation. Bryan looked back across and beyond the flarepath, using its glow to orientate himself on the airfield he already knew so well. Content that he'd found his bearings, he turned away from the brightness, ducked under the wing past the softly snoring observer and walked away into the gloom.

As his eyes adjusted, the fire glow behind him separated shapes from the darkness. First the horizon from the sky, then the landscape below the horizon, and finally the blocky shapes within the landscape. Bryan walked with purpose, enjoying the warming pulse of blood through his limbs, blood that beat through his veins in arhythmic counter-point to the swooping roar of the Beaufighters that dropped in to land one-by-one behind him.

As Bryan crossed the perimeter track, dark blocky shapes consolidated against the darker sky, taking the familiar shape of two block-built storage huts. Bryan approached the nearest, stepped through its doorless entrance and paused to allow his eyes to adjust to the denser darkness within.

Paint cans littered the floor and a sack-barrow leaned against the wall. In the far corner a pile of canvas tarpaulins lay piled on a wooden pallet. A sudden surge of weariness flowed into Bryan's muscles. He dropped his case to the floor, approached the pallet and threw back the first few folds of canvas from the stack. He clambered onto the pile and pulled the layers of canvas over his body. He laid his head against the rough fabric, breathed deeply of its oily scent, pulled his knees up to his torso and abandoned himself to sleep.

*** 

The truck from Xara Palace lumbered to a halt just inside the gate at Ta'Qali. Ben Stevens climbed down from the passenger seat, called his thanks to the driver and followed the pilots who spilled from the tailgate down towards the readiness tent. New shapes arrayed across the field snagged his eye and he paused, shading his eyes against the newly-risen sun, to appraise them.

'Beaufighters.' He whistled to himself in appreciation. 'What beautiful ladies you are.'

Men bustled around the big fighters, lifting thin, bladed rockets from a trolley and slotting them into racks under the wings. The urge to go and help, or at least go and watch, to be closer to these aircraft was strong. But Ben knew his first job was to receive the orders of the day and deal with any business the adjutant might have for him. He trudged on towards the dun canvas bell-tent, hoping there'd be nothing that would detain him for too long.

The pilots settled into the rickety chairs grouped under the makeshift canvas gazebo next to the readiness tent. The canvas tarpaulin that formed its roof undulated gently atop its corner-posts in the light breeze agitated by the warming touch of the sun upon the rocky interior of the island. Ben walked into the tent, where the adjutant was already behind his jerry-built desk.

'Some new arrivals on the field, I see,' Ben said.

'Yes,' the adjutant said. 'They arrived in the early hours.'

'Where from?' Ben asked

'Egypt,' the adjutant said. 'From one of the landing grounds south-west of Alexandria.' He picked up an oil-smudged slip of paper. 'I've got a note here that they brought in a passenger.'

'Top brass?' Ben speculated.

'It doesn't say.'

'I wonder where he is now?' Ben said.

'Perhaps he went looking for a suitable hotel,' the adjutant chuckled. 'I'll go down and see if anyone in the Beaufighter squadron knows.'

'No.' Ben said. 'I'll go.'

He turned and left before the adjutant could answer. He wove through the seated men and trotted easily down the slight slope towards the dispersed aircraft. As he arrived at the first Beaufighter, the armourers and fitters were finishing their work and aircrews were moving around preparing to board their aircraft.

Ben stumbled to a halt in front the closest airman, interrupting their chat to ask about the passenger.

'I don't know anything about it, mate,' one of the men said around the stub of his cigarette. 'The squadron leader is over there.' He pointed towards an aircraft standing about one hundred yards away.

Ben sprinted across the hard ground and arrived just as an airman ducked under the Beaufighter's nose and began fiddling with the clasps on his access hatch.

'Excuse me!' Ben skidded to a halt, breathing heavily from his sudden exertion.

The man turned and regarded Ben, annoyance creasing his features.

'What is it?' The man asked. 'We're taking off in a few minutes.'

'You brought a passenger in this morning,' Ben said. 'We don't know who he is, and we don't know where he's gone.'

The man emerged from under the fuselage and stood beneath his aircraft's nose, flanked by its stationary propellers. He scratched his chin and stared into space.

'It was a pilot,' he said. 'I only spoke with him once. I think his name was Bernie, or Barry. I think that was it. Barry Hughes. Or something like that.'

'But, where is he?' Ben asked.

'I was busy after we landed, but I saw someone walking away, it must've been him. He was going in that direction.' The man pointed back the way Ben had come. 'In fact, that looks like him, there,' he added.

Ben turned to follow the pointing finger. Beyond the readiness tent, further up the gradual slope, two stone storage sheds sat squat in the sandy earth. A figure stood in front of them, holding a suitcase. As Ben watched, the figure set down his suitcase and went behind the sheds.

Ben shouted his thanks over his shoulder as he lurched into a loping run back across the field, over the perimeter track and past the readiness tent. As he arrived at the storage huts, the man emerged from behind them, re-buttoning his fly.

'At last, the reception committee,' Bryan said. 'Was the band not available?'

Ben stood in open-mouthed surprise for a moment, then surged forward and hugged his dishevelled friend to his chest. Breaking the clinch, he stood, straight-armed with his hands clasping Bryan's shoulders, scanning his face to banish his disbelief.

'Where have you been?' Ben asked.

'Up to my arse-crack in hot sand, mostly,' Bryan said. 'The bastards wouldn't let me go until they'd settled an argument with some bloke called Rommel. Even then, I wouldn't have got here had the Beau boys not been transferred for invasion duties.'

'So, it's on,' Ben said. 'There have been rumours. God, it will be so good to be on the front foot for once.'

'What *I'd* like to be' – Bryan scratched absently at the side of his torso – 'is in some clean water with a scrubbing brush.'

'Of course,' Ben said. 'Let's show your face to the adjutant, and then we can get back to the Palace and get you settled in.'

Bryan picked up his case and the pair started down the gentle slope towards the readiness tent.

'Do you know' – Bryan sniffed in disgust – 'they even offered me a bloody desk job.'

'No!' Ben exclaimed. 'The absolute bastards!'

***

The truck ground into the yard of Xara Palace and the two men dropped from the tailgate and went inside.

'There's an ensuite bathtub in my room,' Ben said. 'You're welcome to use that.'

They started up the stairs.

'Can I get my things first?' Bryan asked.

'I'm afraid we sent your things back to your parents,' Ben said.

Bryan cast a sidelong look: 'You did what?'

'We thought you were dead,' Ben said. 'It's procedure when someone dies.'

'Well, that'll be a lovely surprise for my old man.'

They topped the stairs and walked along the corridor.

'And my room?' Bryan asked.

'There's someone else in there,' Ben answered quietly.

'Uh-huh,' Bryan muttered. 'Of course there is.'

They arrived at a door. Ben unlocked it and Bryan followed him in, looking around at the large room.

'This is very pleasant,' Bryan said.

'They said I should have it' – Ben narrowed his eyes as if expecting a blow – 'when they made me squadron leader.'

'Well, congratulations.' Bryan went into the bathroom and set the water running. 'Rank hath it's privileges, they always say.'

'I told them I'd accept it as *acting* squadron leader,' Ben said. 'I believed you'd make it back.'

'And then the first thing you did was send my personal effects back to England.' Bryan's disembodied voice drifted in with the steam from the bathroom.

'Well, you're not a fish are you, Bryan?' Ben said. Who would've bet on a submarine popping up from nowhere?'

Bryan appeared at the doorway, his feet bare, unbuttoning his shirt with grimy fingers.

'Absolutely no-one,' he said. 'Least of all me.' He retreated into the bathroom.

Ben sat down on the bed; the weight of the words he was formulating caused his shoulders to sag.

'So, as squadron leader, it fell to me to break the news to Jacobella,' he said. 'I found her at the church and... I told her you'd been lost.'

Bryan reappeared in the doorway, naked except for his stained and grubby underpants, his face stony with concern: 'You put her straight when you heard I'd been picked up,' he said. 'Didn't you?'

'I went back to the church to do that.' Ben looked up at his friend. 'The priest told me she'd stopped attending. He didn't know why.'

Bryan stared with unfocussed eyes into space as the possibilities behind that revelation paraded through his mind.

'Damn it,' he hissed. 'What a fucking mess.'

'I didn't know where she lives,' Ben said quietly. 'I'm sorry. Perhaps I should've tried something else, but I never got the time to even think about it.'

Bryan's eyes snapped back into focus: 'It's done,' he said with sudden resolve. 'And what happens now is you' – he stabbed a finger at Ben – 'go and find me a set of fresh clothes while I scrub this desert filth off my body.'


### Grand Harbour, Valletta

The bus juddered to a halt and Bryan stepped down onto the pavement, standing back as the vehicle jolted back into motion and belched black smoke from its rattling exhaust. He cast his eyes around the harbour, the broken buildings, the piles of sandstone rubble and the submerged hulks of sunken merchantmen. He drew in a deep breath, exhaled it with a sigh, then turned to go in search of the things he'd been forced to leave behind.

He measured his pace as he walked into the city; but the sea breezes that funnelled through the streets and tickled against his newly-clean skin cooled him with a nuance missing from the oven-fridge duality of the desert.

He arrived at St Augustine's and paused on the steps, eyeing the doors for a moment before pressing on up Bakery Street and dog-legging onto Mint Street. His steps slowed as he climbed the steeply sloping pavement, moving closer to his epicentre, closer to his fulcrum.

He turned onto Windmill Street and his heart leapt with relief to see the houses standing undamaged; one dread was dissipated and his step quickened. He found the familiar door, still peeling curls of blue paint to the elements. He pushed it open, stepped into the hallway and stood before Jacobella's door. He waited for a moment, listening to the silence, then reached up and knocked.

Sounds of a shuffling movement bled down the stairs behind the door, then a stair creaked under the weight of a footstep. Bryan stepped back as the door opened.

The old woman's wrinkled visage puckered into a scowl and she screwed up her eyes to squint at the man before her. Then recognition softened her brow and the hint of a smile curved her thin lips.

'Jacobella!' she called, without shifting her gaze from Bryan's face. 'Visitor!'

The old woman brushed past him and left, chuckling to herself as she stepped out onto the street. Bryan stepped forward into the open doorway and looked up the stairs. A small girl appeared and looked down at him.

'Bine?' she said.

The girl's mother appeared next to her daughter, her long dark hair tied back from her face. Her features trembled in shocked disbelief.

'Habib?'

'Sorry I'm a bit late.' Bryan's voice caught in his throat. 'May I come in?'

### Sunday, 8 November 1942

The flow of people along the pavements diminished as tardy citizens hurried along to join the congregation in St Augustine's. Bryan turned the corner onto Bakery Street, close behind the tardiest of the stragglers. Lučija

169

sat on his shoulders, twiddling her fingers through his hair. Bryan grasped the girl's ankles, and beside him, Jacobella walked, her hand resting in the crook of his arm, her long black hair framing her numinous smile.

They climbed the steps to where a verger stood at the church door, drab in his sullen black robe. The man regarded Jacobella, his eyebrows knitting with disapproval. His gaze to flitted across to Bryan's face for a moment, before his eyes dropped at the message he read there and he stepped back. Bryan lifted Lučija from his shoulders, placed her down at his side, and the trio walked hand-in-hand into the church.

# Postscript

## Saturday, 14 November 1942 – London, England

Jenny stood at the living room window looking down at the sparse traffic that flowed up and down Balham High Road. Her temples throbbed with the vague portent of a headache and she breathed through her nose to suppress the sigh that frustration was building in her breast.

She turned back to face the sofa. James sat there, his head still in his hands. The call up papers lay on the coffee table in front of him.

'You must have *at least* half-expected it,' Jenny said.

'No.' James let his hands drop from his face, and his gaze settled on the letter. 'I was stupid enough to believe that working at the ministry came with an automatic exemption. Apparently not; it seems no-one is safe.'

'Perhaps they'll be glad of your expertise,' Jenny suggested. 'Maybe they can use your skills away from the fighting.'

James threw her a disdainful glance: 'I'm an architect, Jenny. Armies don't construct buildings; it's their business to knock them down. No, they don't need *expertise* – he chewed scornfully upon the word – 'they just need the numbers. You've seen what they're doing in Algeria. Very soon, they'll be looking for the next beach to storm, and then the next one.' He picked up the papers and crumpled them hard in his fist. 'This is just to get the numbers.'

Jenny straightened her already-straight skirt and drew a deep, silent breath.

'Getting agitated on a Saturday morning is not going to help,' she said. 'Calm down and leave it be until Monday. We can look into everything then. Remember, we're visiting my parents this weekend; we need to be getting ourselves sorted.'

'Cancel it,' James said.

'Absolutely not!' Jenny's voice hardened. 'It's their wedding anniversary, mother is cooking, it's been arranged for weeks.'

James remained silent.

'Alright, James,' Jenny continued. 'You can stay here and sulk if you want to, but I'm going to the party.'

Jenny walked out of the lounge and down the short corridor to the bedroom. She pulled her overnight case from the top of the wardrobe and started to pack.

**Sunday, 15 November 1942**

Winston's decree had slipped her mind, but as she helped her mother clear away after a late breakfast, the distant carolling chime of church bells crept into the kitchen. Victory at El Alamein had set clapper against bronze for the first time in three years.

Jenny excused herself, grabbed her coat from the hallway and skipped from the house into the crisp winter air. The reckless clanging drew her along the lanes and down the hill to St John's church where the congregation were already milling around the church doors.

Jenny stood and let the clamorous noise ring through her head, delighting at the echoes that bounced from the buildings up and down Church Row. When the clappers stilled, she closed her eyes and strained to follow the final reverberation back to silence.

Her cold cheeks ached with the smile that filled her face. On a whim, she walked down the side of the church to the rectory that adjoined it and knocked at the door. A woman with a quietly placid face, wearing a flour-streaked apron opened the door.

'Hello, Mrs Hale,' Jenny said. 'I'm a friend of Bryan's. I came to listen to the lovely bells and I thought I'd drop by to say hello.'

'Come in, dear,' Mrs Hale said, stepping back and holding the door open.

Jenny stepped inside and Mrs Hale closed the door.

'Come through, dear.' Mrs Hale led the way into the kitchen. 'How did you and Bryan become friends?' she asked.

'We were in the same class at school,' Jenny said. 'Then, a couple of years ago, we bumped into each other in town, and one thing led to another, and we went out together for a while.'

The older woman's face showed no sign of absorbing this information.

'Have you heard from him recently?' Jenny asked.

'Not *from* him, dear.' Mrs Hale's cheeks sagged, drawing watery red lines beneath her eyes. 'But we have heard *about* him.'

Jenny's vitals chilled, and she lurched to the nearest kitchen chair, lowering herself onto its seat without ever taking her eyes from the other woman's flaccid jowls. When Mrs Hale breathed in to speak, Jenny dropped her eyelids to avoid seeing the words emerge.

'He was lost on the fourteenth of August.' The words twisted as they penetrated. 'They told us he was defending some cargo ships and never made it back to Malta.'

Jenny took a breath and opened her eyes. She focussed on Mrs Hale's impassive face through the first swirling of tears.

'Malta?' Jenny said. 'I didn't know. I'm so sorry, Mrs Hale; I didn't know any of this.'

'That's alright, dear,' Mrs Hale said. 'You were his friend. It's right you should be told.'

Jenny stood up, pressing a clenched hand against her belly to steady the churning.

'I should leave you be,' she said.

'They sent us his things,' Mrs Hale said. She led Jenny back into the hallway and pointed to a small suitcase resting on a side table. 'Take a memento if you like,' she said. 'I'll only put it up in the attic when we get the Christmas decorations down.'

Jenny approached the case and opened the lid. She ran her fingertips across the clothes folded there, and the growing tears finally escaped from her eyes and dropped in soft spatters onto the fabric. Wiping her eyes with the heel of her hand, she noticed an envelope wedged next to the clothes. She pulled it out, and it brought with it a lock of beribboned hair.

The names on the front of the unopened envelope seemed distantly familiar. She picked up the hair in her other hand and turned to Mrs Hale. But the bustling noises of cooking coming from the kitchen indicated that Mrs Hale had forgotten her. Jenny put both items into her coat pocket, closed the suitcase lid and let herself out of the front door.

The November air chilled the moisture on Jenny's cheeks as she crossed to the lane that would take her past the parish graveyard and home. She paused by the iron railings to gaze at the statue on a tomb; the verdigris angel who forever held a dying woman in her protective arms.

'Oh, Bryan,' she muttered through quivering lips as her tears brimmed afresh. 'I hope that you found your angel in the end.'

\*\*\*

Reverend Hale climbed the steps into the pulpit and swept his sombre gaze across the congregation, quelling their fidgeting and coughing.

'We had not heard our beloved bells for a long time,' he began. 'But the peals that summoned you to worship this morning were rung for the most

173

joyous of reasons; our army's great and glorious victory at El Alamein. And we were commanded to ring them by no lesser authority than the Prime Minister himself.

'But joyous though this victory may make us today, it comes with the shadow of a sorrow that, for many, will long outlast this day of celebrations. Indeed, that shadow has fallen across my own door; my own son paid the ultimate price just three months ago while protecting the vital island fortress of Malta. It was the dogged refusal of Malta to buckle that allowed our victory in the desert to come to pass.

'Now our allied armies march on, through Morocco and Algeria, and their future victories will avenge the thousands of families across this land and the empire beyond, who, though they celebrate with us today, harbour a lasting sadness in their hearts. Let us pray.'

***

Reverend Hale stood on the church steps just outside the doorway as his congregation filed out. He exchanged a few words, shook a few hands and accepted condolences. As the last few suited men and behatted women shuffled past, the tap of wood against stone caught his attention. He looked up to see the last in line was a man in RAF uniform. He moved with a crutch under his right arm, and his right trouser leg was pinned up behind his knee. He swayed to halt in front of the clergyman.

'That was a really lovely sermon,' the man said. 'Except, you've got it wrong.'

He beamed his smile into the frowning reverend's face: 'You see, Bryan Hale is not dead.'

I hope you have enjoyed reading Firebird and will consider leaving an honest review on Amazon.

Visit my website at www.melvynfickling.com and sign up for the Bluebirds Newsletter for updates on my forthcoming work.

## Author's notes

This is a historical novel based on real events. It is not a history of those events or of the people who found themselves entangled in those events.

Some major historical characters are named for authenticity. All the main characters are entirely fictional. Any similarity these characters may bear to persons living or dead is coincidental.

Locations are real, although the details of real locations have been fictionalised in a sympathetic manner.

The backdrop of events against which the novel is set is well documented elsewhere. I have kept as close as possible to the actual timeline, but some events may have been shifted slightly to accommodate plot requirements. No disrespect is implied or intended to the people who were involved in those events.

## Sources

*The End of the Beginning* – Tim Clayton and Phil Craig

*Destiny in the Desert* – Jonathan Dimbleby

*An Army at Dawn* – Rick Atkinson

*The Decisive Campaigns of The Desert Air Force 1942 to 1945* – Bryn Evans

*Spitfire* – John Nichol

Printed in Great Britain
by Amazon

40181177R00099